Welcome to Yesterday

Welcome to Yesterday

A Novel

Ian Spiegelman

miramax books

HYPERION

NEW YORK

"If your Lordship would be so kind as to give me ever so small a bit of the sky, even a mile would do, and I would rather have it than the best isle in the world."

—Cervantes, *Don Quixote*

Welcome to Yesterday

1

This Prince Business

I'd been on that beat for six years before I finally managed to kill somebody. Sure, it was Lane Martin who'd written the fatal item, but when you have just three people putting out a daily gossip column with a fairly wide reach it's important that they share responsibility for whatever trouble they're bound to kick up—without that sense of camaraderie, it would be a dangerous business.

Lane was famous that morning and radiant in shock. I wasn't so jealous that I could've shaved her blonde head right there in the office, but she might have mentioned me on one or two of those press calls. She could at least have said it was me who'd broken the news to her.

I found out about the dead man while she was going over the story list for the morning editorial meeting with Robert Harris, who ran the page. The two of them were huddled by his desk in the double-wide cubicle next to the one Lane and I shared. Gossip was stationed at an ass-end corner of the newsroom, where the blinking fluorescents in the low ceiling hardly challenged the slim windows that let in the pale gray light of Sixth Avenue's failed spring. Surrounded by the business section, we could barely hear the prattle of the reporters clustered at the city desk in the middle of the office.

I was surfing for pick-ups on the UK tab sites. When England's wealth of soccer and royalty had exhausted itself on me, I checked e-mail, sending the usual response to four or five publicists:

"No sightings need apply. Thanks for playing."

Normally I wouldn't have answered my phone that early in the morning, but Harris was turning around to ask if I had anything for the page when it started to ring. I'd put in four hours at a boutique opening and a book launch the night before and couldn't remember any part of it, but I'd be sticking the paper with the overtime and cab fare just the same and I wasn't up to discussing it quite yet.

There was also the very real risk that should Harris find me empty-handed, he'd assign me one of the dozens of anonymous tips he got each week. Not that going after a blind lead *always* wasted at least a day of your time, I just didn't share Harris's affection for them. Call it whimsy. Harris had spent a quarter century grooming sources as a reporter and an editor at both of the city dailies, but he still had a mischievous penchant for investigating the conspiracies of any syphilitic who managed to dial his number in the middle of the night. I could see it in his face as he looked to me across the cubicle partition—the flashing glee of an otherwise rational anthropologist about to take off on his annual Yeti hunt.

"I've got a good one for you!" he announced. Nodding and holding up a finger, I answered my phone.

A woman whispered, "Hey there, Sunshine."

"Hey," I said, "hello. Who may I say is calling?"

"Oh, Leon, should I tell you? Would that be much better? But then all you'd do is tell on me for it. How are you feeling this morning?"

"Doe-eyed and dizzy—yourself?"

"A little crazy, really. My boyfriend died last night."

"I'm sorry—what?"

"There was blood all over the kitchen to start. There was blood all between the tiles, all in the sink." She was still whispering, her tone an even, steady trance. "It was under the refrigerator. He didn't want it on the rugs. Maybe he thought it wouldn't happen. But how could he really think that?"

"Okay," I said. "What?"

"I stepped in it. I got it on my shoes. There is blood on my shoes. There is blood on both my shoes."

"Okay. Did you call the police?"

"We had it and he broke it," she said. "He threw it away, he broke it."

"Miss?"

"You people think you know what's going on," her voice changing, "but you have no idea."

"I'm sorry, I don't think I—"

"Think, think, think—you're always thinking. But you know what? The party's over, Sunshine. It's all come and gone and you don't even know it."

"Okay," I told her slowly. "Okay."

She let out a laugh—a spinning thing with blades on it—shouted a random construction of obscenities, and went back to whispering. "I always have a choice," she said. "It only takes a second to change your mind, but I always have a choice. Did you think you were going to make me change my *mind*?"

A girl on a suicide hotline once asked me something that had made everything much worse, but nothing else came to me, so I said, "Is there anyone you'd like me to call?"

She shrieked, "Do not *laugh* at me!" and I could hear the hate rolling in her throat, the skin on my forearms pricking up to receive it.

Ducking chin to chest, I whispered, "Sorry"—an old reflex.

Then there was just the woman's breath in my ear, shallow and too fast, much too fast. Lane and Harris were laughing over something. I palmed the mouthpiece.

"Are you holding your breath?"

"What?"

"Are you holding your breath? I don't hear you breathing, Sunshine."

"I'm a quiet breather."

"You shouldn't breathe at all maybe."

They were ten feet away, Lane and Harris, past the empty desk the part-timers used, Harris in his chair pecking the keyboard with two fingers, Lane standing over his shoulder reading from a legal pad. Their backs were to me, I fished a pencil from the old Subway Series mug, thinking to flick it at them or write a note.

"Why so quiet?"

"What does a person say?"

"I'm going to tell you what to say. And you're going to thank me for it. You're going to praise me."

I liked that. I wanted her to say it again.

"Say that again?"

"You're going to praise me before it's over."

"Before what's over?"

"The party!" she giggled wildly, a high school girl playing Blanche DuBois. "Don't you wish you were recording this?"

The ancient tape recorder sat by the side of the phone, the wires that never seemed to fit any socket curling away from it. I said, "Um—"

"But then recording phone calls is for people who don't rewrite quotes, people who don't lie about people."

"Who did I lie about?"

When she was done spinning out another one of her laughs, she said, "So I'd better get a move-on now. I just thought you'd like to know what you did." I asked her what I'd done, and she sang in a bouncy voice, "You killed Kyle Prince, silly! Like as if you had to ask. He slit his pretty wrists last night. Anyhow, bye-bye now, Sunshine, bye-bye."

The floor seemed to fall away and I closed my eyes.

Kyle Prince was our lead that day, a story that was told often enough, about enough people, that it only bore further telling by being a perennial favorite—a cozy piece of boilerplate where any name would do. It also came with enough detail to fill the top section of the page, which was often all any lead had going for it.

Prince had started out in New York as a talent agent with a gentleman's cocaine habit, moved to LA to become a studio VP and a heroin freak, lost that job and booked himself a stay at a Caribbean rehab resort. Returning to New York, he took a fifth-floor walk-up on Sullivan Street and a junior position at his old agency. It hadn't worked out. Security was packing his desk when Lane got the tip from a source in his office: Prince had reverted to the form in which he was most comfortable. If we didn't know he'd make it final, we might've guessed.

The trades and the other dailies later made it out that all of Prince's friends had called begging us not to put it on the page when he'd gotten canned. Fact is only one person had come begging, and gold his word was not.

Robin Saulie's story isn't any fresher than Kyle Prince's, though it would end more entertainingly. As a money manager he'd made millions for about a dozen of the most worshipped animals in entertainment. Saulie did this by casually wiping out the accounts of fifty people you've never heard of. Word of this was just starting to get around when Prince got the axe. It was Saulie who'd called us begging—no one else.

His request to Lane had amounted to: we couldn't do it, we shouldn't do it, that, this one, this was the one that would push Kyle over the edge.

Lane had put him on hold, conferring with Harris and me.

Harris had offered, "Try finding someone who *doesn't* say that. Do we cover community board meetings? How about a nice Board of Ed hearing? Because that's what we've got to look forward to if we start killing stories every time someone cries suicide." Shaking his head, he'd turned back to his monitor, adding, "Bunch of Quakers I've got working here."

Lane had stared down at her phone as if it might not be a phone anymore, but rather something that could suddenly explode or slither from her desk. I'd never seen her rattled before, and that rattled me.

"What the hell?" I said. "Saulie's tickling your ass, Lane. No one's killing himself."

"Then why would Robin—?" Cutting herself off and squinting down at the phone again, she started biting automatically at her thumbnail, which she was prone to do whenever she was chasing down a thought. "Look," she said, "I think I should just hold it for a day."

"Just long enough to get scooped?" I countered. "What's the matter with you?"

"But what if Kyle's really in trouble?"

"Of course he's in trouble. That's why we're writing about him. If we start accommodating these people we're not any better than their fucking publicists."

That line closed the debate, though I'd added to it my suggestion that Lane ask Saulie to fetch a coffin—to which Lane rolled her eyes, giving me the side of her face.

It had ended with her asking Saulie, "If he's honestly in that much trouble, why don't you go over there? Why don't you call the police?"

He came back moaning, asking her where her heart was, but he didn't trouble himself with answering the question. That made it easy to shrug him off as a bluff. People with a reasonable explanation aren't shy in giving it up. Everything else is PR.

I doubt if any of us thought about Kyle Prince again that day, or that night, and I know Lane wasn't pondering his short shot at existence Thursday morning as she and Harris discussed our annual gun-toting-celebs roundup for Friday's page.

"I'll just write it up," she was saying, a dial tone in my ear where the woman's hissing laugh had been. "They're mostly my accounts anyway."

It was Lane who'd taught me to refer to celebrities, flacks, and snitches as accounts, reducing the people we covered and the people we dealt with to a single base commodity.

"And you'd rather do fuck-all nothing today, wouldn't you, Lee?"

I saw her talking to me.

"Leon?"

Lane was considerably blonder, taller and mentally healthier than anything that was my type, but she had a smile that poured down from her sharp blue eyes and flooded the rest of her face to make sure you'd never dump too many lesser memories on top of it. I was staring at that grin, knowing I'd have to snatch it off her face and hoping she might get it back before too long.

"Hey," she said and I snapped to, setting down the receiver.

"Hey, yes—absolutely," I said. "It's all you."

I got up and went around the corner to a row of three secluded cubicles. My latest cell had gone out a cab window the night before and I needed a phone out of Lane's earshot to find out if the call was just some psycho's prank. The woman on the phone had sounded crazy, there was that, but it wasn't any sea of hope—psychopaths tell the truth as often as anyone else.

August MacCalamite never showed up much before three, so I made myself at home at his desk. Mac had a self-named column that was a fever dream of tall tales, cop heroics, and other conservatisms. His cubicle was flanked on the left by Mike Naffin, a TV reporter, and on the right by Marsha Lindgren, who wrote about kids. Naffin was wearing headphones and laughing at something stupid playing on the set on his desk. Marsha was checking out the *Enquirer*.

"Just taking over for Mac," I told her, picking up his phone. "The old man's gone soft on abortion."

"I reckon the old man's gone soft on a lot of things. Will you be long?"

"Ten minutes?"

"I'll just fuck off for a smoke then."

"The Lord keep you, princess."

"I suppose he might," she said, her rear tic-tocking behind her as she went. She stopped before the corner, smoothed down the back of her skirt with one hand, and was gone.

Calling the deputy commissioner for public information, I got a sergeant who believed his office didn't handle suicides. Calling back a minute later, I got a DCPI officer who believed otherwise, but said without stopping to check that no report on a Kyle Prince had come in.

"Maybe call back in a few hours," he suggested.

"You mean after your shift, right?"

"What's that?" he said while I hung up.

The medical examiner's office wasn't as helpful.

DCPI isn't the only headache at One Police Plaza. There is also the Cop Shack, a second-floor cavern where every paper in the city has offices for its police reporters. I've never liked cops, but I'd have rather skipped through a dozen precincts in my frilliest sundress than spend a minute on the phone with our guys at the Shack. Still, had to be done.

Phoning up, there was at least the hope that Colao or Zeidman would answer. They'd only been on that beat a few years apiece and hadn't yet developed the perpetual ulcer, the blind cop-loving, or the penchant for wearing a dainty little revolver on an ankle holster. Because hope was unreasonable, it was Louis Delores who picked up.

"Cop Shack."

"Hey, it's Koch. I need a little help."

"Who needs what now?" I said my name again, said the name of the column, explaining I had a possible scoop. Delores said, "Fucking Koch. Do you know what time it is?"

"About eleven."

"So?"

"So you just asked me."

"I'm not asking you anything."

We played for another minute or two before he let me tell him anything about Kyle Prince. Then we played some more.

"The guy on our page today. In the lead. He might've killed himself last night."

I could hear the paper rustling as he read it.

"I don't get it."

"Ah, fuck," I said. "What? What are you missing?"

"This kid? This kid doesn't kill himself."

"He doesn't?"

"This kid's soft, he doesn't do it. Does he maybe get kind of tired of it? Yeah, sure he could do that, but not all the way."

"Well, a woman just told me he went all the way, the whole thing, said he slit his fucking wrists last night."

"Oh!" Delores said, stretching out the sound until it was something he could put his fist through. "*Okay* then. You didn't mention that a woman told you, no you left that out. That makes everything different."

My throat was warming at the back. I bit down and asked him pleasantly to stop fucking with me. "It's a good story if it's true," I said. "And you can have it, it's all you—I'm just asking you to tell me before you file. It's kind of personal."

Mike Naffin let out a phlegmy cackle to my side and slapped his desk. His TV showed a teenage girl being scared straight, inmates in orange jumpsuits screaming in her face and leading her around by her ponytail while the tears rolled down.

"You don't want a byline?"

"No, it's yours, take it. All I'm asking is if this guy's dead you let me know about it before you call it in to the desk. All right?"

He said he'd get back to me and hung up. Of course I'd never hear from him again; he'd go screaming straight to the city desk with his stolen exclusive. So I went back to my desk and waited for signs of action.

2
Scoop!

A newsroom is a stupor with walls, a few dozen mildly to chronically depressed adults waiting for a plane to crash and instead getting press releases from the City Council—and never enough of them to go around. Between scoops you rot in your seat, listen to the sounds of your own digestion, consider calling your sources, consider the futility of that, reminisce with yourself over fantastic calamities long gone by, and keep waiting.

When news does break, you may as well start shooting up the windows—boredom is shocked away by a sense of impending slaughter and the quiet's chased off by a chorus of panicked shrieks. I'd been waiting on that for an hour when I started getting paranoid.

If Delores had already confirmed Prince's suicide with his cops, he could've filed it and then worked out a deal with someone on the city desk to keep it quiet until he could track down my madwoman and cut me out of it completely. There were any number of secret alliances at the paper, and I might've known what some of them were if I hadn't always treated every section but my own as a sideshow.

I went over to the city desk to see if I could find anything out.

In the nest of interconnected cubicles that made up the desk, various gradations of editors were gazing at monitors, copy kids sorted faxes, reporters chewed on pencils and pens, made phone calls, small talk, surfed. A reporter fingered the knobs on a police scanner. The photo editor and one of his deputies crowded a dusty laptop in the next cubicle, clicking through party shots from the previous evening. A typist sat reading the *Star* while another reporter leaned back on her desk taking notes for a war story off one of the TVs mounted in the wall.

Julian Kennedy, the city editor, had the first cubicle in the nest. He looked up at me coming toward him, an eyelash sticking to the top of his cheek.

"Got something?"

"Borderline schizophrenia, yourself?"

He was still looking up at me. "Seriously."

"Yeah," I lied. "Jezika and Matt Block," meaning the singer and the actor. A story was displayed on Kennedy's monitor, just past his face, but I couldn't make out the words.

"And?"

"I just got a call they're getting married this weekend. No name, no number, just the tip."

Across the nest, I saw Emma Lake and Gary Pornell by the copier beneath the row of TVs. Em was wearing the fitted burgundy jacket that buttoned tight at her waist and let her breathe at her chest over a white blouse, a gray skirt stopping at her knees and white stockings with Mary Jane flats that matched her jacket. Pornell, a thirty-four-year-old assignment fetch who'd moved to Williamsburg after all but the children had fled, was slouching over her, speaking to the side of her face, one hand on the wall above her head.

"We seem to hear that a lot of weekends lately," Kennedy was saying, running his thumbs in circles over his eyelids and adding another lash to his cheek—a gesture he'd been working at ever since his promotion.

"Okay, terrific," I said. "I'll bring you over the press release when they put it out and we can all look at the pictures in the *Star*."

"Do we have a location, do we have a date?"

Pornell was behind Em now, pointing at something in that day's paper. He wore Buddy Holly rims and a short-sleeved hardware store shirt over a long-sleeved *Ghost in the Machine* tour jersey.

"I guess if not Saturday it'd be Sunday," I said. "Unless they add another day to the weekend."

Em smiled at what Pornell was showing her, quickly covering her mouth with her hand, Pornell's fingers sliding over her shoulder. Em's eyes clicked to his hand.

"As far as location, you could get someone to find out what vacation-type real estate Free Tibet owns—Jezika hasn't seen a Catholic church since her first communion, but Block wears his religion like a leather gimp mask."

"He also wears a leather gimp mask," Kennedy smirked, flicking the lashes from his face and putting his shoes up on the corner of his desk. Em slipped her shoulder away from Pornell. Over their heads, a newsreader said, "It wasn't like it used to be in Jupiter, Florida, and it won't be for a long time to come."

"So what you're basically telling me," Kennedy said, "is that you have an anonymous tip that could or could not pan out and that you don't intend to make any of the calls on it yourself."

"If it pans out you'll just steal it for up front anyway."

"I've always admired your team spirit."

"Ah, Julian," I said, "I've got team spirit to the eyes, that's why I'm letting you farm it out. I find bylines to be pedestrian."

Kennedy shrugged and did the eye thing again. "You don't

want to do it, don't do it. I can't remember the last time you made the wood, but somehow I never wake up thinking about it."

He meant getting a story on the front page, but I never woke up thinking about it either.

Another newsreader was talking in that voice that couldn't tell one thing from another—"The rain that threatened to cool down this parade failed to lower the temperature"—and Em put a stack of papers in the sorter, Pornell putting his hand on the wall over her head again, slouching, his nose just above the back of her hair.

"I've never made the wood," I said, "but who's counting? You want to see what I think of the wood? Watch this—hey, Gary!"

"Don't."

"Gary!"

"Koch—"

Em was stacking her copies, Pornell mouthing slow and easy at her ear.

"Wake up, Gary!" He looked over at us, head toggling over his neck like the two hadn't been properly introduced. "What do you know about Jezika and Matt Block?"

"Asshole," Kennedy said into his vest.

"Who do I know about what?"

Em walked out from under him, disappearing down the aisle with her copies, Pornell watching her go. He came over to Kennedy and me and I laid out the bogus tip for him.

"You'll want to see if you can find out where the Dalai Lama's at," I said. "Block couldn't tie the knot without him. Also, Jezika's got a Santeria priestess she rolls out for special occasions—she'll be in the clips."

"I *broke* that Santeria story," he said, which was the kind of thing he'd have to believe.

"That's why I'm asking you to give me a hand on this."

"You know I'm up to my neck on this MTA thing," he told Kennedy.

"That story's been dead a week," Kennedy said, really damaging his eyes now.

"But I've got a source."

"You don't want to do the wedding? Don't do the wedding. No one's doing the wedding." Kennedy stood up, fingers rough through his hair. "There is no wedding!" he told the room. "Wedding's off, folks! Bride's got a dose of hepsie and I've got no reporters!"

Empty faces peeked out from behind monitors.

"No," Pornell said. "I mean, I didn't mean that . . . Okay. I mean, yeah." We waited for more, but that's all he had.

When Pornell had gone away to his desk, Kennedy said, "The Dalai Lama, Koch?"

"He's not completely out of the question—metaphysically."

"Metaphysically," shaking his head. "This is what puts the fucking tick in my eye."

"You don't have any tick in your eye."

"All right, then my whole fucking face is ticking and my eye's standing still. Look, you just handed Captain Clip-job a fairly large break and I don't think I get the joke. But if you were to do some digging on this—"

"So take him off it if you want to. Put him back on harassing copy kids. What're you, afraid of breaking his heart?"

"Just make some calls."

Em passed behind Kennedy, crossing her eyes at me.

"I'll ask Lane to. Jezika's her account. Her publicist doesn't think much of me for some reason."

"All right, then Lane," Kennedy said. "Have her at least track down if they're in town or in LA or what."

If Delores had confirmed the suicide, he'd have had to call it in to Kennedy. As much as Kennedy liked to play a hardass, he wouldn't be talking about putting Lane on a wedding story if he knew that she'd just put a man in the ground.

He asked me, "Have we gotten any sightings on them lately?"

"We've been deleting sightings as fast as they come in," I said, walking away. "None of us can figure out how they keep getting on the page."

I knew that Jezika and Block were in town. Block's ex-wife, Maria Shockley, was in a remake of *Antony and Cleopatra* that was premiering that night, and Block attended all of Shockley's premieres—his status as the perfect ex was one of his publicist's most inspired illusions. And if Pornell wasted a little time trying to figure that out, well, it couldn't be helped.

I went over to the desk the copy kids used and crouched beside Em's chair. "You know, you can advise that lumpy prick to fuck off when he bothers you."

Her eyeteeth jutted slightly past her incisors, twisting her smile crooked. She covered it with her long, smooth fingers, nails ballet-slipper pink.

"He wasn't bothering me. Was he bothering you?"

"Yeah," I said. "Yeah, he was."

She turned the hinge of her jaw to me, took me in with one squinting eye, grinning with half her mouth. "Yeah, he bothers me too." Her whole face showed again, the full bloom of her smile, her eyes.

"Then why do you keep putting up with it?"

"I may not say anything, does that mean I'm putting up with it?"

Her eyes were a vast, shimmering auburn, laced with flickering bands of amber and gold, charged with something that always scanned me faster than I could look away from it. I always had to look away from it. It was the vastness that scared me. There was something impossible in it, something in her gaze that could change the things it settled on. And I believed that that thing would be ruined if it ever truly settled on me.

Watching her Mary Janes, I told Em, "I don't know what it means."

"Then maybe you'd say I'm encouraging it?"

"I couldn't tell you if you are. But I'd hope not."

"You'd hope not—why?" She crossed her ankles and the back of one of her shoes popped away from her heel, revealing the shadow of an impossibly high arch. I stood up. Em's foot slipped back into her shoe. "No answer?"

"You just got here," I said. "You don't need to get yourself mixed up in anything stupid so quick. Why don't you just wait a while, have a look around first?"

"I don't know. I think if I'm going to do something stupid there isn't any good reason for me to wait for it."

"I didn't say you were going to. Do something stupid, I mean."

"I think you did, Leon."

There was a certain level of tension that Em could always save me from if she felt like saving me. I waited. Laughing, she shook out her curly brown hair, her sideways squint now accompanied by a pitying smirk, as if the most obvious joke had just blown by me.

"Honestly, though," she said. "I think you tell me I'm going to do something stupid more often than anyone has in a long time."

"Then I'm sorry."

"And that's what else you do—you say you're sorry. What are you even sorry about?"

I wasn't sure who was at fault for taking the conversation there, but I was sure that was where I'd leave it—it wasn't any time for a truth-telling contest. And I didn't have the nerve for one anyway.

"I don't know," I said. "Do you need to know everything all at once?"

"Gosh, that's clever. Whenever we talk, half the time all I ever get from you is something clever. Two months isn't long but it's more than long enough for some things, Leon. For instance, it's long enough to figure out that being clever in New York only makes you common."

"Oh come on, Em."

"'Oh come on?' Now that's not even clever—that's just simple."

"I'm not trying to be clever."

"Then what are you trying to be?" she said, pushing two thick spirals of hair from either side of her face and tucking them behind her ears with her thumbs. One of them popped back out, swinging over her eye and across her lips, but she didn't let it distract from her stare.

I told her, "I don't know," a throb beating up through my neck.

Em didn't say anything, neither did I. She was looking up at me, scanning through the tops of her eyes, when she shook out her hair again, laughing into her hand. I crouched down beside her again, touching the arm of her chair.

"You feel like coming to a party tonight?"

Her fingers fluttered at my hand on her chair, brushing it away. "Just hardly."

"Come on, Em."

"There's that 'come on' again," giving me the squint and the smirk. "Go away and let me think about it."

I was going away letting her think about it when a city desk operator called out, "I've got Louis Delores holding for you."

Kennedy took the call. He listened, jotting notes, then put the receiver to his chest, asking me, "Is Lane at her desk?" I shrugged and Kennedy was out of his seat. "Lane!" he shouted, looking over the office, neck craned and head flinching side to side like a meerkat sniffing danger. "Is Lane Martin in the office?"

The rest of the desk staff was looking at Kennedy as I walked away from them, the dolor subsiding before the frenzy. I could hear it building behind me as I went down the aisle. Soon they'd organize—editors shouting for reporters and photographers, reporters screaming for copy kids, half the office trying to get their names on it, looking for sources, back-ups, officials, clippings, the Lord of Abraham . . .

I heard them rumbling down the aisle toward us as I sat next to Lane, the footsteps coming for her, the voices calling out her name.

"Lane?"

She had her headset on, she was typing. I touched her elbow and heard "Roxanne" humming out of the earplugs as she took off the headset.

"What's up, Lee?"

"Lane!" one called and "Lane!" called another.

She looked past my face, a twitch in her smile and her eyes going small, homing in on them as they came for her. They were still calling out her name, and everything she needed to know was in the frantic sound of it. Then she focused on me with something in her expression that I couldn't place, something serene and exotic in the deep blue stillness of her eyes—sympathy.

She nodded faintly.

I said, "Kyle Prince is dead."

She nodded again, closing her eyes.

3

Enter the Dragon

He smelled of ten-thousand-year-old desert plants, of too- wildly realized potential, of the furnace at the core of the earth. Like one of Lovecraft's ancient gods, only the outermost part of him was visible in this world, only his most ragged fringes.

The hook of his nose and what remained of his Mediterranean complexion suggested Hebraic or Arab blood. If you mentioned it to him he would boast of the Jew who'd been mayor of Dublin and of having learned to drink at the elbow of Bloom himself—which wasn't entirely plausible—but I never tried to prove or disprove his stories for the same reason I'd always kept myself from finding out his actual age. I knew, however, that August MacCalamite was as much an Irishman as his father and grandfather, both of whom were Tasmanian.

After the smoking ban went through he'd taken to drinking in the basement of the bar around the corner from our office, where he fed off the heat of the boiler and where the inspectors and their snitches couldn't get a whiff of his Parliaments.

The manager unlocked the door and we started down the walled-in staircase. Lane said her usual "How does he get up and down these things without breaking his neck every day?" without the tone of awed amusement that would normally have carried it. I had a line about getting the lights fixed in the stairwell, but I wasn't in the mood to deliver it.

Keeping a glass table candle at arm's length, I took each cement step slowly, thinking of low-hanging spiders, and put my free arm around Lane's shoulders. She didn't necessarily need it by then— she seemed to have left the worst part of her shakes back in the office—but we were alone there in the dark.

I heard something crunch under the toe of her boot and felt a quiver go through her shoulders, her arm tensing beneath her sweater and the twitch sending a buzz through my fingertips. Until that morning, I had never actually touched her before except to shake her hand—and I'd only done that the first time we met. It had been a cold hand, and it had not let go of mine until Lane had finished saying, "Pay attention around here. The sooner you can do this, the sooner I can quit!"

Over the next six years it had never occurred to me to touch her again. As partners, we developed a sort of natural and unspoken bar against such things as kissing hello if we ran into each other at night. When our crawls crossed paths, Lane would cheek-peck three men in a row and then greet me with an amused and somehow confidential lift of her thin yellow eyebrows. It was a kind of closeness that made kissing hello seem emotionally frivolous, and shaking hands feel stupidly mannered. So we never did either.

When I'd told Lane that Prince was dead she'd held it in a moment, closing her eyes and grabbing her elbows. Then she started to cry. I put my hand on the top of her arm—I hadn't thought not to—rubbing a circle into the muscle with my thumb. She let go of herself, putting her arms around my chest, her face tucked into my shoulder, sobbing, her hair tickling my face, wet breath against my neck, the tears going hot through the front of my shirt and the gasping jolts of her shoulders moving up through my arms, my neck, humming into my face—I hadn't felt anything like it in a very long time.

When we reached the bottom of the steps, I let go of her and we turned the corner, the palm of my hand dancing with pinpricks.

His table was in front of the boiler at the far corner of the first room, a steel door and a black cast-iron sink in the opposite corner. Without MacCalamite lording over it, the table looked like a museum piece—frozen under caged yellow bulbs and laid out with newspapers, pads, the vestigial black rotary, a yellow and green diamond-shaped ashtray that was a keepsake from a soccer match no one had survived, a liter of Beefeater, a quart of tonic, a rack of stemmed cocktail glasses.

Underneath the table was an ice bucket and a gray busboy's tray containing four empty glasses. A glass on the table held a pinky's width of liquid and a sliver of ice. I picked it up to add it to the empties in the bus tray, as if to summon him.

"You will unhand her," he said before the steel door had opened wide enough to admit his silver pompadour. "You will unhand her unmolested, my young merdivore, or you will force me to educate."

"You can't unhand a thing unmolested, August."

"Oh just put the fucking glass down, you schmuck—there's still a drink in it."

His stride had a long, sharp grace that was hardly undercut by him zipping his fly. Stopping, he snapped his fingers in front of his face, turned and went to the iron sink, rinsing his hands and patting them on the bottom of his blue blazer, crisp and immaculate beneath a fine coat of ash.

We sat around the table, Lane's black leather pants squeaking beneath her, August taking three glasses from the rack. I shook my head and he put one back. Once it was poured, Lane sipped her drink from the table until the top was off, then took the glass in both hands and drained it. August watched her with a smile that lifted the hoods away from his eyes—as yellow as they were blue. He put Lane's empty glass in the tray under the table, took another from the rack, filled it, and she took it away with one hand.

When we'd all lit cigarettes, August said, "Something brings you to this depth in broad daylight. So? Speak. Here is your confessor," flicking the crest on his blazer, flakes of ash swirling away from under his long, manicured fingers.

It took the rest of her drink and then another for Lane to get the whole thing out, choking on a detail now and then and shivering over her glass. At the end of it her face was wet, her thin, white-blonde hair sticking to her cheeks. I thought of smoothing the hair away for her and lit another cigarette.

"I just had to get the hell out of there," she was saying. "The way everyone was all over me, like I was a story they were trying to break."

"Nurse no delusions, my child. That is precisely what you are. You can't blame the boys for teaming up on you—you're the most exclusive item they've got." He laughed, coughing smoke, a cackle like throwing rocks at the walls of a cave. Wiping his lips with a red handkerchief and stuffing it into his breast pocket, August continued.

"It means nothing that you didn't actually *cause* the young man's death, it matters only that death came and that it has got your *name* on it. You know very well that the best-told stories begin and end in death—death is our engine, our engine is death."

She put her face in her hands, shaking it side to side. Through her palms, Lane said, "Mac, what are you *talking* about?"

"I am talking about the news—the news you're in, Miss Martin. Because you are concentrating your energies in exactly the opposite of what might do you good. All of this 'Did I or did I not kill the man?' is piss in the Pacific, Laney. This fellow, this . . ."

He made a "fetch" gesture with his fingers and I said, "Prince."

"No, the other one, the dear friend."

"Saulie."

"This Saulie, this man who was so wracked with fraternal love, where was he in all this?"

"That's what I've been thinking," Lane said, wiping her cheeks with the sleeves of her sweater. "If he was so fuck-all worried about his friend, why didn't he go to Kyle's apartment? Why didn't he call the police?" She stopped, under a shudder. "Why did he leave it to me?"

Blowing smoke into the caged bulbs, MacCalamite said, "He who we loveth best, and so to pieces shred."

We said, "What?"

"Consider the burden of such a friend, consider how many times he's required saving. A person like that, a man who seems only to get up to fall down again, there is one place he's heading, one place only, and you might expect those around him to get reasonably sick and tired of waiting for it."

My pulse put an ache into my forearms that closed my fists.

"No," Lane said, taking the bottom out of her fourth gin and tonic. "No, if Saulie wanted him dead, why would he have called me? Why would he have warned anyone?"

"Partly out of guilt, partly from habit," giving a small shrug of his shoulders. "But I suspect the largest piece of it was to have a whipping boy, or, in your case, girl—someone to carry it for him. This Prince's life demanded an ending, this comedy required a corpse, and your man saw fit to hang you with the final credit. Have you honestly lived this long to expect more of the human being?"

She put an unlit cigarette to her lips, held it there. "So what do I do now?"

"You won't have a minute back at the office before the boys are on you again—they're confounded. Having one of their own play a part in a story indicates some kind of exclusivity, and they'll be mining their brains to figure out what it is, how they might flesh out this boon without appearing callous—you know, 'We get action.' Your job is not to help them."

He put two more empties into the tray and made another pair of live ones. Lane looked at hers like it might jump up and grab her.

"Maybe I'd follow you better if there weren't so many of you sitting there," she said. "I'm not in any condition."

"Stay with me, child," reaching across the table and patting her wrist. Until then, I couldn't have imagined Lane tolerating anyone, least of all the old beast, calling her "child" and patting her wrist, but Lane didn't seem quite Lane anymore. I wondered how much Prince's death had already changed her, and what it might do to me.

"The only smart play," Mac was saying, "is for everyone to keep their ridiculous mouth shut. This is a story for every paper but our own and there's nothing left but to let them have their way with us and leave it to memory. It's a tiny thing, as scandals go."

He leaned back, luxuriating in his chair, eyeing the drink at the end of his arm.

"Now the trouble," he continued, after savoring a mouthful, "is that an exclusive is such a damned redoubtable machine. Yes, of course, mass murders, riots, and the occasional pandemic will always have their charms, but, for the seasoned journalist, covering events that so many of his brethren are covering tends to remind him that these events will occur whether he's there to report them or not. This threatens to wear his sense of self down to a fine mist. But, if you're, say, the only man in town to discover that the comptroller's brother-in-law has a fetish for the female armpit—how like a god!"

"August," I said, but it was too late.

"Mickey Brenner, who was a photographer at the *Telegraph*, he understood what's what. That is, he went after the scoop, as was his job, but never allowed it to delude him. You'd ask the man if there'd be rain tonight and he'd tell you, 'That might be. Because, if it decides to, who'll stop it?' Now," pouring a fresh one, "it's funny you should mention suicide."

Lane's drink remained untouched on the table and she watched MacCalamite with wide open eyes, as if she were trying to make the performance sober her up. Me, I couldn't have been more sober—and I'd never been his audience in such a state before.

"Mickey was engaged to a girl called Marina Leticia, who was an Argentine soprano with the Sydney Philharmonic, when it came back to Mickey that Marina had done him dirt with a young tenor. So of course there was nothing left but to feed said tenor to the sharks, which is a thing they absolutely did back then—just ask me where Georgie Barrister is."

I didn't dare, Lane's head listed to one side.

"But then with Barrister there were politics to consider. You see—" MacCalamite stopped, a dove into a pane of glass. His eyes retreated into the shadow of his brow as he tracked down a thought.

Lane and I would've troubled him for more details, but it was clearly going to be a hazardous expedition, and we couldn't assure our party's safe return. We snuck to our feet, Lane taking our little candle from the table.

Mac called after us when we reached the bottom of the steps.

"I do hope that you children haven't had trouble following me," he said. "See if you can follow this." The hoods lifted from his eyes with a grin. "Your names belong on top of your damned stories. Not inside them."

4

Them

"*Y*ou're supposed to stop him before he gets to Mickey Brenner."

"I tried, I said, 'August'—didn't you hear me?"

"I heard you. What an effort."

I could smell her in the wind, the alcohol evaporating through the pores across her nose.

"Besides, I don't mind it. I like his stories, with everyone dropping dead in twos and threes and none of it coming to much of anything, everything so far back and so painless."

"We should've been back upstairs half an hour ago."

"They'll cut you any slack you want today, they've got no choice. Anyway, we can go up right now if you want to."

"I don't want to. Couldn't we say that we got sick or that a car hit us or that August was attacked by some animal?"

"We can say anything you want, I'll do whatever you want."

The two of us were crouched around the Bloomberg in front of the bar, flicking ashes in the sand.

"Will you?"

"Yeah."

"Then tell me the truth. Did you really think Kyle wouldn't do it?"

"I don't think I really thought about it at all."

She stood up, she stood over me—I stayed where I was.

"Is that the truth or are you just talking?"

My face was hot in the wind, sweat cooling over my ribs.

"No it's not the truth," staring up at her as she scanned me down the bridge of her nose. "I thought that he might or he might not and I didn't care about it going either way. I didn't care if he lived or died and I don't care about it now. I don't care if any of them do."

"Don't get yourself started on that. There's no them."

The toes of her boots were scuffed and the heels worn down—I'd once told her that she should wear better shoes and she'd laughed at me. "Get relevant!" she'd said.

"These millionaires," I was saying, "these pretty rags, these rapists—they say we make our living off of them but they make their living off of everyone else, everyone in the world. You see them laughing about it, you see them picking out girls . . ."

The stories were starting to come, they always came too fast, with too many pictures—I closed my eyes on a high school girl kneeling under a desk, opened them gazing up at my partner, needing her to be herself again. Standing, we were eye to eye, and I took a step back from her.

"That's too easy," she said, dropping her cigarette in the bucket between us, the coal dying out in the sand. "How do you factor in that you actually like some of these people? Some of these people are our friends."

"No they're not. They're just, I don't know, next to us." I named the head of a record label that Lane hung around with. "He's some-one you do the crawls with, you have dinners, you were at his wedding—when he's got a story he always comes to you first, right? And then he tries to fuck your little sister."

"Why not? You do it all the time."

"I'm not pushing sixty and I've never offered her four thousand dollars for it. If it were anyone else in the world you'd have never spoken to him again."

"He was just drunk," hiding her hands in the sleeves of her sweater. "And it was more a joke than anything."

"It was only a joke after she said no. But what about all the jokey propositions they make to people who can't afford to say no? The ones who are afraid to?"

"Keep your voice down," she said, gesturing with her chin at the flow of tourists streaming past us, heading to and from Times Square. "You're harping on one isolated incident."

"They all develop the taste soon enough. We make them into it, we pay them attention until they start hurting people and then we pay them more of it. We're ruled over by surgically enhanced sociopaths wearing the latest design by the latest homosexual."

She looked at me like I was carrying a pair of elves on my shoulders, her eyes red along the rims.

"They're just people. You won't admit it because you're in that zone of yours, but when you catch your breath you'll know it's true. You've been doing this job long enough to know that they're only as shitty and only as good as anyone else and we don't have to go shoving them off cliffs every chance we get."

"And maybe you've been doing it too long," I said. "If you can't see that they're not people at all anymore—they're creatures, they're creatures who can do anything they want to anyone they want to do it to. There's never any way to put a check on them."

"We put a check on them," smiling for the first time since she'd heard the news. I should've stopped to enjoy it.

"We may slow them down, but we never stop them. We embarrass them a little, but we never stop them."

"Well we sure as fuck stopped one today." She wasn't smiling at that.

"I wish we did, I wish that was really us."

The wind was blowing her hair away from her face and I wondered if anyone could guess her age by it.

"What are you talking about?" She took out a smoke and we huddled around the flame of my lighter.

Watching her eyes past the coal of her cigarette, I said, "I wish we could pull a suicide out of them more often."

Her face didn't move. "There's a pudgy little corpse out there who might say we've only just started."

"Prince had been killing himself all his life, all we did was put out an advance. But think about actually causing a thing like that, if we could make them feel shame like actual humans feel shame—they'd have to stop doing the things they do, wouldn't they?"

"Lusting? Whoring? Bullying? Coveting? Has anyone ever stopped doing that?"

"Everyone else is made to answer for it. But if we could pull off a Kyle Prince every couple of months—think about it—they might start behaving the way everyone else has to. They think they're gods, Lane."

"You're forgetting entropy."

"I never forget entropy."

"They're never around for more than five years, Lee—be a good boy and let them fade away."

Her smoke blew back into her face and her eyes watered, still red around the edges. She sat down on the steps in the doorway of the bar, her elbows on her knees, rubbing her eyes with the balls of her hands.

"You know Kyle wasn't like anyone you're talking about. He was this pale, eager little guy who had dandruff—he could barely speak to a person without going off on some nervous rambling jag."

"He was an agent, Lane. Are you leaving that out on purpose?"

She flicked the butt of her cigarette in the Bloomberg. "He was just this chubby, sweaty little boy who got in trouble all the time."

"He was an agent, Lane, a movie star agent. And from what I've heard he could be pretty ferocious about it."

Looking down, she smiled. Her nose began to run and I wanted to wipe it for her. "We were in LA once and he bum-rushed a valet in front of the Ivy," she said, taking a wad of tissue from her pants pocket and blowing her nose. "But that freaking valet was such a goon. He just kept ignoring poor Kyle while he stood there trying to give him his keys; this bouncer-sized goon giving Kyle his shoulder and Kyle's head doesn't even come up to it—and with his whole party watching."

I sat on the step beneath hers, drew a circle on the toe of her boot with my fingertip. "I'm not defending the valets of Los Angeles."

"I just keep thinking about him alone there in some shitty little burnout apartment. You're talking about gods? What kind of a god is that?"

Her shoulders started in, shaking, and a choking sound came out of her mouth. Then there was a long sniff, her hands through her hair—she straightened up, looking down at me. I touched her hand and she did something no one had done to me in years: she grabbed me by the front of my jacket and pulled.

She pulled me and I twisted toward her on the step, faced her, my knees meeting the cement. I was kneeling in front of her—close enough to taste the liquor on her breath, her knuckles pressed against my chest and the stair hard under my knees, cold. I thought of all the things she might say.

"Look at me."

That was good enough, that was perfect.

"Okay," I said, sliding my hands behind my back.

"Did you mean what you said?"

I'd said a lot of things. I'd said that I would do whatever she wanted—that's all that was coming to me now, her eyes were bottomless.

I kept my mouth shut, waiting.

"Answer me. Did you mean what you said?"

"What do you want me to mean?"

She told me that she wanted the truth. Of all the things an adult might say, it was as silly as announcing that you wanted to be happy. We'd always taken it for granted that what we told each other was the truth, and now we were reduced to asking for it out loud. Now I was groveling for her in the afternoon and enjoying it, the toes of her boots touching my thighs—

What would the tourists think?

Lane bit her lip, letting me go, smoothed her hands down the front of my jacket.

"I'm sorry. I have no idea what I'm doing." I could have stayed there—I did stay there—tilting my head like a child as she fixed my collar. "I'm sorry. I'm drunk and I'm scared and . . . and I don't even know what I am."

"You're okay, Lane, you're okay."

Smiling, she patted my shoulder. Then I got up.

Slapping the dust from my jeans, I picked a bit of gravel off one of the knees, rolling it between my fingers.

"I still want an answer."

"I'm sorry—what was the question?"

"Pulling a Kyle Prince every once in a while—did you mean that at all? I know you're crazy, Lee, but it's usually good-crazy, but if . . . I mean, this other business."

"How's it go? Absolute power obstructs absolution?"

Crossing the street to the back entrance of our building, I could still feel the cement trembling against my kneecaps.

"You know, Leon, sometimes you make it very hard to be amused by you."

"Oh, you're not even trying. Look, all of this ends when you end it. Let it go, it'll fly right out."

"Every time I let it go I see a picture of poor fat Kyle Prince in my head, all alone—it's the middle of the night and he's all alone."

"He wasn't alone," I said. "Does that help?"

5

That Golden Feeling

"Why didn't you tell me?" she said. "Why didn't you tell anyone?"

We were still at the back entrance of our office building. I'd told her all about the madwoman, everything she'd said to me.

"I was waiting to see if Prince was really dead."

"You knew that as soon as Delores called the desk."

"I told Delores about the woman—why didn't he tell anyone?"

"How much did you tell him?"

"That a woman gave me a tip."

"What about the rest of it? She used your name, she *threatened* you—what did she say? She'd make you praise her? You shouldn't breathe? Did you consider mentioning that?"

"Not really," I said. "It didn't seem like anything Delores needed to know, and I was in a kind of a hurry."

"Well, how long were you planning to keep it to yourself?"

"When was I supposed to tell you? When you were crying?

Down there with the old man? I don't really need him spinning that yarn for the happy hour crowd, do I?"

"No, I guess you don't."

"I wasn't going to keep it from you, it wasn't anything like that."

"Okay, good. But aren't you going to tell anyone else? What about Robert?"

"Maybe Robert, but not the rest of them. I want to keep this to myself."

"What for?"

Back then, sometimes, when I was very drunk and not doing much of anything except trying to cook dinner, I used to laugh and cry all at the same time. Then I'd say out loud, "Oh God I'm confused." That's more or less what I told Lane, I said, "Ah fuck, Lane, I'm confused."

"You're confused?" she said. "What is that? What does that mean?"

I didn't know what it was, I didn't know what it meant.

"All I know is that she didn't call anyone else, she called me. You had to hear her—it's like she picked me out, like she chose me for something. That makes her my business—not the paper's business, not anyone's."

"What?" she said. "You think you're protecting a source?"

"That's what it feels like, yeah."

"There might be a few people upstairs right now who'd beg to differ."

"Look, I'm sure that asshole Delores and his fucking cops are already looking for her and there's probably a whole 'nother crew of reporters on it by now. Nothing she said to me is going to help them find her, so why shouldn't I keep it to myself?"

"Go tell them that."

"I don't owe them any answers. Hell, neither does she. She saw him dead, her boyfriend, she sounded like she saw him fucking do it too—do you know what that is? The way she sounded, it's like she still had it in her eyes. What do these people upstairs know about that? What do cops know about it?" I felt myself about to go too far, then I went there. "And what the fuck do you know about it?"

Lane started to say something, then closed her mouth and shook her head. She turned away from me and started walking. I caught up to her, apologized, said I was sorry as we showed our IDs to the body-armored Emergency Services Unit officers at the revolving doors. "Please, Lane, I didn't mean to—Lane, please, I'm sorry, I—"

"Just shut up!" she yelled. "Shut up! Shut up! Shut up!"

As far as our conversation went, that was that.

When we got into the newsroom, Kennedy told us we were wanted in the editor in chief's office.

"I'll go in first," Lane said. "I think Leon needs a little time-out."

"They want you both."

"I'll go in first," she said, turning her back to me and walking off.

Kennedy began to say something—I left him there with it.

Back at my desk, Harris said, "Well, this turned out to be quite a morning," and I nodded my head, holding on to the arms of my chair and measuring my breath.

Checking voicemail, there was nothing from her, nothing to say if anyone had found her yet, nothing even to say she was still alive.

"Get any calls about this?" Harris asked.

I shook my head no, the shake spreading down into my body. Harris told me to refer any press calls to the paper's publicist, his triangular eyes trying for a look of seriousness but falling immediately to the laugh that always lived behind them. His shoulders were as calmly squared as ever, his dark blond hair as neatly parted, and his perpetual pirate's smile still toasting all the world's rich variety. I was watching my hands go at it, clenched together, yellowish-pink in my lap, vibrating there like they were someone else's.

There'd been three messages reminding me about a lunch

date I was half an hour late for. That seemed like a better risk at the moment than the roomful of inquisitive people waiting for me at the other end of the newsroom.

On my way past the city desk, Kennedy called out, "Didn't we just go over that the Editor wants to see you?"

"Call my cell when they're done with Lane," I said. I was interested to know who would answer it.

Of course I never made it to the elevator. I turned around, went back to my desk, waited my turn. Since starting at the paper I'd worked under three different editors in chief. Until that day, the latest of them hadn't had occasion to haul me into the office, but there was little reason to expect that this one's employee relations technique would deviate from what Corporate indoctrinated all its upper operatives with—namely a lot of red-nosed yowling about *Our Brand* punctuated here and there with "Are you just stupid?"

Gazing at my monitor, I started to think about it, waiting for it, and ground an ache into the hinge of my jaw.

It wouldn't be just the Editor in there, but the whole management crew, the whole Tasmanian Landing Party, and I'd have to sit there and take it. It meant all the old trouble—the sweaty little palms, the little kid palms, little kid eyes and little kid throat, throbbing, hot, wanting to close themselves. All the old bursts of light, the yellows and reds, the black spots in between, opening up on a forever of nothing.

It had been a long time since I'd seen those spots, the gaping wormholes that used to suck me out of the real world when it got too scary to live in. Everyone I'd loved had gone through those holes, and a lot of them had ended up staying there. We were all very young then and people had done what they wanted with us. Anyway, I'd never be that young again.

Lane came back without a word for me and it was time. I walked the length of the newsroom, my pulse making ocean sounds in my ears, now and then looking over at the cubicles to my left to see someone eyeing me from behind a monitor. I thought I'd get into that glass-walled corner office, flip the silly mahogany desk onto someone's legs and let them shout about that–let everyone watch that, let them talk about that.

A wad of paper bounced off the side of my head.

Em crossed her eyes at me from the copier, showing me her perfect, crooked teeth. I felt the tick of a smile coming on, the heat seeping away from me.

They were arranged around the desk, the Editor at center with the lesser elders fanned out in chairs to either side like some kind of tribunal–the editorial director, the managing editor, the features editor, the Sunday editor and the photo editor, all of whom had been slipped quietly into position over the last couple of years. A major American newspaper run by a group of transplants from the South Pacific–at least, we often said, they weren't British.

I sat directly opposite the Editor, eye to eye across the mahogany sea. What annoyed me most about that desk just then was that it was hiding her legs–they were magnificent. I was trying to catch a glimpse of ankle when she started in with, "Right. Tell me everything you know about this anonymous woman of yours."

"Right," I said, snapping to. "I don't know anything."

The skin on her face was dull and it sagged darkening beneath her eyes–the wages of her first New York winter. When we'd locked our dark tired eyes an instant too long I looked away, to one of the others, who spoke right up.

"No," he said. "This woman didn't call you, say, 'Here's something you might not know,' and hang up. It doesn't fit. It isn't logical."

Like so many editors, he clearly hadn't worked a reporter's phone since college, if ever. In any case, he was fishing–Lane hadn't given them anything to fuck me with.

"She didn't sound very logical," I told the Editor. "She sounded stoned out of her bird, she mumbled and slurred everything. I could hardly make out a thing she was saying."

"It sounds like you made out well enough," she said. Her shoulders shifted as she crossed her legs beneath the desk—I could hear the fabric of her stockings sigh against itself. "You knew Prince cut his wrists. You knew where he lived."

"That's all she said, that he cut his wrists. And I know where a lot of people live."

Her eyes tightened. "And of course you got none of this on tape."

"She was done talking before I could even hit the button, before I really even knew what she was talking about."

The Editor leaned forward. Her eyes were the kind that had always given me the most trouble—black with a living shine but no quiver, no doubting tremor of hesitation. She was good at it, better than I was, but I had a strong defense against the truth-seeking stares of most women: pure, warm-blooded submission.

I opened my face to her, tilting my chin down and letting my eyes go wide and empty. You had to think true things and let them out through your eyes, you had to be a child, your eyes pouting with terror and hope. They never knew exactly what I was thinking, but they always looked away. That expression was my best impersonation of being in love.

When the Editor dropped her eyes, my mind was still enjoying itself, playing games beneath that big black desk.

"From now on," the photo editor spoke up, "I'd say it would be a good idea to hit record as soon as your telephone rings. Do you agree?"

"Absolutely."

"And whatever else you find out about this," said another one, "you'll bring it to us directly—no more furtive arrangements with your friend at the Cop Shack."

"Delores? He's not exactly a friend."

"We know," the Editor said with a smirk. "I fired him an hour ago."

Nodding quietly at the threat, I drew a breath into my stomach and said, "That so?"

"I had him in to chat about a certain hole in the story he filed, and when he couldn't explain it, I suppose I went off on a bit of a whinge."

"That certain hole would be—"

"If a man dies in his flat and no one's there to see it, how does a cop reporter find out before the bloody cops?"

Delores, she explained, had actually written the line "Police discovered the body of . . ." Sounds reasonable enough until you consider the police discovering a corpse snug in its own apartment that hadn't been a corpse long enough to stink or be reported missing.

"Well," she went on, "after Delores tried out several piss-poor excuses, he finally decided to let me in on this mysterious caller of yours."

"Hey, look," I said, "I told him all I knew about her. I haven't seen what he filed but I didn't have any reason to think he'd leave her out of it."

"I didn't fire him for leaving her out. That there may have been someone else in the room is certainly worth noting, but obviously the real *get* is, who was she? What did she see? All the nasty little details of those last desperate hours. I wouldn't blame a reporter for wanting to find that on their own—no one wants to share a byline. I didn't even fire him for lying to me about it."

"Then why'd you fire him?"

"I fired him," dazzling me with the shine of her eyes, "for telling the truth."

"Excuse me?"

"The man broke like a *sweat*. Cracking after a little five-minute chat—I mean, that really is pathetic."

And it was good politics, too—killing off a dinosaur every now and then who'd had too fat a contract and too much pride—but that wasn't any of my business.

"Duly noted," I said, "duly noted," and I may even have bowed my head.

6

Treatle's Case

Meredith Fields was malice in thousand-dollar shoes. She was also my most valuable account. I'd inherited her from Lane when Lane had decided that Meredith's information wasn't worth the cost to her spirit anymore. Me, I had no problem with people like Meredith—provided they showed a certain enthusiasm, looked a certain way, and were female.

Despite what people believed and what was printed in the papers, Meredith didn't officially represent a single celebrity. What she represented were the nightclubs and the restaurants where they played and the products they endorsed. Using that proximity, Meredith would befriend the famous, insinuating herself into their lives until she became their de facto publicist. There were no contracts, no confidentiality agreements—with Meredith, it was all about friendship.

She amazed these friends with her ability to keep people like me from writing gleefully mean-spirited stories about them when they got into trouble. She amazed people like me with her ability to keep feeding us sweaty reports from her friends' bedrooms without getting caught.

The only pay she needed for all that good work was power. Besides, stealing money from nightclubs and corporations was easier on her accountants than stealing it from individuals.

Meredith was the lunch date I'd blown off for the Editor's little chat. When I'd gotten back to my desk, Harris had already written most of the column for the next day and Lane was taking press calls as a friend of herself. That is, reporters would call for her reaction to the Prince suicide and instead of referring them to our PR man, she'd say, "I'm having a pretty fuck-all bad day." Tomorrow her quote would show up in the other papers as, " 'She's having a pretty bad day,' says a friend of Martin."

That she was ignoring August's advice (and the Editor's order) to keep her mouth shut wasn't unusual—we were gossips. Anyway, no one was asking my opinion—no one was asking me much of anything—so I called Meredith and asked if she was still hungry.

"Oh my God!" she said. "I'm starving!"

Lunch was in the front room of a restaurant on East Fifty-fifth Street. It was past two, so there wasn't much to look at. Meredith had her own table, but the only person sitting at it was a pretty teenager who looked vaguely familiar, sporting an *Outlandos D'Amour* T-shirt, olive clam-diggers and blue suede clogs. I figured him for one of the toons from her office and went to the bar. When Meredith came in she told me who the kid was.

"Well," I said, "this'll be pleasant."

"He's what I wanted to talk to you about in the first place, stupid." Her blue-streaked black bob swished above her eyes as she shook her head at me, saying, "My God."

"What about him?"

"Oh I love you, you idiot—you never know what's going on. You're going to fix his career."

"Am I?"

"Oh, you are," taking my wrist and patting the top of my hand, her rings sending cold into my skin. "Now let's see you act like a grown-up and behave." She tightened her grip on my wrist—nails sharp against tendon and vein—and led me into the room.

Meredith had a preternatural talent for leading people where she wanted them. As soon as I'd started working with her, I realized that she regarded everyone around her as nothing more than aspects of her own imagination. It was a quality I'd been attracted to—until I'd been alone with it at night. That it turned her on to pitch stories to my competition while I went down on her was the sort of thing I'd expected. That she would immediately pitch to me what the competition had just rejected was something else.

When I'd suggested the separation of business and pleasure, Meredith shrugged, saying, "Don't pretend you don't know me."

The kid at her table got to his feet quickly enough when Meredith introduced us, but his handshake suggested that he would rather not have bothered with the ritual.

"Billy," he said, "Billy Treatle," his tone over-casual and his eyes on something just above my ear—a toon's move, a plus-one's way of showing you that he could just as well have been invited to the party in his own right.

Nodding, I said, "Great," and dropped his hand.

"So you guys had a little drama today, huh?" Meredith said. "Anyone getting fired?"

"Of course not—we're the story of the week, raises for all." She didn't seem to know if I was kidding or not, and I didn't seem to want to help her figure it out.

"You're not freaking out?"

"You know the saying—we get action."

She watched me for a moment, not changing her face. Then

she started to laugh, pointed a fingernail at her clear brown eyes and said, "Oh my God, I'm crying!"

"You know," Treatle said, "no offense and all, but it's, it really is sad. If you think about it, it's just so really sad." He dragged out that last *sad* until it might have meant something, his eyes watching it come out of his mouth and float away somewhere in a bored gaze. "This whole business is so sad."

"You were friends with Kyle?"

"Who?" he asked, zapping back to the living.

"The dead man."

"Oh . . . Oh. Well, I mean, not close or anything. But just, if anyone can do that, I mean, kill themselves? If anyone feels that way—anywhere—it just kind of kills me. I could never do what you people do."

"Have a little more faith in yourself," I said. "You've already proven you're capable of some pretty astounding things."

He gave me a smile that no one had told his eyes about. "Oh," he said, "that."

Billy Treatle had just started to get a name after four months as an editorial assistant on one of the better weeklies when he'd been fired. It'd been a cush job, writing up quotes and descriptions to wrap around a page of party photos every week. His caption copy wasn't just bits of snark; some people said it neared poetry, and some other people started to notice. That's how he got caught.

When he'd described Toni Cazdraeder's "perfect counterfeit of ease" at the launch of her handbag collection and readers pointed out the line as Fitzgerald's, Treatle's editors chalked it up to subconscious cannibalism—he was, after all, fresh out of NYU. They let him off with the same excuse when the color of Maria Shockley's dress at the premiere of *Kabala Blues* was Amis's "the blue of sex or sadness." A week later, attendees' faces at the Starlight Children's Foundation gala were "streaked with light and full of pity," as were the drive-in movie angels in *Jesus' Son*, but Treatle's employers still didn't see a need for any immediate action.

If Treatle had stuck to biting off morsels of undergrad lit, there's little reason to believe that anyone would ever have bothered about him. In the debate that followed his dismissal, one of his former editors—a woman who'd come to New York directly from the London *Mirror*—commented on a media blog, "The poets of ancient Greece and Rome borrowed phraseology from one another like so many cups of sugar. I dare suggest, if it was good enough for them . . ."

It was Treatle's switching to more recent fare that got his ass tossed curbwise. Complaints started coming in from journalists who thought a line or two of Treatle's more than closely resembled something they'd published just a month or so before. Treatle seemed to have had a particularly sweet tooth for "Sunday Styles."

In Treatle's defense, all reporters everywhere sound pretty much the same. But the magazine he worked for couldn't contend with the bad press his accusers were starting to generate for it, not to mention a blogger at Hunter College who'd taken to googling Treatle's copy every week to see what it matched up with.

As far as Treatle went, that was that.

He was twenty-two but looked seventeen if you didn't look too closely—a bit awkward in the face, like the features were still growing into their adult form, not a hard angle or crease anywhere and every feature equidistant from the others, eyes and lips enormous, in full bloom. He had a long, jangling body, somewhat less feminine than it was masculine, the muscles in his forearms and calves apparent but not blatant, still smooth, just hinting—his outfit showed them off.

We were somewhere in the middle of his story when the waiter brought our food. I asked for a Red Label on the rocks. Two minutes later, I asked for another one. I had a rule against drinking during the day, but it was that kind of story.

"But it could also work as a screenplay," he was saying. "I don't know, you can get all suede with a screenplay and, like, beautiful, putting your passion into visuals, but it's not enough—I don't know—it's not enough . . . *you*."

There's no joy in life that can outrun being a well-employed alcoholic catching a buzz in broad daylight. I felt the anesthetic seeping numb into my lungs, the warmth spreading out through my chest and into my arms, calm down to my fingertips.

"Oh, yes," I said. "Absolutely."

Meredith was munching a French fry and Treatle was saying, "It's your passion. It's your, you know, pain and blood—like your blood itself is suffering, like blood-suffering, down in you, down in the *down* of you . . ."

"Mare," I said, "did you do something to your face? You look so pretty."

"Got my cheeks out. I decided I'd go natural—do you like?"

"Oh I love."

"That's so sweet," sipping at her Bloody Mary. She smiled at me around the stirrer, Treatle's face going side to side between us. "But Billy's talking to you, so don't be rude."

"Sorry. Go on, Billy."

"Well, so the problem I have is, if you put it in a screenplay and then there's no *you* in it . . . I mean, like *I*. Like there's not any *I* in it."

I said, "Eek-eek-eek."

"What?"

"Monkey talk."

"Leon."

"Shh!"

"Did I just get shushed?"

"Never! Waiter?"

He brought another and I sucked the top of it into my empty stomach, cubes clicking against the fronts of my teeth.

With Meredith's encouragement, Treatle continued to speak, his hairstyle—a shiny blond exercise in radical geometry that I'll describe some time when I can make a day of it—bouncing in the corner of my eye through an easy golden mist. I slid down in my seat to see Meredith's legs under the table. They ended in pointy white mules and I shook my head at them. When I looked back up she was eyeing me across the bread basket.

"Okay, so, a memoir," he went on, "would easily bring in, you know, the whole talk show circuit thing and I'd get, at least—there's the consultation thing when they do the pic, but that whole business is so . . ." touching the front of the hairstyle with the backs of two fingers, "artificial. I mean, do I really want to expose *art* to that?"

"You'd better not," I said.

Under the table, Meredith had her mules off and was pointing her toes at me—ten neat, purple nails. Above the table, she was sucking Bloody Mary from a celery stalk and giving me a look: be nice.

The waiter brought another.

"Dude," Billy Treatle said.

"Yes?"

"You really like to drink that much?"

"Billy," Meredith said.

"Do I ever!"

"No, don't get me wrong, I understand. I get like that too, like you want to just drink until, I don't know, until you get that, like, like—that click."

"That's *Cat on a Hot Tin Roof,* Billy."

"I know, I know—I just mean it's kind of sad." His eyes bunched a little, and I couldn't tell if he was about to smile or cry. "This whole business, what it does to people."

"I think people do what they want to themselves," I said. "And I think that there's no such thing as a good motive, but if you've got one you'd better get to telling it because I can't keep drinking like this."

Something happened to his face, the perfectly taut skin suddenly going slack around the overly symmetrical eyes and the eyes clicking side to side as if he'd gone REM without shutting his lids. Then he fixed his gaze on a spot in the ceiling. The look was concentrated and imbecilic at the same time, like he was trying to identify a thing he'd never seen before by staring at it harder, boring into some bit of fine-printed code that would never reveal itself to him.

"No one here," he said, looking at me again, his eye skin tightening back into place, "no one here ever stops to appreciate, like, beauty. You don't know, no one here ever stops to think about it, about how much beauty there is in the world. And there was beauty in what I did."

"What did you do?" bracing myself for the answer—because he'd have one.

"I was trying to teach people about how phony all this is, like an experiment. You take these parties everyone cares about so much that no one'll ever remember and you mix them with all these great *words* that live forever. Then, then when they notice you, what you did, it's this whole other game. And you know what in the end happens?"

I shook my head, tired and anxious for any part of the rest of the day to make this part stop happening.

"Remember a second ago? When I said no one stopped to appreciate it? But think about it. They're talking about me. A few months ago nobody knew my name and look where I am now."

"People know your name because you stole from them, Billy."

"I didn't steal from anyone, not really. They were influences, you have to have influences. It was just some of their words—like part of my style. Most of it was mine, all of it really. In ancient Greece, in Rome, the poets—"

"Yes, I know."

"Stop it, Leon." Meredith had only the vaguest suggestion of eyebrows, but what she had was pushing a V between her eyes. "Let him finish."

Treatle's hands wrapped themselves around an invisible neck in front of him on the table, eyes centered hard on the face above it. "People need to get it," he said. "They need to think about it. I made them talk about me, they know my name, but they need to know my story—how it's just so stupid and all, being famous, how it doesn't mean anything. I can show them how it doesn't."

The thing in his hands was dead now, so he let it drop, spreading his fingers around his plate.

"And of course you have to get famous to do that."

"Yeah," he said to his spot in the ceiling, the backs of two fingers returning to his hair. "That's the only way it can work."

"Isn't it brilliant?" Meredith said, her voice flat and her face daring me to say anything but yes.

"Sure," I said. "But I can think of something else that'll work."

"Yeah?" Treatle said.

"Yeah. You can go home. You can go back to school or get a job and you can grow up for five minutes. This isn't the place for your learning experiment."

Nothing budged in his eyes as the dead grin slit his face and he leaned close to me.

"Listen," he said, "are you going to work with me or not?"

I turned away from him and, without thinking, took a bite from the untouched hamburger in front of me. Truffles, short rib, caviar, and gold flake oozed onto my plate from inside the burger. Managing to choke the bite down, I stepped lively to the men's room and let it back out with the truest possible urgency.

7

A Hard Bargain

*L*ight-headed, face tingling, but not anything you could really call drunk, I came back from the bathroom and found Meredith alone at the bar, drinking another Bloody Mary. I ordered a scotch and sat next to her.

"I sent Billy home," she said. "There was no sense putting him through any more of that."

"If you want another just like him, wait here and I'll fetch you one."

"You didn't even give him a chance. You didn't listen."

"I heard what was coming out of his mouth," I said. "Look, where's the money in this? That kid can't do anything for you."

"Not everything is business, Leon."

I had never heard her express even a remote approximation of that sentiment—I had never heard her express a sentiment. I watched her face a moment; she lowered her eyes.

"Oh for fuck's sake, Meredith! Are you fucking kidding me?"

"He's young, Leon, he's still trying to figure out what he did—

why he did. But I honestly believe he didn't mean to do anything wrong."

"You *honestly believe* things now?"

Her eyes clicked on mine and I watched the hate behind them, the thing that always made them seem so close together.

"Is that what you think of me?"

"You don't care what I think of you." In the silence I sipped my drink until Meredith was beautiful again, and hurt. I wanted to make it better, to say I was sorry and that she was beautiful, but I shook it off, telling her, "Stop fucking with me."

She stared ahead of herself, into the blinking white lights of the back bar, holding something down.

"I am not fucking with you, Leon." She turned her face to me. "Just let us keep this professional. I want a favor. You don't owe me any?"

"You, sure. But not your little friend."

"Then you can do it on my behalf."

"At my expense," I said.

"What?"

"I've written lies for you before, but this one bothers me."

"You're *bothered*, Leon? Since when do you care what you put on that page?"

"Since when do you fall in love?"

I wished that I could put that back in my mouth, but it hadn't seemed to come from there. The sensation was of things changing and closing in, all of them much too fast. I'd felt it first with the madwoman, then Lane, now Meredith. None of it felt like doing business. I needed to focus on something clinical, something I was sure of—and I was sure that I hated Billy Treatle.

"You want me to put it out there that agents are tearing their throats out trying to sign this kid and the story of his beautiful, tortured vacation in medialand, right?"

"Why not?" she said. "It's happened before. My God, it seems like it happens every day."

"I've got nothing to do with that. I can't stop these people from happening, but I don't have to help them."

"What a noble boy you suddenly are." I didn't say anything, thinking of what to say. "He's not like those other people. I'm telling you—he's different, inside."

"Down in the down of him? In his blood-suffering?"

"He's just trying to find a way of putting things."

"It's no wonder he had to find other people's ways of putting them."

"The reason he did it is what's different—what matters. You know me, Leon, you know I'm a good judge of character."

She was tapping her fingernail against the side of her glass, counting down the dare.

"Look," I said. "We don't get good characters to judge. We don't deal with good people and I've never known you to have your head up your ass about that. You know who we deal with, what we do, and you've never kidded yourself about it. We both know that we've launched some very fucked-up people together—I know that, I don't mind it—hell, it's been fun. But there's too much about this one that I don't like."

"I don't care if you like him."

"You wouldn't like him either if you weren't thinking with your body."

She held her drink under her chin, a tremble running through the rim of the glass.

"He's ambitious," she said. "I'll give you that, but it's only be-cause he has so much enthusiasm. Didn't you feel that way when you were his age?"

"It's a pedophile's enthusiasm, Meredith—people like him are the same age all their lives. Their lies get better and the pathology stays the same."

"I should've planned on you being like this. You hate every-thing and you think it makes you cool," she said, looking down at the napkin and twirling one corner into a point. "I know what that's about." A blush seeped into her cheeks. "But maybe I don't always want to be cool, maybe I don't want to be cool at all anymore. It's true what Billy said—no one here ever stops to see the beauty in anything."

"That's a crock of shit and you're smart enough to know it. If a fat lady in Birkenstocks said it instead of some pretty child with a pretty mouth you'd laugh in her face."

An itch broke out in my forearms and I started to sweat, trying to think my way through the anger. When I felt the fear underneath it, I backed my mind away and the room seemed to darken. Meredith touched her chin to her chest, took a breath and sat up straight, the blood cooling away from her cheeks.

"Don't tell me what I think," she said. "Don't do it again."

"Then we'd better change the subject."

"No, I think I'll just leave."

"I'm sorry," I said. "Just wait a second—please, I'm sorry." She put her purse under her arm and her watch slid down her wrist—I touched the warm imprint the band left in her skin. "I need to ask you about something. Please?"

She nodded, guarding her chest with her purse, and sat back down.

Over another drink I told her all about the madwoman, the sound of her voice, the blades rolling under her laugh. I asked Meredith to help me find her.

"Gee," she smiled. "And you think Billy's got problems?"

"We don't know what this woman's problems are."

"I wasn't talking about her."

"All we know is that she somehow found out about Kyle Prince killing himself before any of us did and that she sounded like it'd hit her pretty badly. Everything else is a guess. I think what she said was true but I can't be sure about that. I just need to find out who she is."

"Why?"

I didn't know. There was something there, in the madwoman's voice, but I couldn't get close enough to it.

"The whole paper's all over her," I said. "The cops'll be too. I want to find her before they do."

"I know that. That isn't what I asked you—I asked you why. Don't make me ask you again. You know how I get when you lie to me."

That, I knew—like I knew how she got if I stared at her knees when she wanted an answer. I said, "I feel, I don't know, responsible for her."

"You're responsible for a lot of things, Leon. Why does this girl you don't even know get such special treatment?"

I kept my mouth shut, lowering my head and gazing up into the hate behind her face. It could've been a minute we stayed that way, trading up in the silence, it could've been seconds—I don't know.

"What's going on in that funny brain of yours?" she said. "That you're going to help her? Is it fantasy time in there? You think you're going rescue her from something?"

I waited, trying to find something else to say. There wasn't anything else.

"That's how it feels, yeah."

"Then God help her," turning away and finishing her drink.

"Please, Meredith, I just want to know who she is. Someone out there's got to know who she is. Two people can't have something without someone else finding out about it, it can't happen that way—people talk, they can't help it."

"Some people can help it," she said, looking at my glass.

"No one we know."

"What if she's not someone we know? Maybe she just wants to be left alone."

"Then she wouldn't have called me."

"Maybe she regrets that now."

I picked up my drink, put it down again without taking a sip. Meredith was watching the lights of the back bar.

"You know who she is."

"Keep your voice down," she said, her eyes dead ahead of her. "I don't know who she is, but I know what it's like when something falls apart on you. People do stupid things and then they regret them."

The bartender took her glass away and she waved him off when he went to pour her another. She crossed her legs, I watched the shadow shift in the muscle of her calf.

"People have a couple of drinks and forget what really happened," I said. "You never even liked me."

"I told you not to tell me what I think. Were you born knowing everything everyone thinks or did someone have to fill you in?"

"Meredith."

"Fuck you," she said getting up. "Fuck you and fuck me and fuck everyone." I sat still, taking it. "I'll find your crazy girl for you, I can do that—I know everyone, don't I? I'll find your girl and you'll give my boy his stupid little item and everything will be nice and clean between us."

She was opening her purse, throwing money out of it.

"No," I said. "Treatle doesn't get that item. Trade me something else."

"I don't have anything else!" The room turned to see her. She winced away from all the stares and breathed herself calm again, leaning close to my ear. "I'll ask around, I'll get her for you, and then you will write exactly what I tell you to write for Billy. That's the deal."

I knew better than to make deals when I'd been drinking, like I knew better than to drink during the day.

"Okay," I said. "But he gets nothing before you find her, not a fucking word."

"Fine."

The soles of her feet made pink flashes at me as she clicked away on her mules, and I wondered which one of us was kidding ourself about what we'd been to each other. It had started so easy, just another part of doing business, and it had ended that way. I wondered which one of our minds was more likely to be changing things around after the fact, or if we were pretty much the same that way, and why it had suddenly started to matter.

As I left, the manager came over and handed me an envelope, saying, "So long as you're here."

That envelope would keep his place in sightings for another month. I don't know how other gossip columnists make ends meet—we don't even have a union.

8

Cleopatra'ed Out

On the way back to the office I bought a new cell phone hooked up with the number of the one I'd lost the night before. Soon as it powered, an ad for the Brazilian bar across the street from where I was standing filled the screen, announcing happy hour specials. I clicked away the ad and it was replaced by another for the remake of *Antony and Cleopatra*, and I thought of Gary Pornell and the wedding chase I'd sent him on.

When I managed to get into voicemail I deleted most of it—Charlie Gaines, who had my position at the other paper, asking if I was at the party we'd both been at when he'd called, various publicists telling me who was drinking at the spots they repped, the city desk wanting to know if an actress I'd never heard of was at an event I hadn't been to.

There were two voicemails that I didn't trash—one from Em wanting to settle a bet with her roommate at 1:56 in the morning. The other had been left at 4:17.

It started with a breath. There was traffic behind it, far away, the whine of brakes and a horn. The coal of a cigarette sizzled through tobacco paper and I could hear smoke being blown past a receiver.

"You made me smoke," she said, her voice smooth, even. "You're making me smoke." She took another drag, a long one. "You can't do this, I won't let you," her tone hardening, the words speeding up to match it.

"You should be here, you should see what you made him do, you should have to look at it! You won't do it to me, I won't let you change my mind—you won't!"

Her breath shivered in my ear, then her voice went calm again.

"There's always the choice," she said. "It only takes a second to change your mind, but you always have the choice. You can't take it away from me, no one can take it away." After another pause, there was that sound that had been murmuring through the dome of my skull all day, that seething pulse with a laugh rolling over it. "You think you can make me change my mind, Sunshine? Maybe I'll make you change yours first."

It felt like every cell in my skin was opening up, sending and receiving some psychic hum. I tried to shut it down, focusing on the words.

The rest of the call was harder to make out. She'd started whispering—to herself, it sounded like—the same thing over and over, a chant. At first I thought she was telling herself to breathe, then I thought she was saying, "Please, please, please . . ." I had to play it back four or five times to get what it was.

"Breeze," she was saying. "Breeze . . . breeze . . . breeze . . ."

I called my office voicemail—nothing from her. Listening to her message on the cell again, trying to find clues, I felt stupid—and scared, overwhelmed. She's standing there in the middle of the night over a man's carcass, a pool of black, and she's thinking about me.

I had the aching sense that she and a lot of other things would stop being anonymous any second now—and that I wasn't even close to being ready for it. Hell, I might've given her the number myself some night, looked right into her face and said—*what?*

I'd always tried to keep my mouth shut about myself, stick to other people's secrets, but the end of the crawl was always a truth-telling contest, an AA meeting with free booze, all I could stand and all that I couldn't. Secrets can bond people together at certain times and certain places, but at that time, in that place, a secret was worth what it could be traded for.

My throat went hot as I felt my mind leaning over the precipice of a thousand forgotten crawls, all those nights, all the people I could've pissed off—wondering if the woman had asked one of them for my number, just last night, and if she'd told them why.

The thing now was to stop, hole up at the bar, have another bracer, work out what I had so far—small problem being that I didn't know what I had, and fuck me if I had any idea how to "work out" any part of it. I didn't even know what that meant.

I may have been drunker than I'd let on to myself.

Still, though, for the nerves . . .

The old blind guy with the knotty black hair was taking up a corner of the bar across from the office when I went in, so I went back out again and sat on the steps by the Bloomberg.

Lighting a cigarette, all I could conclude about the situation was that I didn't belong in it. Before starting that beat, I'd never known the rich, never known what they cared about or imagined that they cared about anything. Manhattan had always been just a dull blue battleship across the East River, twenty minutes away and never worth the trip. Even after six years of being right in its business, I was still sitting on its doorstep, watching it dumbly from the abandoned warehouses on the wrong shore.

But there was something between that woman and me—a

feeling that the job had never stirred in me before. I didn't know who she was, but I knew her. She was terrified, alone in the dark. She felt like home.

I used to believe there was a house for people like us, all of us, on a mountain somewhere. Sometimes I still thought it was up to me to build it.

The sky was flat gray with no end to it and the wind was strong but moister than winter air and I could already smell something sweet in it, new leaves, the two rivers warming up, things waking back into life.

Breeze ... breeze ...

Someone would quote *The Waste Land* at Kyle Prince's funeral. Whoever spoke after that would have to wing it.

◇   ◇   ◇

The ESU cops mulled in front of the building, MP5s slung across their chests. I showed one of them my ID and went in.

"*Yojimbo,*" I told Em in the newsroom.

"Excuse me?" she asked, not looking away from her monitor.

"Your bet last night—I just got your message."

"Just now?"

"I'd lost my cell phone."

"Oh, yeah—you were ignoring me."

"At two in the morning, angel?"

"Anyway, you're wrong," she said, clicking away with her mouse. "It was *Red Harvest.*"

"Well," I said, going behind her and checking out her screen. She was scrolling through pictures in Merlin, the paper's photo archive program. All the shots were of Jezika and Matt Block. "How's Gary doing with that wedding story?"

"He found out they're in town and he's feeling pretty darned spiffy about himself."

"Of course they're in town, they're going to that premiere tonight, that Cleopatra thing. Block's got a soft spot for sandal epics."

"And women's sandals," Em said, turning around with her wriggling smile. "You could've told—" Her face changed. "Gosh, what happened to you?"

My shirt was soaked through from the pits to the bottom of my chest. I put my jacket back on. "Little bit of a rough afternoon," I said. "Are you coming out with me tonight?"

"Could be. Where do you want to take me?"

"You want to try that Cleopatra thing? I'm sure it's a holy piece of shit but we can skip it for the after-party."

"But I want to see that movie."

"It's no good seeing a movie at the premiere, Em—everyone's watching each other."

"Not when the lights go off. And I've never been to one."

"Do you know how long it's been since I sat through a movie in a theater?"

"Two years. You told me." She crossed her legs and folded her hands on her knee, eyes wide and steady—her patience pose. "I think it's about time for you."

"Ah, fuck," I said. "Okay."

"Am I dressed all right?"

I flashed to see her in the Cleopatra pose, stretched out on a funerary couch, on her side, a golden sheath drifting away from her thighs, firelight along her skin, playing in the amber bands of her irises, eyelids traced thick with kohl . . .

"You're beautiful, they'll be dying for you."

"Yay-rah," giving a sarcastic little cheer with her fist. "Sure you're okay?"

"Please."

"How did it go in there?" she asked, tilting her head toward the Editor's office as one bright incisor dented her lower lip.

"That? Just the usual yellow discipline, a little whinge—no trouble at all."

Back at my desk, Harris told me he'd sent Lane home for the day. "Are you looking for something to do?"

"I thought I'd try to figure out who this woman is that called. Prince's girl."

"How do you intend to do that?"

"I have no idea."

"Oh boy, oh boy," he muttered, his default response to all trouble. "Go through the pictures," he said. "If Prince had a girlfriend one of our guys got a shot of them together."

"What makes you say that?"

"These people gotta *eat!*"

I logged in to Merlin and queried "Kyle Prince." A scrolling grid of thirty-two thumbnails popped up. Ignoring the shots of Prince alone or with other men, it still felt about as hopeful as getting a list of every woman he'd ever known and trying to find out where they'd been last night. But anything beat the wait, anything that cut through that frozen nightmare feel of someone coming after me.

I said, "You too, huh?" clicking open a shot of Prince with Dani Mouchar on the red carpet for *Brown-Eyed Girl*, a movie about a woman who rapes men that was some director's homage to the Michael Douglas canon. Mouchar's publicist was Linda Klier at PMK-HBH, one of Lane's accounts, who always seemed to resent it when I called. I told her that Mouchar had been seen late last night at a bad Italian place on West Ninth that was popular that season, sucking on the thumb of Simi Chase, who was that season's girl.

"You heard what?" she said.

"What, I have to say it twice for you now?"

"I thought Simi was in rehab."

"Everyone always thinks that. Care to comment?"

"I think, um . . . Is Lane there?"

"Nope."

You could tell Linda was torn—Mouchar hadn't made anyone's page in months. Eventually, she admitted, "Dani's shooting in Greece."

"A Cleopatra flick?"

"Nefertiti."

"Thanks for playing."

The publicist Claire Nussbaum was pushing sixty with both hands and feet, but the team that maintained her kept her alluring in an aggressively feline sort of way, not to mention that she was a poisonous bitch—some men go for that. There she was on Prince's lap with her heels digging air at a Grammy after-party.

"What," she said, "you do publicist sightings now?"

Her voice wasn't giving anything but annoyance, but that didn't count her out. I hadn't heard enough of the woman I was looking for to know what she'd sound like in normal conversation—this being normal.

"Well," I said, "when I hear that you flung a Manolo Blahnik at a bouncer's head at Resort last night, I think it's worth a little more than just a sighting."

"Didn't you little monsters have enough fun killing that poor Kyle Prince today?"

"Don't say things you'll regret, Claire."

"I've grown incapable of regret," she laughed. "But let's you get one thing straight—I don't wear Manolo Blahniks. And if you ever find me at Resort, my God, I pray you'll leave me there."

"My source is pretty sure it was you."

She laughed again and a shiver slid through my chest. It could've been the madwoman's sharp, trilling cackle. But it could've been anyone's. How do you mark the laughter of strangers?

"Well," she said, "if your source is pretty sure then I'm pretty sure you're going to write whatever on earth you want to write. Now just you hurry up and write it, little one—it sounds marvelous."

Nussbaum was still laughing when she hung up on me. I wrote her name on a legal pad, thinking, *little one* and *Sunshine*.

Cintra Bale had one arm around Prince and the other around Trina Tam at a gallery opening in Malibu two years back. Everyone knew that Bale was pulling a pilgrimage in Tibet—it was her turn. Tam's rep was Linda Klier.

"Jesus Christ," she said. "Did someone put me on a list?"

"Some people are born lucky," I told her, and she assured me that her client couldn't have thrown up on a bouncer at Okay-Shiny last night because she was in Toronto being scanned for a CGI role.

"Why do I get the feeling you're taking potshots today?"

"Why do you want me to tell you why you feel things?"

The further you scrolled down through the grid, the more recent the photos became. There was one from last summer of Jennifer Morales and Prince on opposite sides of a silvery horse at an East Hampton polo match that had preceded a charity screening of *White Monkey*. Beneath the animal's neck, Prince's hand rested on Morales' bare shoulder and nothing in her face suggested that she noticed.

"She's unavailable," Kevin Rose told me. Like Claire Nussbaum, Rose had been doing it since they were called "press agents." Like Nussbaum, he didn't fuck around.

"How long has she been unavailable?"

"I know you think I'm some crazy old piece of shit," he said, "but if I tell you the truth and you tell me you'll go easy on her, will I be reading tomorrow about her courageous recovery or will I be waking up with your fucking prick in my ass?"

"I'm not going to write a word," I said. "It's part of something else that I'm not going to tell you about."

"I must be right out of my fucking nut, talking to you. She's been there a week and a half, since last Sunday."

"Voluntary?"

"If it was court-ordered you'd've heard about it."

"I mean, could she walk out if she wanted to?"

"Sure she can. If she wants my shoe up her cunt."

"Okay," I said, moving away from it. "In-state?"

"Sure. Do you think for a minute I'd have her at some fucking cunt-ass West Coast holiday spa? That's strictly for the cocksuckers and we know this. The girl gets clean or she dies trying. Besides," he added, "she has family here."

"Thanks," I said, adding Jennifer Morales to the list.

Half an hour later I'd found two more women Prince had been photographed with and who couldn't be placed out of town when he'd killed himself. There was the artist Vivian Hunter, whose studio manager was pretty sure she hadn't broken a champagne flute on Simi Chase at Love, but who hadn't been able to track her down all day. She said she'd call me back and I started working on the next prospect.

Antony and Cleopatra had been three weeks on location in Tunis the previous September when a Molotov cocktail took out craft services and production wrapped in Toronto. Prince had been in Tunis, crouched beside Maria Shockley on the doorstep of her trailer, speaking into her ear with the desert blurring behind them. Whatever the little fat guy had said made her smile.

I thought I remembered some mutterings about Shockley and Robin Saulie at Sundance a few months back, a little wisp of a rumor involving a hot tub. Lane would know more about it than I would, since they were her accounts, but I didn't figure she'd want to hear from me just then.

Shockley's rep was Terreya November, one of those sporty things that'd flown in from Miami and LA over the last couple of years, starting up boutique firms as a hobby.

"Oh she did not," Terreya said when I told her that Shockley had been spotted doing coke off Simi Chase's thigh at a Chelsea after-hours around four in the morning.

"Oh she did too," I said.

"We dropped her at the St. Regis at like one. I walked her all the way to her room. Trust me, she wasn't going anyplace after that."

"You can't be sure."

"Maybe, but if you put it that she was doing coke—"

"What choice do you leave me if you can't even vouch for her whereabouts?"

"Crap-crap-crap!" she said. "You are a freaking nightmare, do you know that, Koch?"

"It's been suggested."

"Look, I seriously can't get to her before the premiere—can't you just please wait a day?"

"What," I said, "and get scooped? Get Maria, tell her what I'm writing, and she can call me herself if she's got a problem with it." She kept making I-can't noises. I said, "What is so fucking hard about that?"

Nothing from her end. Then she whispered, "Can I tell you something?"

"Sure."

"My whole office has seriously been over there for like hours— no one can even get her out of bed."

"Ah," I said. "I see."

"Yeah. So we're all just a little Cleopatra'ed-out over here."

I told her to call me by six whether Shockley got out of bed or not, saying, "Tell me the truth one way or another and I won't write anything. But I'll find out if you lie to me, and then I'll write everything."

"Okay," she said, making a noise like she was clearing a hair from her throat. "I just want to go home."

"Me too," I told her, adding Shockley to the list and continuing to scroll.

Prince was coming out of the Soho Grand with Tamara Brookes, a singer who'd overdosed that Christmas—a month after the picture was taken. They'd also gotten a shot of Prince at her memorial service, walking into the Riverside Church with Lisa Wei, an actress who was supposedly still recovering from the car crash she'd had on New Year's Day. I wrote Wei's name on the legal pad, but didn't call her publicist—Claire Nussbaum.

I called Celebrity Service instead, looking for a connection between Prince, Brookes, Nussbaum, and Wei. The operator told me that Prince had been Wei's agent when he was still in Los Angeles but that he'd never repped Brookes, and Nussbaum had never been Brookes's publicist. Our librarian ran a NEXIS search for me that didn't bring up a single clip mentioning Tamara Brookes in the same story as any of the other three.

I made notes:

Tamara Brookes OD Xmas.
Kyle Prince, Lisa Wei @ funeral 12/29.
LW DUI 1/1. Still in hosp?
Jennifer Morales in rehab 4/9.
KP suicide 4/18.
Vivian Hunter MIA 4/18.
Maria Shockley OD? 4/18.

I considered cross-referencing all of them against one another, all the possible combinations, and an ache started moaning in back of my eyes. If addiction was a connection, the whole city was family—I might as well have started whittling candidates from the phonebook.

Taking another look at the Merlin grid, it felt like a thick, damp hood had been tossed over my head and I lay my face down under it, tucking my nose into the hinge of my elbow, the ache pumping behind my eyes as I closed them. It was too big, there was too much of it—an empire of addicts, psychos, snitches, all of us so interested in each other, each other's business, each other's bodies, every whisper repeated, every orgasm an item, all of us clawing to the inevitable, the breakdown—

We're all just a little Cleopatra'ed-out . . .

It occurred to me, there in the dark, that I could walk away from this, boycott the whole thing in my mind until it blended into the past, that mist that makes everything the same—people love you, people degrade you, people die on you: you put it away, you move, you keep moving.

Maybe you get revenge.

The last thumbnail on Prince's grid wanted me to click it open and stare into it. I'd seen it in the corner of my eye, a speck of red and white in my periphery, and then I'd put my head down.

I clicked the thumbnail open.

It reminded me of my friends stoned behind the 7–Eleven when we were kids, the way it leaned back against the refrigerator with its head slung down, its left leg straight out in front of it and the right leg crooked up with one wrist resting lazy on the knee. All it needed was a cigarette and some clothing.

I thought of something I'd heard a cop say once: "You could only tell it was human because it still had some clothes on." He'd been talking about my best friend, at the hospital after he'd killed himself with a car. They seemed to think I couldn't hear them, that I was in shock from having seen it happen. I don't know—it had felt the way endings always felt.

At least Prince still had a facc. You could only see it in profile, the closed eye, the open mouth, the skin that weird blue of an August dawn. Some beat-walking hump might've snuck the photographer past the police tape for beer money, but they hadn't let him prance around for the best angle—you couldn't see the gashes that had draped everything from the waist to the knees in blood, the right forearm flush with the thigh and the left forearm pressing into the side of the stomach.

His left hand cradled his penis.

I knew automatically that I would be closing my eyes on it every night until something came to blur it out. I thought of the woman who believed I'd turned a man into that, that sculpture of a chubby adolescent playing with himself on a kitchen floor, and who wanted to pay it back to me.

There were things I'd waited all my life to pay back and never anyone to pay them back to. Before I was old enough to think I'd discovered that even the lowest humans could always find some little scrap of power to get off on. Unfortunate, should you happen to be the little scrap that got them off.

That I'd ended up where allegiances changed in less than seconds—in a psychic tick you couldn't really call time—well, you understand, it suited me. There was ego without true emotion, animation without life. Everything was someone else's story, someone else's trouble, and nothing in it could hurt me.

I didn't care about rescuing Prince's woman, protecting myself, breaking a story. All that mattered was what her revenge would look like, what she had in her mind to punish me with, to snatch the ache and the dead from my eyes. She would wake me up, tell me what I was, or what I'd become.

Staring at Prince's open mouth, the fear rustled like a match flame and died. Seeing what she saw, I could feel her in there, the shudder of her breath in the dark, the futility of an open mouth, the nothingness of two people in a room. It was all the sense we would ever make.

She would come after me. I wouldn't have to do a thing, she'd come after me. All she needed was to find the coldness in herself to follow through. And I knew she could do that now—she'd have taken that from the room.

9

A Beautiful Friendship

Whatever it would be, we'd be alone in it. There was something that loved a closed system, something in us wanting it. Two people can keep a secret if one of them is dead, but she'd started telling it to me, bringing me into it, in jagged bits and pieces, her hopeless laughter, even before Prince's body had gone solid—why else would she want me to know?

It kept coming to one thing in my mind—that she wanted what everyone wanted, the simplest thing, the saddest and most tawdry: to get something back. If she'd decided I had a part to play in that, then I wanted in. Let me be simple, tawdry, let me be sad—I wanted in. I knew a suicide case when I saw one; she was a danger to the both of us, one of Mac's death engines. But she turned me on.

Every threat from her mouth, all the sounds underneath them . . . A tribe went missing once and spread across the world—you were in it or you were outside of it.

Imagining what she'd want from me, my first thought was that I'd already betrayed us, I'd already gone talking. Fucking amateur. Keep the outsiders out, she'd be saying, keep them out and out of the way and keep their mouths shut.

There was Lane—she wouldn't go talking. There was Meredith.

"But you told me to ask around," she said.

"Now I'm asking you not to. Things changed."

"Uh-huh," she said, and that was it for a while. I waited for her. "I sent the whole office home. I was sick of their voices. Remember when you used to come over? How you used to come over and there was no one else here?"

I said, "Meredith, did you hear me?"

There was the muffled squeak of Meredith pulling on a joint, then her breath across the receiver. "Remember, Leon? How I used to smoke a joint? And you'd go under the desk and there was no one else here?"

Harris was on the phone with a profile writer from one of the glossies, saying, *Light to heavy petting, mouths opened or closed. Though open-mouthed is certainly implied.* The interviewer said something that made Harris laugh, the square of his shoulders shaking up and down over the back of his chair.

"I remember," I said. "Of course I remember. Can you do this for me?"

"Do what?"

It doesn't appear in your dictionary? Well it appears in mine. Of course, I have a very old dictionary.

"Kyle's girl, don't talk to anyone about Kyle's girl. Don't ask around, don't do anything."

When we have something more specific we're going to use it. We had a sighting last week for instance, a guy tickling Serena Bishop's feet at Okay-Shiny. I believe that was from my colleague Leon Koch, who I believe has a thing for tickling. Or is it feet? Hey, you probably should leave that out.

There's the pull quote, I thought.

"Wasn't it fun?"

"What?"

"How you used to—"

"Of course it was, of course it was fun. But I'm trying to talk to you now and I need for you to concentrate."

"Believe me, Leon, you've got my attention. All I've thought about since lunch is you and poor Kyle. Do you know what he told me once?"

"What?"

"He said he didn't mind so much that he couldn't stay in Hollywood. He said it wasn't any good being in Rome if you weren't a Caligula—said it made people crazy."

"And this is where he came to find sanity?"

"He hadn't lived here in years. I guess he got sentimental and forgot that we're just a bunch of Caligulas too."

I shook my head, saying, "The sentimental agent."

"Don't be crass, stupid. I just mean that he wasn't like he was when I'd see him in LA. He used to look at you like you were hiding something from him that he just absolutely had to have or he'd just die. But he came back here, I don't know, gentle. Serene?"

I was taking it in, the broadening picture of the man we'd killed, when Meredith said, "So what about Billy?"

"What about him?"

"You said if I found out who Kyle's girlfriend was you'd give Billy his item. Now you say you don't want me to find out. But we had a deal, Leon."

It needed to be set down lightly, it was delicate—Meredith was made of tiny red wires.

"Billy's dead," I told her. "Deal's dead."

Something clacked in my ear, sharp and hollow. I could see it, her eyes tightening beneath her bangs as she snapped her mouth shut, waiting for her composure to return.

You'd have to prove malice, Harris was saying, *and for that you'd have to show a pattern.*

"Why don't you want me to find that girl?" Her voice was faux-curious, a casual tease.

If I'd thought it through before calling her I might've had a decent lie prepared. I might also have thought it through before bringing her into it in the first place. Now there was nothing left but the truth and her mercy, and there'd be as little of both as possible.

I said, "I want to do it myself."

"And why is that? Are you in trouble?"

"I don't know. Maybe."

If we do have a pattern when it comes to some of the people we cover, the best word to describe it would be Byzantine—we weave when you think we're gonna jab.

"Why are you always in trouble, Leon? Do you ever think about that?"

It's up to them to maintain their privacy, and most of them just aren't any good at it. If they were, hell, we'd never fill the freaking page!

"I think about it, yeah."

"I don't want to get you in trouble, Leon. We've always worked so well together."

"I know that, Meredith."

"But you're forcing me. You *do* see that you're forcing me, don't you?"

I'd heard her doing this to other people, casually pushing the nails in, me under her desk, so impressed by her sense of purpose, casually pushing the nails in.

"You don't have to do anything," I told her. It was feeble, but it was all I had. "You've always got a choice."

"Don't pretend you don't know me," she said. "It makes us both look silly. Don't I always keep up my end of a deal?"

"You always have."

"Then why are you making me do this?"

What was between us was quiet and ugly and we sat there with it.

I'm not aware that there are any vendettas over here and, if I was, I wouldn't be at liberty to discuss them.

"What am I making you do?" I didn't need to ask, I just wanted it out of her mouth already.

"You're making me force you. You tell me these things you shouldn't be telling me and then you refuse to do me the littlest favor. Look at the position you're putting me in, look where you put me. Did I ask you to tell me your secrets?"

There was a cardboard box under my desk marked DO NOT REMOVE, full of paperwork from a story the page had gotten sued on. It had been there since before I took the job. I stared at it, the red letters squirming against one another.

"Did I?" she said. "Did I ask you to tell me?"

"No," I mumbled, and it burned coming out.

The clack of her teeth snapped into my ear again, echoing through her small dry lips.

"I didn't need to know, but you just had to tell me. You just loved telling me. You put yourself where I have you and you loved it—you're loving it right now."

I thought that it might be true and stopped thinking about it. Then I apologized—Meredith hated that.

"Don't get emotional with me," she said. "This isn't therapy. Do you know what you do when you break a deal, Leon? You make the other person look silly. Do you think you can make me look silly and then send your *regrets*?"

"We could pretend it never happened. We could make it a do-over. We've done that before."

"This isn't about some ridiculous client I can write off. You're forgetting Billy."

"What about him?"

"I love him."

"He's making you look silly, Meredith."

"How do you think you're making yourself look? Do you love the girl you're looking for?"

"I don't even know the girl I'm looking for."

"That makes it so much easier for you, Leon—I've been inside that head of yours."

"Then you have a thousand other things you can use against me. It doesn't have to be her."

She said it again—"Don't pretend you don't know me"—and I apologized again and she screamed. With what we had for logic, her argument was sound.

"I'm treating you the way you're making me treat you," she said, "and you think *I'm* the one who should feel bad about it?"

"This kid, this kid you're doing it for—I wish you could see what he is."

"And I wish you could've been my friend."

The argument had gone as far as it would ever get. So had we. And I wondered if we'd ever been friends.

"You win," I told her, feeling an appetite for the first time that day, a tiny thumb of hunger pressing up into my diaphragm. "Send me the item. You win."

"It doesn't feel like much," she said, and I could see the roach whimpering in her ashtray, nudged by a shiny purple fingernail. "I'll send it tomorrow. I'm too tired to write anything today."

"Okay."

"Leon?"

"Yeah?"

"I'm not a whore."

"I know that, Meredith, I know you're not."

"I'm sorry it had to be like this."

"It's fine like this, it's good—we've got no more questions between us."

"I guess," she said. "Anyway, thanks for playing."

10

Hood

When I got called back into the Editor's office I knew at a glance that shadowy forces were colluding to slam me in the ass. Everything was wrong. Aside from the Editor, none of the Landing Party were present, and there were two blue-suited droids from Corporate sitting at the coffee table by the windows, a male and a female. The glass front wall was lightly tinted and I could see us in it. Lit by one frosted lamp behind the Editor's desk, the deep sparse room was dark in the glass.

So was the cop in it.

He didn't look like anything I thought of when I thought of cops, but there was nothing else he could've been—this black reed of a man in an awkward beige suit with the jacket sleeves showing too much shirt cuff and the pants slouching over his shoes. There wasn't a hair on his head or his face, as if it had all fallen out at once or had never grown there to begin with. He was hard to look at and I figured he must've been sick a long time once.

When he introduced himself—Detective Hood, homicide—I took a seat in front of the Editor's desk before he could offer his hand.

"So you're a gossip columnist," he opened, and I told myself to be cordial.

"Yes," I said. "Are you the asshole that let the photographer into Kyle Prince's apartment?"

The Editor rolled her eyes across the desk.

"You people had a photographer in there?" Hood said.

"Ask my fearless leader."

The Corporates opened their mouths as if to commence lawyering, but neither said a word.

Hood shrugged it off.

It was all wrong—I'd never heard of a cop investigating an obvious suicide and I'd never seen a cop without a partner. But there he was. I thought of asking to see his badge, but he'd have already gone through the courtesies with the Editor. I asked him, "Where's your partner?"

"Excuse me?" taking a green leather notebook from his suit jacket.

"Your partner—they don't let you people go running around on your own."

For a second I worried he'd take "you people" to mean blacks instead of cops, but he shrugged that off as well, saying, "I have a partner," and leaned himself against the edge of the Editor's desk, giving her his back—I'd never seen that before either. "Do you have any other questions?"

"Sure I do."

"Fine," he said, "that's fine. You know, you don't exactly match my idea of a gossip columnist. Kind of more raggedy than I'd have in mind."

"It's been kind of a day."

"What kind of a day is that?"

"It doesn't matter," I said, "it's over now—I've got big hopes for tomorrow."

"It's not over yet, Mr. Koch, not just yet." He had mellow gray eyes that collapsed at the corners and that someone could've taken for sympathetic. "Now," he said, "who was Kyle Prince to you?"

"To me? He wasn't anyone to me."

"You knew him," placing the notebook beside him on the desk. "You've written about him."

"Lane's written about him. He's her account."

"Her account?" The corners of his eyes drooped a bit farther into his cheekbones.

"Her account, yeah. Like her contact, her man, her problem. You should talk to her."

"What kind of relationship did they have?"

"I wouldn't call it a relationship—it's just work."

"A working relationship then."

"Maybe you should be talking to Lane."

Ignoring me, he picked up the notebook, tapped it on his thigh, and set it back on the desk. "You have working relationships with all these people, movie stars and such?"

He could've been thick or pulling some game or just sadly curious—everyone was always curious about all that. At least they pretended to be. Wherever he was going, I couldn't see the end of it.

"We've got nothing to do with movie stars," I told him. "If I say, for instance, that Matt Block is my account, what I mean is his publicist. So if someone on the page hears that, say, Block caught hepatitis off a midget hooker, I'm the one who gets to call his publicist. But, you understand, that's just rhetorical—Matt Block isn't my account."

"And neither was Kyle Prince?"

"Nope. This is why you should be talking to Lane."

He didn't say anything and the Editor locked eyes on me over a steeple of two index fingers pressed against her lips. I looked at the lawyers, then at Hood, saying, "What's your deal? Why's a homicide cop running around about a suicide?"

Hood glanced over at the droids by the windows, the last light of the flat dull sky washing out what was left of their faces.

"You're one of these people who loves to miss a point," Hood said. "The bigger the better, too."

"Kyle Prince wasn't any murder."

"Then what reason have I got for being here, friend? You heard me when I said homicide, did you not?"

"Now this'll be the fourth time I'm suggesting you talk to Lane," I said, "and the fourth time you'll stand there paying it no mind."

Hood grabbed the notebook again. "Let me walk us back a few steps, just a couple," standing away from the desk and running a hand over the back of his head. "You said Kyle Prince wasn't your account, you didn't know the man—"

"Sure I knew him, Detective—why shouldn't I've known him? That doesn't make him my account."

"Why not you? Something wrong with you?"

"Ah fuck," I said and Hood eased himself back against the desk with a fast, slick smile to say he was happy to wait and wait. So I explained. "The people we cover, we try to build up a rapport with them, get a little trust going, some kind of consistency. For that you've got to match up personalities if you can, have the same person calling them every time—make them *feel* like they have a relationship with you."

"So what is it about this Lane that Prince felt so easy with? Why not you?"

"Why do you keep trying to connect me to him?"

"Why do you keep ducking these easy questions?"

"I'm not ducking anything," I said. "But I don't know what went on between Lane and Prince and I wouldn't tell you if I did. I wouldn't tell you Lane's business and she wouldn't tell you mine—I've got a partner too, Detective."

Hood grinned confidentially, some sweet evil spreading itself between us, the gray eyes flickering to life. "Good enough," he said. "Good enough. What if I could tell *you* something then?"

Past Hood, the Editor's face was rigid with patience, bearing up against the specter of a little stranger running her office without so much as looking at her. Only the darkness beneath her eyes challenged the strength of the mask—I was staring into it when Hood shifted his body to one side, blocking her out.

"Now see," he said, "I've been eating and breathing Kyle Prince all day—talking to his friends, tracking down family, the people he worked with, just trying to find anything to tell me why that particular tub of troubles had his problems solved last night. Do you want to know what I found out? Are you a curious kind of person?"

"Sure," I said. "Curiouser and curiouser."

"Shit. I haven't found shit. Now, for me, that problem's for real."

"I can appreciate that."

"I have gone through that man's inventory in *full* and I haven't turned up anybody who claims to know fact one about his personal life. Most of them didn't even notice when his little habit had kicked up again—he didn't start messing up at work until about a week ago. Now that's kind of quick, don't you think?"

"I don't know. How long did it take him the last time?"

"Now there's a point worth raising," Hood said. "That's exactly worth raising. When it happened in LA he didn't end up dead. There was something else going on with him here—what was it?"

"Who knows? Maybe it's worse the second time around, when you know what you've got to look forward to. Most people, if they really knew what they were staring down the barrel of, don't you think they'd buy out?"

"Maybe," Hood said, leaning his face toward me. "But I already told you I'm looking at a murder, so do me a favor and put suicide out of your mind when you talk to me. You can do that, can't you?"

"No," I said, "I can't. But I can pretend to."

"Good enough," he said, "good enough—you just go on and pretend for me." His face froze and he stood away from the desk, gazing a threat down the length of his body.

"Was there a question?"

Smoothly, deliberately, Hood put his face so close to mine that he might've curled himself up in my lap, his hands on the arms of my chair and an antiseptic scent coming off his skin. "What was the man's secret?"

"I don't know," I said. "His sense of timing?"

When he spoke again it was in the controlled, weary tone of a middle-aged man unsurprised at finding his trophy bride laying the masseur.

"He had something that no one knew about him, something he kept just for himself, and I think you know what it is. I don't think Lane knows it, I think you're the one. And I think you need to be telling me."

"That wasn't even a question."

Nodding, Hood backed away and I watched the newsroom beyond the dark soundproof glass, the stupor of the first night shift settling in beneath the clammy white fluorescents.

"Fair enough," Hood said, "fair enough," the sweet-evil smile returning to his face, his ass returning to its perch on the Editor's desk. "Looks to me like we've got ourselves a case of the irreconcilable differences, you and I." He opened the notebook, clicked the button on his pen—him just getting started and me just starting to get nervous.

The Editor's face was still set at neutral. Her hands were folded on the desk. I listened for the sound of stocking against stocking, watching the steady black of her eyes.

There was only one reason for Hood to be asking me questions, one reason for having me in that office, and in all the chatter he still hadn't gotten to it. He didn't want to ask me straight out about the madwoman, he wanted to pull the cop move and dance me into it, talk me around the room until all my shady answers put me into whatever shadow he meant to put me in. There's no way to win that game with a cop, so I called it off.

"I'd have an easier time talking to you," I said, "if you weren't trying to talk me off a bridge."

"Oh, you're in the mood for some truth now, Mr. Koch? A little clarity?" Hood closed the notebook and set it on the desk, clicking the button on his pen up and down, ticking off seconds. "I might be straight with you if you'd do me the same simple courtesy."

It was so poor, so cute, that it could only mean he wanted to keep playing, be entertained. So I told him, "I'm thirty-two, I've been audited three times since I took this job, I have no wife, no ex-wife, no girlfriend, no ex-girlfriend, I own nothing and I'm sitting in a room with a cop, my boss and two lawyers because some psychopath made a phone call this morning and you haven't even bothered to mention her yet. I wouldn't be straight with you for all the ass in the five boroughs."

Laughing with his eyes closed tight, Hood rocked forward and rapped me on the shoulder with the side of his fist. "That's straight enough," he said, "straight enough," and I could still feel the contact spreading down through all the fibers in my arm. Hood grabbed a chair from the Editor's side of the desk and dragged it around next to mine, taking a seat.

"Let's have all three of us in on this conversation," he said, adjusting the chair so that he was facing the Editor and me at an angle, cutting the lawyers out of my sight with the line of his shoulders. "You want to talk about Prince's lady friend? Well let's talk about her, let's talk ourselves stupid—I'm all for that."

◇ ◇ ◇

It felt good, feeding Hood the same nonsense version of my conversation with the madwoman that I'd given the Landing Party that morning. He wrote it down as I spoke without taking his eyes off me.

"Okay," he said when I'd finished. "Is that everything?"

"That's everything." It was a good lie, I liked it a lot. And lying to a cop for an anonymous woman who'd made threats against me—I liked that even more.

Turning to a fresh page, Hood said, "Let's just go over it once more."

He had me tell it five or six more times, prodding me with questions here and there that never came to anything. Then he read over his notes for a while. It was dark out and I was pretty sure we were done with each other when he pulled his Columbo.

"That'll about do," he said. "Last question."

"Ah, fuck."

"Who is she?"

"Are you fucking kidding me, man?"

"Robin Saulie calls Lane, Kyle Prince was her account, but this lady calls you. Just explain it to me."

"I can't."

"There are three names on the top of that column and she picks you. You didn't write the article, you didn't make the calls, but she picks you—just explain it to me."

"Maybe she tried all three of us and I was the only one to pick up the phone."

"Or maybe she knows you and maybe you know her."

"There's a lot of maybes floating around in your head, Detective."

"True enough," he said, "true enough. Here's another one for you—it's a tough one, it's a killer. This woman is sitting alone with a dead body, that dead body used to be her man, but what's on her mind is you."

It felt like someone was coming up behind me, and I tightened my shoulders against it, telling Hood, "You don't know where she was, you don't know where she called from or if she was ever there at all." He put his hand up to speak so I spoke faster, trying to make words outrun the sudden tremble moving into my chest. "You don't even know for sure that she's the one who saw it—someone else could've been there and told her, who knows what other people have a part in it? What are you even saying she did? You think a man'll sit there breathing while someone cuts his wrists for him?"

"Maybe he was high beyond all sensation and didn't have a clue what was being done to him."

"And maybe she was high beyond all sensation and didn't have a clue what he was doing to himself. You're not the only one who's been running this through his head today, and every word out of your mouth is telling me that there are at least a few possibilities you're not even looking at."

"You are going to let me speak," he said, shifting to the edge of his chair, each plosive wet against the side of my face. "And the only possibility we'll be looking at is the one that I want us to be looking at."

"Go ahead," I told him, getting up and walking to the slim, floor-to-ceiling windows. Hood's voice, the din of the office, all of it was at my back, blending into the hum that humans and machines never stop making, that twists inside your ears until all of it's the same, until all of it goes elsewhere to stop mattering.

The possibility Hood wanted me to look at—I didn't need him to tell me what it was. But I kept my back to it a few seconds longer.

The woman had gone to the trouble of calling from the dead center of her own personal holocaust. Then she'd disappeared.

"Now," Hood was saying, "there are any number of scenarios

you could dream up to explain that to yourself, any number of them. But we both know the one I'm talking about."

I watched the jagged skyscrapers looming over a dim orange halo of streetlight, thought of Prince's mouth hanging open to the dawn—

It only takes a second to change your mind . . . You think you can make me change my mind, Sunshine?

Turning away from the window, I said, "There's nothing else I can tell you."

"Either you know who she is and you know what happened to her," Hood said, "or you don't know who she is and you don't want to know what happened to her." Something changed in him, he took his eyes off me, staring down at his open notebook like it was the only thing in the room that could hold him together, the ball of his pen shivering against the page. "Either way you look at it comes to the same thing."

I thought of Em, the shine of her, that health, and it scared me. She didn't belong in my mind with the madwoman, the cops, the suicides—any of them. She didn't belong in my imagination. But there she was.

I sat across from Hood, the darkness under the Editor's eyes spreading over her face as she watched me, wearing away the mask.

Hood folded the book closed and looked at me. "You're not much to me," he said. "Not much at all."

"Okay."

"You saw that man. You saw that mess. You looked right into the dead end and still you can't find the good sense or the good grace to *do* some good while you have the chance."

He touched my shoulders, or was about to, and I shot up from the chair, turning. "Don't touch me," I said. "Don't get behind me and don't touch me."

The gray eyes charged, went vivid. "You're a jumpy sort of a man, Mr. Koch? Do I smell liquor coming off you?"

I let go a breath, sweat itching over my ribs and the adrenaline shock tingling in the pulp of my teeth. "Don't get behind me and don't touch me."

"Oh you do shit some silk," Hood smiled. "From fabulous creation to straight out your mouth."

"She didn't kill herself," I said. "She wouldn't."

"And how would you know that?"

"I can't explain it to you. I just know it."

He put his notebook in his suit jacket and took a raincoat from the rack in the corner behind the desk, slipping it on, never looking at me.

"She's not dead," I said. Shaking hands with the Editor, Hood thanked her for her time and nodded to the lawyers. "Just listen to me," I said. "Just hold up."

The glass door swung shut behind him. I watched him make his way down the aisle and I turned to face the Editor. Her eyes narrowed with an appetite for whatever she was about to dish out. The office was suddenly foreign and severe, a hostile distance—the way things always look just before you lose them. After a few seconds, the Editor said, "This better work itself out to the good, Leon."

Breathing through a grateful blush, I told her, "I know."

"All right," she said. "Go get him—scram."

I caught Hood at the elevator bank, saying, "Don't you know better than to interview a reporter in front of his boss?"

11

One More Thing

Out on the plaza, far enough from the building that its lights didn't reach us and the audio feed from Corporate's news network was lost to the wind, I told Hood, "There's nothing I can do to help you find her."

"Well, shit, man, you walked me out here to tell me *that?*" he said, buckling the belt on his raincoat.

"And I don't believe that she killed anyone, either. But even if I did, it wouldn't make me want to help you. Kyle Prince was no one to me and if he got himself killed it's none of my business. And I'm sure as fuck not about to make it my business."

"Oh hell, motherfucker, nothing in your business is any of your business. What I ought to do, I ought to bust you right here on the street for obstruction, let you spend a night getting your head clear."

"I guess you could, but I guess once I got out I wouldn't feel too much like talking to you if this woman came looking for me."

"Are you saying you'd get in touch?"

"She's not coming looking for *you*, that's the only thing I'm saying."

He seemed to be deciding whether to deck me or walk away. Stepping to me, he reached out and grabbed my arm. I tried to pull away and he yanked me sideways into his chest, holding me around the shoulders with his free arm.

"Get off me," I said, but I doubt if it sounded like English, more of an animal growl as my body began to quake against his.

"Just hold still," he was saying, closing his hand hard around my wrist, pressing the ball of his thumb across the veins. It felt like a blood pressure cuff as he gripped more and more tightly, until I could feel the pulse pumping right into the surface of my skin.

"You feel that?" he said. "Do you feel that?"

"Yes."

He held my wrist up between our faces, scanning me through my own wriggling fingers as they curled into themselves. "You feel that blood? That beat? Never stops–day and night and it never stops. You can feel it the second you think about it, feel it in your damn earlobes once you think about it. You ever think about it, Mr. Koch?"

"Yes."

"Hearing it, feeling it, never any let-up–like a goddamned clock in your head, am I right?"

I could feel his pulse matching mine, the sweat on my skin where he was touching me, watching his eyes watch mine–we were alone in it.

Nodding my head, I said, "Yes."

His face creased all over and the eyes were deep in his head. "Gets at me sometimes," he whispered, "gets right at me. Ever get at you?"

"Yes."

His eyes were lit with something that had hurt him and changed him, something that had become his engine–I saw it flash,

I got dizzy and he let me go. I felt the rush peak and pan out in a calm, shallow pool. My head cleared. My arm was electric and numb.

"If you don't think this girl is a for-real threat to you, to herself, to anyone else," Hood said, wiping his hands on his jacket like I was something he wished he hadn't touched, "that's fine. That's fine. You know, though, what was interesting about Kyle Prince's wrists wasn't just those nasty cuts." He handed me a card. "Found some rope burn, too. You have a good night now."

Watching him walk away, I rolled that little nugget around for a while, first considering the possibility that Hood was full of shit, then thinking up several ways Prince could've gotten rope burn that didn't include getting murdered.

In the end I decided that even if she was what Hood made her out to be—a woman who'd tied a man up in his apartment and killed him—I could be okay with it. I mean, you understand, it's not like I was ever going to be alone in a room with her. It wasn't like some part of me was hoping for that, not giddily, not gratefully . . .

The cell bleeped in my pocket.

"Are you done with the police?" Lane asked. "I called to check on you and Robert said you were talking to a cop."

"I just watched him walk away in the dusk. It was very noir."

"Listen to me, Lee. I know what you're doing and I want you to stop. It doesn't matter who that woman was. It isn't your problem. Whoever she is, she's dangerous."

"Lane? What happened in Los Angeles?"

"What do you mean?"

I watched the gray canyon stretch out on either side of me, unable to picture that other city.

"Kyle had the same thing happen to him there, but it didn't kill him. What was different there?"

"I don't know, Leon. Sunshine?"

I felt my face darken at the word.

"It doesn't matter anymore," Lane was saying. "Just promise me you'll leave it alone now. It's dangerous. You have to trust me."

She was still looking out for me and I was grateful for that. And I'd have been happy to do what she wanted, to walk away from this, to return to our old routine. But I could never leave a mess half-made.

"I do trust you," I said.

Not that it mattered anymore.

12

Casino Bestiale

Maria Shockley wore wraparound gold-rimmed sunglasses and a short gauzy dress of shimmering purple with high-heeled spaghetti-strap sandals to match. On the backs of both calves were bruises the shape of thumbs. Her feet were dirty. It was night, with nothing sweet or humid in it, just the bare metallic harsh of winter wind.

This was the after-party for the *Antony and Cleopatra* premiere. Normally, I'd have gone right in, but Em had insisted that we hang around out front to watch the arrivals.

The flashes caught the gold highlights in Shockley's brown feathered hair and the glitter across her equine cheekbones until one paparazzo noticed the grime on her toes and aimed his camera at her feet. The rest of the mob followed suit. Shockley didn't seem to notice through the strobe-lit screech of the carpet walk.

"Maria!" one called and "Maria!" called another, snapping away across the carpet from where Em and I were standing, the reporters with them leaning over the ropes to beg comment, notebooks and recorders bruising the velvet.

There was business on both sides of the red carpet, but ours was the side going in. Em's eyes could barely decide what to focus on as we stood there, flicking between the publicists at the door at one end of the carpet, the pair of movie stars getting out of a limo at the other, and Shockley posing, flanked by bodyguards, in between. Those auburn eyes were wide with all the magic that was supposed to be in an event like this. But I could count on a premiere like this at least every Thursday every week of every year, and I would have liked to recall when any of them had made me feel even a part of what was showing on Em's face.

Shockley's choice of bodyguard had gone out of style seasons ago—young black giants in identical bandannas, blue jeans, T-shirts and sneakers. They formed a loose six-man scrum behind her. Rank amateurs, they were dangerous, and I was keeping us off the carpet until they passed.

"Why are they taking pictures of her feet?" Em asked.

"That's where the dirt is."

"That's just mean."

After Shockley had arranged her face for a few more shots that no one took of it, the guards enveloped her in a body-wall and walked her through the door of Okay-Shiny.

As they were going in, a photographer shouted, "Maria, why don't you wash your feet?" and one of the bulls turned, eyeing the crowd until he spotted the offender by the fear on his face and the stares of his colleagues, who were moving away from him in a wave.

They screamed *First Amendment,* they screamed for the police, they screamed *lawsuit*—all as the bodyguard reached across the rope, got his hands around the man's neck and squeezed. The photographer's camera bounced against his chest from the strap around his neck, his fingernails scraping at the guard's wrists and his cheeks going a deep red verging purple.

Suddenly the monster let go, spun away from the rope with a yelp, and cradled one hand to its chest. A reporter had jammed her pen into it. His eyes danced with fried circuitry as he watched the reporter. She was maybe five feet tall, a hundred pounds, trapped against the velvet rope by the writhing throng behind her.

Stepping toward her, the guard cocked a fist as he reached his other hand across the rope. Then something happened to his face and he grabbed with both hands to see what it was, spinning away from the rope again and squealing into his palms as he knelt on the carpet.

"Hold your breath," I told Emma, taking her hand and ducking us under the rope onto the carpet.

"Koch!" Charlie Gaines called out, catching up to us at the door. He slipped a little black canister into the breast pocket of his suit, saying, "Gonna stand around here all night, guy?"

"I think not," I said, and we went into the club as the guard got back on his feet and you could hear the choking coughs from the pepper mist spreading over the crowd. I was glad it wasn't me who'd maced that guard—I planned on getting near Shockley at some point and he might've had a gift for faces.

"What the heck just happened back there?" Em said as we walked into the lobby.

"They don't put their hands on us," Gaines told her. "They're just touring through—we live here." I knew who he meant by "they," but his definition of "us" was harder to pin—it wouldn't normally have included a reporter pulling carpet quotes.

"Is someone going to call the police?"

"What're you, nuts?" Gaines said. "We just got here and she wants to have the place arrested. Who is this gal?"

I made the formal introductions, grateful that Gaines hadn't drunk enough yet to start tossing around *dame* and *broad*, and we got in line at the check-in. Gaines folded his overcoat on his arm and Em eyed his suit—it was from the same Gene Kelly movie as his dialogue.

A line of people as long as the lobby and almost as wide waited for a squad of studio PR girls in full headgear to check their names against the list. Gaines made a "scoot" gesture at me to jump it and I gave a sideways nod at Em, shaking my head—she'd find it tacky.

That was a mistake. The way Gaines was looking at her then, I could tell he was marking her for a toon. Leaning to my ear he whispered, "Where's LaLane?"

"You don't have to whisper," I said. "Lane's not up for a party tonight."

"Not up for a party?" he chirped. "That's crazy talk."

"You hear about this Prince thing?"

"What? All this fuss over *that* fat fuck?"

"Keep your voice down."

"Why? You think fat boy's gonna hear me? He doesn't even know he's dead yet. LaLane did him a favor."

Em's lips went rigid as she gave a stinging pinch to the spot between my thumb and forefinger and I decided she needed to thicken her skin a little.

"Okay," I said, "that's about it for me and this line," gently tugging her toward the front of it, deaf to a few stray complaints from the herd.

"Are you sure?" Em was saying. "Is it okay?"

"We're working," Gaines said. "These jokers are just here to chew the grass."

Neglecting to stop for the formal check-in, we let the PR girls see our faces before we went through the metal detectors in front of the stairwell at the end of the lobby.

"Where's Tonic?" I asked Gaines, meaning his partner, as we got in line at the coat check.

"Toxic's probably already inside terrorizing the place. They had to let Matt Block give one of his speeches when the movie was over—you know, thanks for showing up—and Toxic wouldn't sit for it. She really said that. The little nut gets up right in the middle of the speech and says, 'I don't have to sit for this,' loud enough for Mattoid to hear it."

"How'd he take it?"

"With some K-Y and a prayer. He goes, 'I understand that peace might not be a very popular position right now,' and you can hear the whole audience cracking one-liners about his popular positions. Next thing we're all laughing so hard the guy can't finish."

"That's great—you using it?"

"Listen to yourself. They're gonna take it up front, probably make the wood if nothing too big got blown up today. 'Course, they'll have to leave out that Toxic started the whole thing."

"And tomorrow we'll say you left it out and do a story about your paper's rank lack of professionalism."

"That's fair. Wait'll you see what they cooked up for LaLane tomorrow—I wouldn't want to eat that breakfast."

"Assholes. They leave me out of it?"

"You? You got lucky. Robin Saulie swears you said something about a coffin."

If I'd been drinking something I'd have spat it out. Instead I took a breath and swallowed it.

"I said what to him now?"

"He'll be along, you ask him. Anyway, the city desk thought it was over the top—they don't know you."

I calmly flicked a finger across my chin, which was a meaningful public gesture I'd been developing. "I thought Lane had him on hold."

"That's what Lane thought."

"Who's Robin Saulie?" Em asked, and my lip twitched when I opened my mouth so I closed it again, trying once more to remember anything substantial about Saulie and Maria Shockley. I'd have called Lane, were I not in the middle of breaking the promise I'd made her. My mind pricked at a tiny wire, tickled it, and came out in a room somewhere. Then it went away.

"Saulie was a friend of Kyle Prince's," Gaines was telling Em. "He'd like to throw your date here under a bus."

"He isn't my date—he didn't even take me to the movie."

"Come on, Em."

"Yep," she said. "He had to get drunk."

"I'd get drunk if I was him."

I said, "What're you talking about?"

"Saulie's gone psycho for you, guy."

"How so?"

"Ask Saulie, he'll be along."

We paid our way through the coat check.

"Saulie's not the only one going psycho for me today."

"How so?"

"Ask Saulie, he'll be along."

It was right up ahead of me, twisting itself out, blooming like a forest fire, a mirage—all I had to do was walk into it.

◇   ◇   ◇

Fingering the four-in-hand knot on his silver tie, Gaines screamed, "Try to keep up, sister!"

Em had been saying something as we'd walked through the doors before she stopped dead, taking it in. She started speaking again but I could only tell from watching her mouth, the music pounding our faces in crashing waves of bass.

Okay-Shiny's main floor was a scaled-down Circus Maximus, or a gargantuan roller rink, looping around a sprawling oval bar of reflective black stone—six bartenders working either side of it. The pink marble walkway, or Promenade, that looped the bar was hemmed in by glowing red enclaves of banquettes around shin-high black tables.

"What's Okay-Shiny supposed to mean?" Em yelled in my ear.

"Nothing! It used to be a warehouse for a Korean import-export—the new owners kept the name!"

The new owners were Brazilians who'd made their money in scat and rape videos and were over here trying to clean it, but I didn't mention that.

Wincing against the staccato blare, Em asked, "Will it be like this all night?"

"Not for us!" Gaines told her, pointing a finger toward the ceiling.

The main floor was a bulk corral—if you didn't know you were being kept there, that's why you were being kept there. Doming the corral were five concentric terraces, each one a tighter circle than the one beneath it, each one with a VIP list to match its size.

At the center of the dome was a black skybox that could fit maybe forty people at a time. They called it the Credit Lounge because the people who got inside had their drinks on permanent credit, people who'd go to hell before they'd go anywhere they were expected to pay their own way. It didn't matter who was paying for the party in the rest of the club on a given night—there was no doorman at the Credit Lounge, no PR girls and no list. A black keycard fit an electric lock; either you had one or you didn't. The fun twist was that if you lost your card you didn't get another, and if someone cut you open and took it from you they'd be just as welcome there as you'd been.

Whenever someone complained about the setup, Florio (who didn't quite own the place, but was sure enough in charge of it) would tell them, "God made the rules, Darwin wrote them down—all I did was to pay attention."

Okay-Shiny was never hated quite the way people had hated Soho House before the fire—Florio wasn't British—but there'd be no shortage of volunteers to light the match when its season was over.

The party had only started, but already the bodies clogged the loop in swarming tides. I took point, weaving our way through ad-sales folk, production assistants, food editors and other fringe elements, Em trailing on my wrist and Gaines keeping step behind her.

The faces as we passed them, some looked confused, some depressed, disconnected—all of them seemed to be waiting for something. Some made the course in frenzied little zigzags, as if chased by invisible plagues of gnats, while some rounded it with a kind of maniac's deliberation, chasing imaginary flags. Others drifted off to the flickering banquette caves to die by candlelight.

Fame, for them, the world had none—nor suffered. We cut through them as fast and as unobtrusively as we could.

At the back of the corral was a velvet curtain that opened on a publicist perched on a bar stool beside a bouncer. She nodded to the bouncer, he opened the steel door for us, and she whispered something into her headset as we passed.

The music cut off like a phone slammed home when the door swept shut behind us.

13

Il Sorpasso

When we stepped onto the first terrace, two stories above the corral, Em said, "Gosh, it's freezing in here," and hugged her elbows.

"No one really ever hangs around down here but they pump in the AC as if they did," I said. "There's never enough bodies to use up the cold air. That's one theory, anyway. It'll get warmer as we go up."

"Then let's go up."

"A drink first."

"Now you're speaking English," Gaines said.

Making our way to the bar, an old man with an Asian child in a stringy red gown blocked our way, saying, "If it isn't my son Leon! What's the good news?"

"The good news? You're in it, Alden, you're in it—mind if we play through?"

"Certainly, of course," he smiled with a certain desiccated grace, but he didn't stand down. He put his hand on the tiny girl's shoulder, edging her forward. "This is my friend Yuki. Yuki, this is Leon and Charlie."

She smiled hopefully, gave a tiny bow of her head, shivering, and Alden took his camera from inside his suit jacket. Alden Lott was one of the few photographers allowed inside the events, because he was considered such a classic little gentleman.

Before we could stop him, he had Gaines and me huddled around the cheap digital, showing us the evening's take. After he'd clicked through a few shots of celebrities in the lobby of the Ziegfeld, Yuki appeared in the viewer—in a bathtub with the faucet going full-blast between her legs. I hoped the water hadn't been too hot.

"Now how did that get in there?" he said, laughing an old fuck's laugh with old fuck's breath through old fuck's teeth.

"You get what you pay for," Gaines said and Alden stopped smiling, letting us pass.

I considered half the crowd at any event to be some version of Alden's arrangement, even if they were simply interns or assistants who showed a certain enthusiasm and had a certain look, and I didn't like the prospect that someone might take Em for one of them. I wanted to get her out of there and far away from it, but that wasn't possible. We were only going further up, and deeper in.

◇   ◇   ◇

Halfway round the second terrace we came upon a pride of models arranged around a table of hors d'oeuvre trays. We'd almost gotten past them when Massimo Ciccone, their booker, spotted us and insisted on introductions.

We suffered those pleasantries well enough, and Em was happy to see that I'd been right about the warmer temperature. The models had whatever names you want them to have; I forgot what they were as soon as they got out of Massimo's mouth. Well, all but one.

"Ziortza's a beautiful name," I said, gently cradling her fragile hand as it trailed chicken grease across my palm.

"Yes it should be," she said, taking back her hand and wiping her lips with the back of it. "Massimo gave it to me."

"Leon," Massimo said, getting a thin hard arm around my shoulders. He was a small, tightly bundled package of a man, and I didn't like being so close to the nervous energy of his anxious little muscles. "Sit with the girls," he was saying, "talk to the girls. Please, please—everyone."

Gaines had already installed himself at the center of the models' couch, talking to their elbows and jawbones as they fed—models were his niche. Massimo ushered Em and me onto a daybed across the table from them, seating himself between us.

"What is this?" one of them said, pushing a forefinger into a pile of syrup-tinged golden-fried pastries. It sprayed her forearm with a fine purple jet that smelled of cloves and mildewed incense. "This attacked me!" she shrieked happily as the girl beside her sucked the crust from her finger.

"The girls," Massimo whispered, "I have to wire their jaw shut sometimes, yes?"

"You try?" asked a girl with a pink faux-hawk, nudging one of the trays toward us. It was shrimp, split open and wrapped around some kind of meat and bits of yellow fruit, tied together with strips of bacon.

"Vegetarian," I said and "Vegan," said Em.

Faux-hawk shrugged, popping one into her mouth tail and all. She chewed on it a little, swallowed hard, and spat a perfectly molted tail shell onto the tray.

Ziortza snapped the shell right up, crunching it luxuriously in her mouth, white shards of hair swaying above her head. Lowering her eyes at Em, she flashed her teeth, saying, "I love the bones," and Em's head moved back.

"Leon," Massimo said. "You have a walk with me?"

Em's eyes went small.

"Massimo," I said, "you just got here. People will get jealous."

He laughed, telling the group, "I never know what he says," and there was that hard Roman arm again, lying across my shoulders. It pulled me to my feet. "I want to clear the water between us—don't worry, the girls keep your friend company."

"Oh, most *yes,*" Ziortza said, snapping her teeth on another discarded morsel.

"I'm giving him three minutes," I whispered to Em. "Just sit tight."

"Yep," she told Ziortza. "I guess I'm your hostage."

"Can we do that the other way around? I don't love giving orders."

Em's head went back again. Then she smiled her half-smile and held her glass toward Ziortza with a bright giggle. "Okay. Fetch me another one of these?"

"Only if I can take you with me."

In a second, the two of them were up and bouncing away together and I could almost hear it tearing—the fabric of what I took for reality. I would've called after her, but I didn't know what to say, and wouldn't have said it in front of anyone.

"Why do you never call?" was Massimo's opener, the two of us leaning our elbows on the padded leather railing, watching the folks in the pit do their rounds.

"Me? You're in Charlie's wallet, that's a whole 'nother paper."

"So I am friends with Charlie. I can't also be your friend as well? Everyone is my friend. I am everybody's friend."

"Why is everyone always saying that?"

"Eh?" Turning away from the pit, he put his hands on the tops of my arms and I told myself that people were going to stop playing grab-ass with me someday. "I want that you make Robert Harris to stop fucking me."

"Keep your voice down," I said. "I can't make Robert Harris do anything. Why don't you call him yourself?"

"He never returns my calls."

"He never returns mine either."

"Every day the attacks, every day—every day I am doing these things to the girls."

"If you don't want Harris to write that you're fucking your girls, maybe you shouldn't fuck them so much."

Massimo's lips curled back and his eyebrows were a pair of vampire bats. Past them, across the pit, I saw Em and Ziortza walking away from the bar.

"These are not children," Massimo was saying, his hands making a lot of dramatic European gestures in the space between us. "This is not illegal. Any of the girls will tell you, for the, for the record—these stories, they have no truth. You could write that, yes? You could quote the girls?"

"They'd be lying," I said, and there was another flurry of sign language.

Em and Ziortza stopped walking and Em disappeared behind a red column, Ziortza laughing and reaching a hand toward her.

"You," Massimo said, "no one can talk to you."

Ziortza's hand was behind the column and she was still laughing. Even her white spikes were laughing.

"Maybe not," I said and started walking toward them. Massimo got my elbow.

"We can have business. You don't like me, this is very crazy, but we can work together, yes?"

I asked him what he had to trade, he told me he was suing someone, I said I wasn't interested. Massimo noticed my eyes and followed them.

"You maybe are interested in something else?" he said after a second, gesturing across the pit. "Ziortza, she likes your friend, maybe you like Ziortza—"

"Ah, fuck," I said. "Don't tell me you're not a pimp and then wave your fucking pimp-hand at me—it's too honest."

His face weaved slowly side to side, trying to find my eyes again. "You, eh—did you . . . Leon, did you just call me a fucking pimp?"

"I think I just taught you English."

He smiled, fondled my shoulder, dug a thumb into it and made a threat. It was all getting very gay. I told him that I didn't want to fight him any more than I wanted to make out with him, but that if one of the two needed happening he should hurry up and pick one.

"You have no head for business, Leon," his hands dropping to his sides as he walked away.

I was glad he hadn't offered me money. My rate for image re-hab could be anything from a kind word to a couple months' rent, and if he'd had that information he'd have used it. If he'd had that information it wouldn't have cost him a cent to use it. I'd never done business with pimps, but it's not like he'd have taken that for an answer.

◇ ◇ ◇

"We're in love!" Ziortza announced when she and Em got back from their tour.

"She's from Louisville," Em explained.

On top of each other, Em said, "She's coming with us," and Ziortza said, "We're going upstairs."

The lovers were trotting off, Gaines and me following after them before Massimo could reopen negotiations.

Strolling the third terrace, Ziortza spotted a banquette that was empty except for a few coats, so she dodged over and sat on them. The coats' owners might get their garments back, but never that territory.

Ziortza was longer than Em and made of bones, but they could've been from the same place—if you took away Ziortza's wig, washed her face and put some clothing on her. She wore white eyeliner shadowed hot pink to her temples, a halter top that matched the eyeshadow except there wasn't as much of it, black PVC hot pants and pink stiletto T-strap sandals.

I divided my attention between her and Em and the crowd cruising around us, wishing I knew what the hell I was doing.

"I'm going to get a drink," I said, and both girls jiggled their empty glasses toward me.

When I got back to our table, Ziortza was telling Em, "You don't mean that! Not literally."

"Literally!"

"Did you know Emma was a virgin?"

I paused on that, Em giving me a shrug. "I did."

"Now that's the kinda sugar poppa likes," Gaines said, rubbing his hands together. Literally.

"Did you take the pledge and all?"

"No, you don't swear to God about something like that. At least I don't."

The virginity of Emma Lake had fascinated me for months, and here we were chatting about it, just Em and me, and the competition, and one of Massimo Ciccone's molls—it should've been plenty to hold my attention, but the room was nagging me again.

I kept trying to see something in the faces going by—who I was up against, or why, or if I was really up against them. They flashed by and flashed by, making their rounds, always the same faces, always in new arrangements—the media columnist Michael Pedansky with Jim Vonning, who until recently ran a men's magazine, Claire Nussbaum with Cora Heart, the sex novelist, Pedansky with Linda Klier and Trina Tam—who Klier had said was in Toronto—

Vonning and the Chase sisters (Simi and Westphalia), Nussbaum with a soap star, Simi Chase with Cora Heart, Westphalia and Klier and the soap star . . .

As my information stood, that set included three hardcore addicts, a kleptomaniac, two schizophrenics, a lifestyle Domme and a rapist. For the first time on that job, the information didn't give me any sense of security. Watching those faces, those sullen fucked-out eyes, all I figured out was that I wasn't supposed to be sitting on my ass watching them fade around the terrace.

"What about you?" Ziortza was asking me.

"What about what now?"

"How old were you when you lost your virginity?"

Her eyes were too widely spaced and too pleased with the question—I looked away from them. She had long flat feet that were mostly toes and looked like they'd swoop down on a meadow to snatch a leaping hare if they got the chance.

"Don't you remember?"

"No, I don't remember. When's the last time you lost yours?"

"Leon!"

"Oh that's starving. Here we were all being so honest."

"I'm sorry," I told Em. "It's just making me grouchy sitting here—I can't just sit here, okay? I've got to move around."

"Geez, Leon, we're just catching our breath."

"Come on, Em, the whole point is to walk around a little."

"Listen to yourself," Gaines said. "We just got this real estate and you want to give it up? We get up now and the next time anyone's sitting down it's in a cab."

"Hey, I'd keep this little salon going all night if it were up to me," I said, "but I'm supposed to be working."

"What're you gonna do?" Gaines laughed. "*Interview* someone?"

"Why not?"

He looked at me with all the credulity of a bail bondsman—

none of us had interviewed a celebrity at a party in years. It felt beneath our dignity, getting some publicist to drag you to some star or starlet's table to have them drop the same agent-approved anecdote that had died on Leno and Letterman a week before.

"I think I'll look around upstairs," I said, and Ziortza snorted out a piece of her drink.

"You mean the pigpens?"

"It's all rappers and anchors up there," Gaines said. "And there isn't room for half the ones they let in."

"They're just trying to scare you," I told Em. "There are no anchors up there. Will you come with me?"

She said she would but to give her a minute. I set off to the bar for another round. I'd just gotten the top off it when someone trilled, "Hey, booger!" at the back of my ear. I turned toward the sound and Tonic Blackwell tapped her cheekbone into mine, dabbing my jaw with her lips. "You have got to tell me what's going on about Lane."

"There's not a lot to tell."

"Okay, I'm calling her right now," she said and her cell phone appeared at her ear through some sleight of hand. She was talking into it and I never saw her hit a button.

"Okay, Laney? I'm here with Leon," she was telling one of Lane's voicemail accounts. "He said I should call you—"

I let her go on, Lane would know what to do with it.

"I know you must be totally freaking out but you have got to call me, okay? Robin Saulie is in a butt-load of trouble, sugar—it is frickin' gi-normous. Okay, I have another call. Call me . . . Hello? Hey, booger!"

I didn't get too excited about Robin Saulie's butt-load of trouble. It was probably a figment of Tonic's imagination or a tease to get Lane to return her call. It was just as likely to tease me into asking about it.

Tonic was once Tonique, but she may also have once been Tonia and she may also have once been white. I'm not sure what she was by the time I met her, but what it was suited her.

Tonight she was blown-out blonde, but her eyes were still the same warm chestnut with the subtle squint that could go from endearing to menace in less time than they took to blink. Nothing was subtle about her body, and she'd dressed for it—a black leather bustier top with a green silk skirt that showed most of her right leg and none of her left, and square-heeled slouch boots in black suede.

"Listen, fuck-show," she was saying into her cell, "if you *ever* call her again I'm going straight to your fucking wife and telling her everything. I'll let her listen to the fucking tape if she doesn't believe it."

There was no anger in her voice, she was reading off a potential to-do list. But the squint in her eyes was at full destruct and I wanted to get on my knees and pull the skirt away.

The cell disappeared and a tiny black purse clicked shut. "So what's going on?"

"What's that about Saulie being in trouble?"

The purse clicked, there was a cigarette in her mouth and the purse was under her arm again. "Light."

I lit it for her and took out one of my own, Tonic leaning over the railing and flicking ashes into the pit, me using the carpet. A waiter passed by, telling us to put them out. We nodded at him and kept smoking. We dropped the butts on the carpet and Tonic told me to snuff them out.

"These are suede," lifting one boot toward me.

"I know."

"The soles are *incredibly* thin—you like?"

I nodded at the boot, at the shine of her calf, the gold gleam of her knee. She twisted her ankle side to side, showing off the boot, and the skirt fell away from her thigh. There was hardly a moment to appreciate it—someone was saying my name. Two people were saying my name.

"Leon," said one and "Koch," said the other, each with a little sneer of her own.

Their eyes were anime—dense jittery pupils straining against thin rims of moon-blue iris, none of it seeming to see anything. I wished I'd never left the table, never left Em.

Simi was nineteen, Westphalia was sixteen, and those three years hadn't made a difference. I waited them out as they glowered at me over their cans of Red Bull, wondering if whatever prescription they were on had gotten popular enough to earn a catchy street-name yet—I had one I'd been meaning to coin.

The straw popped away from Simi's mouth and she told me, "You are the most severest cunt." Her sister asked how I lived with myself.

My snappy answer would have to wait, Tonic cutting in, "Behave yourselves, ladies. Leon's a friend."

"Then make him apologize."

"Make him beg."

"I can do that," I said, and nothing moved on their faces.

"Okay, girls, what did Leon do? I haven't seen anything about you all week."

"He doesn't have to write it," Simi told her.

"He's telling all these people all these things," Westphalia explained.

"What things?"

"Everything, I'm in all these places . . ." Simi's lips struggled with the math and Westphalia picked it up.

"He's calling everyone telling them Sim's kissing girls and throwing glasses and spilling stuff—"

"And I didn't even go out last night!"

I said, "How would you know?" and Simi managed to focus her eyes on me.

"I don't like you."

"It's a good day for not liking me—everyone's doing it."

Westphalia stepped toward me, dropped her Red Bull on the carpet, and reached her hand toward my face. I kept my own hands at my sides, waited to see what she'd do. It wasn't something I could've predicted.

Getting a hold of my ear, she began to fold it, twisting the lobe up with her thumb and bringing the top down over it with her other fingers, pinching it shut.

"Westy, what are you doing?" Simi asked.

"I'm boxing his ears!"

"I wanna try."

Westphalia frowned and asked, "Doesn't it hurt?"

"I'm afraid not."

"No, like this," Simi said, taking Westphalia's earlobe and digging her thumbnail into it. Screaming, Westphalia let go of me and slapped her sister's face well enough to get a good sound out of it.

Slowly stepping back, Simi covered the bright pink welt with her hand, closed her eyes tight and began to cry.

"Oh you *cunt!*" she sobbed.

"I'm sorry!" Westphalia shrieked. "I'm so sorry!" Parts of the crowd were stopping to form an audience around us. Westphalia murmured, "I'm so sorry," taking Simi's hand from where her slap had landed and pressing her lips to the welt. "I'm so sorry . . . I'm so sorry . . . I'm so . . ."

The Chase sisters walked away in a wet tender cuddle, the mob parting around them. A second later, Westphalia came back through the crowd and grabbed my hands.

"Are you gonna tell on me?"

"No, Westy."

"Promise?"

"Yes, Westy."

"'Kay." She turned and went back into the crowd. Her hands had been much too cold.

"And I thought my heart would never break again," Jim Vonning said, coming up between Tonic and me. He had Cora Heart with him.

"Do you think . . ." Cora started. "Do those two—I mean, has anyone ever suggested . . ."

We were waiting for the rest of it when Vonning shook his broad stony face, telling her, "For God's sake, get it out already. I have enough trouble finishing your books without you adding your sentences to the workload—be reasonable."

"A friend of mine says he saw them once—"

"That's an urban myth," I cut in, to which Vonning added, "I didn't think you printed anything but."

"Are you looking for a fight already, Jim? You're not even drunk yet. I know that because you're not trying to fuck any busboys."

"Charming," Cora said. She had dark blue pointed eyes and a pointed smile, under eyebrows that overarched the natural line of her brow. "When was the last time you fucked anything at all?"

"You don't need me for new material," I said. "I'm sure there's still a few things no one knows about your snatch."

Cora wrote books about hard independent Manhattan women who died when there wasn't a man behind them, on top of them, or generally in the room somewhere. We'd been friends until she'd gotten married. Her two years with a doctor who'd gone from anesthesia to plastics and finally into the treatment racket had provided a rather wide target for my narrow skill set, and her divorce from him a month back had provided an even broader one.

"You'll have to take pity on young Leon this evening," Vonning told her. "He's heartbroken—he's just lost his dearest friend."

I said, "What are you talking about?" assuming it was just

another lame Prince joke. In a way it was, but there was nothing lame to it.

"Your wicked little alliance with little miss Merry-death Fields fell apart today. She's very upset, young Leon. Maybe you should apologize—I'd like to watch that."

It didn't scare me, Vonning dropping that—it freed up a lot of things. Em was somewhere and I'd find her or I wouldn't, Vonning had something on me or he didn't, the whole Prince thing would come together or apart with me on one side of it or another and I was in the exact piece of the universe I was supposed to be in—I'd been there before, I'd never left it, there wasn't anyplace else to be.

"I think we might've been in love," I said, "but one of us is insane. What's she been saying about me?"

Vonning gave me a smirk that took contributions from every part of his face.

"It amazes me that you haven't learned better lo these many years. Leaving a secret with Merry when she's in a mood is as good as leaving it out in the street—people have been tripping over it all day."

"She talks all the time," I said. "She's wired for it. I'm only surprised that you believe her."

"Some people like her lies better than the truth. Some people like her lies enough to put them in the paper so they can reach millions of tiny little minds attached to millions of tiny little mouths that repeat them until—voila—they become the truth."

"That can happen," I said. "But when I wrote you were getting canned, you got canned. Where wasn't the truth in that?"

"It took two weeks," Cora said. "Do you know what kind of negative word of mouth two weeks can generate?"

"Did word of mouth break up your marriage?" I asked. "Or was it that your husband's a weird old creep and that you're a bit of a slut?" Crow's feet bunched around her eyes, and I wished that I had only insulted her ex.

"I have a date around here somewhere," I said. "If either of you would like to finish rolling out the threat, let's have it."

"Don't you think it's nicer to leave it to his imagination?" Vonning asked her.

"His imagination isn't a nice place to leave anything," Cora said, "but all right."

"Okay," I said, "but you know Meredith likes you even less than she likes me—what makes you think she'd tell you anything useful?"

"What makes you think she told us anything at all? You have so many friends."

The table was buried under martini shakers and glasses filled to various levels with various colors of drink, Em, Ziortza and Gaines huddling over them on the couch.

"Playing bartender again?" Tonic said to Gaines.

"It's no game, sister." I introduced Tonic to Em and Ziortza, and Gaines poured us each something red from one of the shakers, saying, "*That'll* put a dent in your damned sobriety."

Whatever it was, it wasn't for me, so I went to the bar for a scotch. When I got back with it, Em said, "So tell me about your girlfriend Meredith."

"Meredith?"

"That's her name, right? The one who hates you so much she's making friends with Robin Saulie because he hates you too?"

"Goddamn it," I said to Tonic. "When did you find the time to say all that?"

Tonic twirled her lips together tight, nodding her head to say she'd heard me. "I don't know—it gets so late so early these days."

"I want to know what that girl's saying about me. And don't tell me to ask her myself."

Smiling at me, she rattled off another one of her lists: "I mentioned you on the phone today and Meredith said not to mention you anymore. I ask, 'What happened?' I say, 'Leon's a friend,' and Meredith tells me, 'Leon's not anybody's friend.' And you know what she called you? She called you a ghost."

"Ghost?"

"As in your having no soul, except that that doesn't make sense—but when do you expect Meredith Fields to make any sense?"

"Okay, I know she hates me, that's great. Did she say why? What's Saulie got to do with it?"

She put a cigarette to her lips and I lit it.

"The basic of it is that you'd gotten along just fine after the two of you stopped doing whatever it was you did to each other but then, today, she heard how you laughed when Robin said Kyle would kill himself and that you told him to buy a coffin. She didn't like that at all."

"That doesn't make sense."

"Then go work in a morgue if you want everyone to make sense, booger—I'm telling you what she told me."

"But Meredith doesn't give a fuck for Kyle Prince and Robin Saulie put together."

"Then I guess you'll see."

"See what?"

"She says she has something on you and she's going to give it to Robin if you don't behave."

"She tell you what she has?"

Tonic waited over that, pulling on her smoke. "Nope. She just said it was something good."

"How did she know what I'd said about Prince? She's got nothing to do with Saulie."

"Oh how do I know? Everyone knows what everyone said."

"Tonic . . ."

She waited on that as well, letting her name hang over two long elaborate drags. "All right, I told her. But you know I couldn't've meant anything by it—I thought you were still friends."

"It's okay," I said as if she'd asked. "I probably thought that too somehow. Have you told Saulie yet?"

Tonic set her chin at a thoughtful angle. "I haven't seen Robin around tonight, but he'll be around."

"Well," I said. "That was some phone call."

Meredith's ditching me for Tonic was no shock, but using her to messenger a threat so soon was. She should've waited to see if I'd make good on Treatle's item before bringing other people into it. Moving that quickly was rash, it was bad business—I was ashamed for her.

"She's way off her game," I said. "That little toon's really gone to her head."

"What toon?"

"Tell you all about him in a minute. After that you can tell her to forget him. You can tell her he's dead and you can tell her what she's got on me isn't any good anymore—you can tell her I ruined it for her."

So, for the third time that day—if it was still that day by then—I spilled what I knew about the Prince woman.

When you took it all out and laid it down flat it wasn't really all that much: a dope fiend had killed himself, his girlfriend may or may not have seen him do it, she left some threats on my cell phone around the time he'd died and called me at the office to repeat them a few hours later. And then she may or may not have killed herself.

I left Detective Hood and his rope burns out of it, left out that she may or may not have murdered Prince. Even without a murder it was a sad story, but it didn't feel sad coming out of my mouth. It had become information.

I hoped that if she was dead she hadn't been beautiful. Then

I hoped that she had been—I couldn't decide which would make me feel worse, or which way I wanted to feel.

I thought how I could have just as easily suggested that Lane drop the Prince scoop and let it all be on Harris. Or I could've told the Landing Party or the Editor about the woman and leave her to them. I could've told Hood. There'd been so many appropriate opportunities to put her out of my hands.

But I'd wanted so badly to keep her to myself—and I'd done such a good job of it.

As I finished talking, I wondered remotely where I might've been if I'd stayed in straight news, stayed home nights where there was no one to open my mouth to, watching cop movies where there are bad guys and they scream, "Why won't you just die?" Or maybe someone else would've been there with me, but that felt too innocent—thinking of a home at night with someone else in it. Besides, I hated being home at night and I hated being alone in it. Give me all the trouble in the world and all the worst people, just please don't leave me to myself.

Everything had to have gone exactly as it went. It even had to happen that I threw the story all over Okay-Shiny's third terrace, from where everything always spread like the most ambitious plagues.

"I just can't have Meredith trying to push me around like that," I said. "Not on behalf of some boy-model plagiarist with a memoir. As much as it'll cost me, I mean—you understand—there's got to be limits."

Then I told them about Meredith and Billy Treatle and his book of inculpable adolescent sadness.

"So that's the deal on Meredith," I summed up. "Now I'm going up to find Robin Saulie and punch him in his face. Anyone want to come?"

"You're not!" Tonic said.

"I am. I don't feel like myself anymore and it's not entirely my fault. Prince is dead, so it's no use blaming him. I don't know who the girl is, and you and Meredith are just being yourselves. That leaves Saulie."

Standing, I put a military snap through my body, as if to say that I wasn't drunk, that I'd never been drunk. Tonic and Gaines got up as well, so I sat back down to give Tonic her head start.

Gaines said he had to meet a girl about a nightcap, naming a good bistro on East Thirteenth. Tonic said she was exhausted and would be heading home. I don't know why she felt a need to lie. Now we'd have to pretend not to see each other on the upper levels, through what was left of the night. This whole Prince mess really did have to end—it was turning a lot of good people amateur.

They went and I wondered if Tonic would leave it all to word of mouth or if she'd put any of it in their paper for the day after next. The distance between this night and that day seemed like more space than I had enough time left to cover, but there was still nowhere to go except through it.

14

God's People

Maria Shockley's head drooped slowly to the table and back up in a jolt when she came awake, her gold-rimmed sunglasses hanging across her face in a slant. Matt Block held the back of her neck, talking fast at her ear. On her other side was Jezika, stroking the feathered hair from Shockley's eyes and speaking slowly.

I was watching them from across the pit—Em, Ziortza and me leaning over the railing for a breath. Down in the corral, busboys were clearing tables and mopping the pink marble Promenade while the bartenders packed away their stations and counted out their drawers.

There wasn't much area to cover to get to Shockley's table, but it would be tight, sweaty work. The aisle between the banquettes and the railing barely accommodated two people walking shoulder to shoulder, and that fact made no impression on the packs of table-hoppers cramming four and five to a gang as they made their last desperate rounds. Hard-liners, they couldn't give up on a party until someone invited them to sit down or threw them out.

Tonic and Saulie were nowhere on the fourth terrace.

"Why did you quit AA?" Em said. She'd finished the martini she'd brought up with her and was dangling the glass over the pit by its stem. I took the glass from her, set it on the floor.

"I wasn't going to drop it," she said. "I don't really even feel very drunk anymore."

"Do you feel sleepy?"

"Not really, except it's so hot in here. Is there anything else to do or can we go somewhere else? Zee was saying there's an after-hours."

"Yeah," said Ziortza, "this place is all burned out. I want to take her to Siberia."

"She wouldn't like Siberia."

"How do you know?"

"It's in a basement and strange men on cocaine pull down their pants at you."

"I don't mind. We're going to make up names for ourselves and give them fake numbers."

"You can do that here."

"No," Em said, "this place is all burned out already. It really is too hot."

Tiny beads dotted the tops of her cheeks. Down in the pit I saw Simi and Westphalia cross the Promenade and walk out through the archway. Across the pit Maria Shockley was shaking her head and pushing Matt Block away from her. Bodyguards stood up around the table, Shockley's young blacks and Block's middle-aged whites.

"So, really, why did you quit AA?"

"I didn't want to stop drinking."

"Could you, though? If you wanted to?"

"I couldn't want to."

There were other names at Shockley's table—Sport Meyers, the real estate mogul, Andre Blane, who ran Jezika's label, and the plastic surgeon Jerry Best. Two of Block's Tibetans were there as well, dressed in dark crimson robes. They were all filing out to make way as Shockley fought past them with her fists clenched on either side of her face, shoving with her elbows. She stalked shakily away from the table and a small redhead trailed after her. They were heading my way.

"What do you mean you couldn't want to?" Em was saying. "What if you had a good reason?"

"There's no such thing as a good reason."

She shook her head. "I mean, like if you met the right girl."

Shockley's elbows were parting the crowd as she rounded the last part of the curve that would bring her to me. She wasn't ten feet away when the little redhead got up behind her and grabbed her arm. She spun Shockley to face her, said something, and Shockley swung her free hand at her face. The girl caught Shockley's wrist, twisted it into Shockley's waist and held her still, speaking to her through her teeth. Then they walked forward together, the redhead holding Shockley's twisted wrist to her side with one hand and guiding her by the shoulder with the other. As they walked together, you couldn't have noticed that anything unusual was happening between them unless you saw Shockley's fingers changing color in the redhead's hand.

Maybe five feet tall, Terreya November looked fresh from high school in her ribbed wife-beater and cargo pants tied tight above her bare ankles. But she wore them with black pumps that gave her another few inches and some of her age showed in the corners of dark green eyes that brightened when the long loose plaits of her coppery hair swung down around them. The eyes flashed on me, then away, as she pushed Shockley past. I called her name and she kept going, so I called it again, running up behind her.

"Terreya," I said and she stopped. I walked in front of her. "Me and Maria have got to talk."

"Crap-crap-crap!" Terreya said. "Do you really think this is a good time?" Shockley's glasses rode the tip of her nose, showing her swollen eyelids. "I have to put her to bed."

"Yeah, like last night—I know. I'm going to talk to her first."

Shockley leaned forward, watching me dimly over the rims of her shades. "Who's this?" she said, and the glasses fell onto the carpet. I stooped to get them.

"No don't," she said. "I hate them now," her sandal pressing down on them with a crack. The state of her feet hadn't improved any through the course of the night.

"Now Mar," Terreya said, her tone lovingly authoritarian, speaking to a small puppy, "you'll cut yourself."

"Not before you break my arm."

"Well we don't want you to fall down and break that beautiful face, do we?"

There were cigarette burns and smudges of ash in the frills of her purple dress. "What's the difference now?"

"Don't say that."

"No. You tell me."

"Everything's going to be fine. You just need a little sleep."

"You can't do it. You won't make me."

"Leon," Ziortza said, stepping beside me with her eyes on Shockley, "are you ditching us for new friends?"

Em came up behind her, stayed behind her.

"We really have to go," Terreya said, and Shockley shook her head, pulling herself away from her handler.

"I don't have to do anything. I'm going to stand here and talk to these people—who are these people?"

Ziortza introduced herself, pulled Em forward and introduced her, too. I didn't do a thing.

"What about you?" Shockley asked me.

"That's Leon," Terreya said. "He's a friend."

"Everybody's a friend. Hey," she said to Em, "are those for real?"

"Umm . . . Huh?"

"Your rack! Look at that *rack*!" Em covered her chest with her arms, laughing into her hands. "Oh don't be embarrassed."

"I'm not!"

"My God, look at that rack!" she told Ziortza. "Your date's the A-bomb."

"Most yes."

"My ex-husband's at my table."

"Excuse me?"

"He's right there, you see him?" Her hand pointed to nothing in particular and her eyes looked down at the broken sunglasses by her feet. "He just keeps talking to me. No one ever makes him stop."

"I'm sorry," someone said.

"He owns Chinese people."

"Mar . . ."

"Little brown Chinese people. They own him." Her head bowed and came up again, somehow too erect on her neck. "They're God's people, they own God. I'm Catholic. He used to be Catholic but nobody's Catholic anymore."

The sound of her voice was throaty and bleak and it told me nothing. It was familiar, but there could be the movies to thank for that.

"Are you Catholic?" she asked Em.

"I'm Welsh Presbyterian."

"I don't know what that means," Shockley said, and then she was looking at me. "I know you."

I let it sit there, her puffy eyes scanning my face. She looked away from me, back to Em.

"Grown men," she said, putting a hand on Em's shoulder, "wearing sandals with socks—with *socks*." Balancing against Em, she stepped down out of her sandals, picked them up with her fingers through the straps. Terreya took a walkie-talkie cell from a pocket in her cargo pants, whispering into it.

"They're always around," Shockley said, "they're always *whis*pering."

"Who?"

"God's people—I *told* you."

"Honey, please," Terreya said.

"You know what they do?"

Em shook her head no. Shockley pressed the ball of her foot into the smashed sunglasses, grinding it in as if she were stamping out a cigarette.

"They walk in glass," she said, the lenses crunching beneath her foot. "They walk in glass and play with needles. But they don't hurt themselves because they have God. I had God too, you know."

The more she spoke, the more I believed I'd never heard that sound in any movie.

Two of her bodyguards were cutting through the crowd, Matt Block bringing up their rear.

"Here I go," she said. "It's my bedtime, you know."

"It's bad out front," one guard told Terreya while the other put his arm under Shockley's shoulders—she slumped into him. "We got three of them waiting out back too."

"Crap-crap-crap! Let's try and wait them out a little more. I think she'll be asleep soon."

The guard's chin touched his chest when he shook his head. "No good. They're going nowhere they don't see her coming out."

"I understand that. But Mar-Mar's got a case of the talks and I'd rather they get pictures of her carried out half dead than have her screaming God-knows-what at them."

"There's my overtime," the guard said, and Matt Block started whispering something to Shockley as she lounged against the other guard's body.

"I didn't tell them you were a faggot!" she shrieked, delighted. "Don't worry, Matty! I'd never tell anyone that!"

Block slid the sides of his sport jacket back and stood with his legs at a commanding space, hands on his hips, looking from side to side—I'd seen it in a dozen films, but it was still very good.

"You know how you look when you get like this," putting his hand to his forehead in something like a salute, then using it to chop the air above his head as he spoke. "It's unconscionable, Maria, it is un-conscionable!"

"He's not a faggot," Shockley called to us over the guard's shoulder as he lifted her into his arms. "Don't you tell anyone he's a faggot, because he isn't!"

Block's speech was punctuated by hyper little bolts of breath that were something like laughter. "Okay!" he said. "Okay—ha! It's Crazy Town! You want to show me Crazy Town, Maria? Ha! Is that your best? Don't hold out on me, Shockley! Ha! Show it to me!"

You couldn't look away from the intensity of his square blue eyes except to see the intensity of his square white mouth.

"I'll show you my best!" she screamed as the guard took her away. "I'll show you my best!" Block, Terreya and the other guard followed them into the crowd, and you could still hear her screaming—

"I'll show you God! I had God too, Matty! You're going to see it! You're going to praise me!"

Ziortza picked up the twisted frames and put them in her purse.

"Well," I said, "there goes my girl."

15

Siberia

Em didn't know about Okay-Shiny's Credit Lounge, so I was able to get us out of the club without showing it to her. By the end of the night that secret room's plush and guarded elegance was left mainly to trawlers hoping for a glimpse of the players who'd never step foot in it after two AM. Dawn and the haunted hour or two before its arrival were always spent at Siberia, a spot on Fortieth Street and Tenth Avenue marked only by the red light above its door. By all rights, it should have been condemned a decade back, but it went from empty dump to cherished homestead as soon as the rest of the city stopped serving drinks.

The main bar on the first floor was usually rowdy even by after-hours standards, but all the best stories crawled out of the barely furnished basement beneath it. Through there you could also reach the shuttered coffee shop around the corner from Siberia's front door that Tracy, the owner, used as a VIP space, if you knew how to get there.

At the freestanding bar just off the street entrance, Darol Varmanian's dark face and mascara-painted eyes smiled at me over a gold coin that twirled in midair above his open palm.

"Hey there, Koch," he said smoothly, the coin freezing still beneath his chin and throwing dull electric light at the kohl-rimmed eyes. "Steph."

"Hello, Darol," Ziortza said. "Kind of late for tricks, isn't it?"

I expected him to toss off an ugly line about Ziortza and tricks and the end of the night. Instead he let the coin drop and disappear into his hand, saying, "Give a boy a break, Steph. That's my bread and spread."

"Stop calling me that."

The wide dim cement room boomed with "Can't Stand Losing You," a live version from the dozens of bootlegs in the jukebox—it would be that way until dawn. People sat on torn-up sofas, love seats, picnic benches, drinking from plastic cups around the wooden industrial cable spools laid on their sides to serve as tables. A Harley Davidson of some make and model stood in the center of the room.

A deck of cards appeared in Darol's hand and he said to Em and me, "Ziortza hates illusions. The first time I levitated for her she tried to get me exorcized—she's mad superstitious."

"It's good to be superstitious," she said. "People aren't afraid of enough things anymore. But I never tried to get you exorcized— you have to have a soul for that. You're just . . . You're a ghost."

"You don't have to get so rough with me now."

"He really levitates?" Em said. "I always thought that was trick photography."

"He could do it right now if he wanted to. But he won't because he knows you want to see it—he only does things when you can't stand seeing them anymore."

"Rough," he said. "Burn my ass. So what's your thing?" He was looking back and forth between Ziortza and me.

"We just met tonight, at Shiny's, but we're old friends already."

"Wish I'd seen you there. I'd've had a better time."

"Don't count on it."

"Rough, Ziortza, rough." Turning to Em, he said, "So how long've you been in town, Emma?"

Before she could answer, Darol rattled off her address at Northwestern and her date of birth, slipping Em's driver's license out from the bottom of his deck as she felt in her coat for her wallet. He made the cards disappear and handed Em back her license.

"Neat," she said, putting it away. "But don't do it again, please?"

"He thinks it's charming."

"To some people it is—a lot of people."

The bartender stopped the conversation, bringing over a round of yellow shots in specimen cups. I was just looking up to see who'd sent them when Tracy got me in his arms to loosen me up a little, starting with the bones. An avalanche with feet, he lifted me and shook me against his chest, saying my name and asking how I was doing and who was my friend.

"This is Emma," Ziortza said. "Darol's trying to get in her pants because he's too creepy to see she's with Leon. But they don't know they're together either, so it all evens up."

I didn't know what to do with that—I liked it but I didn't know what to do with it. I didn't even look at Em's face. I wish I had.

Tracy put it all under his laughter, a wave of healthy sound that left you refreshed when you came out the other side of it.

For Darol it looked like it'd had just the opposite effect.

"Let's go downstairs," Tracy said, ruffling Darol's hair. "Everyone's downstairs."

"Not this kid," Darol said.

Ziortza watched him go out under the red bulb above the doorway, saying, "I guess I was wrong about him—that's the one trick I wanted to see him do."

"He's in love with you," Em said.

"I hope it hurts."

We all took drinks and went downstairs.

At one end of the basement was a platform half a foot off the ground, maybe six feet by ten, where bands would try to play over the jukebox pumped in from upstairs until the crowd shouted them down and unplugged their instruments—if it was a friendly crowd. There was a pair of turntables at the other end of the room where a DJ could get the same treatment if he wanted it. The basement was decorated in the same aesthetic as the street level, except somewhat less stately and a lot less bright.

There wasn't any kind of a scene, just some shadows moving in the hall behind the turntables and a few people at the far end of the basement, huddling around a spool in the darkness at the edge of the stage. The hallway in back of the DJ stand ended at a storeroom door and across that room was the corridor to the coffee shop/VIP lounge. That is, if the storeroom wasn't locked.

Tracy walked us over to the table by the stage and I was pulling out a chair before I saw their faces.

The night hadn't been gentle to Meredith Fields and Billy Treatle—he was asleep in his seat and her mascara ran trails down her cheeks. Tonic and Jim Vonning seemed to be holding up all right across the table, though.

"Hey there, handsome," Tonic said, and I thought of my face. "And you're still up, sweetie?" she said to Em. "Come sit next to me."

Tracy went back upstairs while Tonic arranged us so that I ended up backed to the wall between Ziortza and Treatle. Meredith and Vonning bookended Em and Tonic across the table.

"I didn't see you at the party," Meredith said. We were face-to-face. "I was sure you'd come looking for me."

I looked around the table with the feeling that a fight was about to start. I pushed it down, smiling.

"I don't always like to do the things you're sure I'm going to do. Someone's got to make you wrong once in a while."

We didn't say anything; we sipped our drinks, everyone sipped their drinks, and Treatle slept at my shoulder.

Once I'd heard Maria Shockley talk about praising her, there hadn't been any reason to stick around Okay-Shiny, but I was glad to see them all now—they were all so harmless. In the morning I'd tell the Editor about Shockley and she could do what she wanted with it, give her up to Hood, put her in the paper. It was out of my hands. Maybe Shockley was a desperate little case, but she wasn't my case. A dead boyfriend, an ex-husband, a crowd of strangers at a club, a stranger on the phone . . . It all came to the same thing— an audience. It was nothing personal. She was a movie star.

Change your mind . . . Praise me . . . Sunshine . . . It was all probably off some straight-to-DVD looping through her head. I'd have rather paid five dollars to rent it than what it had cost me, but her performance at the club would make a nice story, maybe even the wood. Things had worked out fine for me. I had every reason to be pleasant.

Treatle had traded in his cruisewear for an antique tuxedo jacket with velour lapels over a knockoff of Lennon's NEW YORK CITY T-shirt. His head lay back between his shoulders, mouth open just enough to show his tongue against his lower lip.

"You shouldn't keep him out so late," I said. "He's plumb tuckered."

Meredith drank something pink, swirling it in her mouth. She took another sip and spit it back into the plastic cup. "Jim got bored and slipped him a roofie."

"Did you really?"

"Get bored, yes. Drug the boy, no. Have you ever seen anything so earnest?"

"You didn't buy that, did you?"

"Well he wasn't *selling* anything else. It's cute for a while."

Meredith said, "For a while, yeah."

"Well," I said, "I guess that's pretty much that, huh?"

"Pretty much. He looks cute sleeping though, doesn't he?"

"You shouldn't've kept him out so late."

"It's my own fault, working him so hard before we went out."

"That's hard work."

Meredith's eyes grinned under her bangs.

"You don't want to start with me tonight."

"No," I said, "I didn't want to start with you last night. But now it's tomorrow already."

"No, stupid. We've all got to go to work in a few hours. So this is already yesterday."

"And so am I, right?"

"You got it."

"And this was tomorrow?" I said, flicking my finger against the toon's shoulder. He muttered something and brushed a finger across the tip of his nose.

Meredith took another sip, swallowed it, and then I saw her mouth working behind her smile, the cheeks moving in circles. I knew what was coming but I didn't believe it enough to move away. She spat in my face and Tonic said, "Meredith!"

I laughed, pulling up the bottom of my shirt, and wiped her spit out of my eye.

"In front of company, Mare? You're really full of tricks today."

"Don't you mean tomorrow?"

"I don't even know, everyone's been so fucking sloppy lately. But I wish you'd done something else—we're not going to be able to explain this."

"What if I do it again?"

"Better not. Once, I could explain, twice, not so much."

I heard the hard "T" of tongue to teeth and felt the spit spread across my eyelids without turning my face from her.

"Why are you letting her do that?" Em said.

"That's disgusting," Ziortza said, laughing. "I dare you to do it again."

"This is going to be impossible to recover from. It's a scandal, Meredith, a terrible scandal."

"Good," she said, and she did it again and I wiped my face with my shirt again.

"My mother bought me this shirt."

"I'd always assumed you were an orphan," Vonning said, and Meredith did it again.

"Cut it out," Em said. Her voice was cool and serious, and everything seemed to slow around it. Leaning across Tonic's chest, she looked Meredith in the eyes. "He likes it too much."

They went into a fit and I went with them, laughing and slapping the table until Meredith's drink slid off it into her lap and she shot to her feet, everyone stopping to watch her.

"If you can't hold your liquor," she said, taking the drink in front of Tonic, "you shouldn't go touching other people's."

She doused me, Ziortza getting hit with some of the collateral and retaliating with my scotch, most of which ended up clotting in Em's hair—Em repaying that with a drink of her own. The tossing of drinks went on until there wasn't a drink left to toss and Tonic had the hiccups. Billy Treatle woke up and inspected his tuxedo jacket.

"Did something happen?"

"No," Meredith said, fishing ice cubes from her skirt. "We were just talking about yesterday's news."

"Things no one'll remember tomorrow," I said. "Tiny awful pretty things that were fun to look at once."

"Leon," said Tonic.

"That's what my book's about."

It hadn't taken Treatle a second to come to that, and Vonning said, "Amazing."

"Jim."

"But it is amazing. I'm more amazed every time he mentions it—and at what length! Honestly, Billy, has anyone not been amazed by you yet?"

"Well, I mean, it's not me all that much that I find . . . I mean, I find that in people's reactions . . ."

The doll eyes found their place in the low ceiling as the glossed and sculpted head approached its most meaningful posture. I had to look away. Watching the shadows move in the hallway at the back of the basement, two people together in the dark, I lost what little I'd had of a good mood.

"I'm both from here and not from here," he was saying. "I'm part of the scene but I'm also, you know, I'm in with the outsiders."

"Amazing," Jim said. "I sit thunderstruck."

"So I can, you know, avail myself of those different paradigms, all these like new and different unique perspectives."

"Oh thank God. Now promise me you'll do that. Promise me you'll avail yourself of all the new and different unique perspectives and not the same old ones everyone's always availing themselves of."

"Jim . . ."

"But it's important—he's going to avail himself of things unique and different, new things. If we don't encourage him he might forget and not avail himself at all."

Whatever I felt about Treatle, he looked exactly like a little kid once he'd been slapped down enough to know he was being slapped down.

"Okay, Jim," Tonic said, "enough."

"Go forecast some news, Toxic—you're almost as much a dinosaur as I am."

"Sure," I put in, "but she takes it better."

"Take it however you like it—young Billy here's the future. And don't you dare go getting in his way if you don't want him to avail himself of your perspective."

"I'll remember that."

"What a time to be alive. A new perspective, hearths and homes, backyard barbeques, Twister in the basement, papier maché balloons . . . What an era, what times!"

All the little kid was gone from Treatle's face—he looked bored by the conversation and took himself out of it, studying one of his lapels.

"Did Maria go home?" he asked Meredith. "I was interested in talking to her."

I watched the shadows in the back hall, feeling the blood rush in the sides of my neck like fingers closing around it. I could hear it in my ears.

"You talked to her enough," Meredith said. "You talked and talked."

"I was just wondering where she was."

"You were just interested."

"Well, yeah."

"In talking."

The moving shadows explained why we were the only ones in the basement and why Tracy had walked us down himself, though none of that had needed explaining until Treatle mentioned Maria.

She'd probably thought the storeroom door was unlocked.

I got up as Treatle was saying, "I can talk to anyone I want— she wanted to talk to me."

"You really think you're in some kind of league," Meredith said, laughing at him. Treatle turned his chin to his shoulder. "Oh did I hurt all those feelings of yours?"

He looked around the table, then up at me.

The blinking eyes didn't appear to know my face and they had the sleepy confidence of deep and permanent disconnection. It was as if he were alone.

He whispered to me, his voice a subconscious reflex of the lungs, the gas-groan of a corpse: "I hate the sound of women laughing."

I left him to the rest of the table, walking off to pull Maria Shockley from the dark.

16
Good Day, Sunshine

*E*very part of that darkness made me happy. It was hot and alive and there was something in it for me whether I wanted it or not. I was at the edge of it when Robin Saulie stepped out of the shadow of the hallway, taking off his glasses. He slipped them inside his sport coat and said, "I'll give you a chance to walk away."

His face was rigid under a back-nine sunburn, his eyes calm and blue behind short black lashes the same color as the military buzz-cut on his head.

"I'll give you a chance to walk away," he repeated, taking off the jacket and dropping it on the floor beside him.

His tight white polo shirt would've enhanced the tan of his arms in better light, not to mention their shape and size. His arms, chest and shoulders were all about the size that makes men feel like they've been up to something. In back of all that sex, I could just make out Maria Shockley crouched in the hallway, her hands over her ears, rocking on the balls of her naked feet.

"Thanks," I said, "but I've been going for this all night."

"I don't necessarily want this to get ugly."

"This is ugly. And I don't necessarily want to talk you through it."

My hands wanted to shake but I made them look casual, hanging them at my sides.

"I told you to leave me alone!" a girl shouted behind me.

I turned to see Darol Varmanian on one knee next to Ziortza's chair.

"Baby, please," he was saying, "just please let me tell you!"

"Get away from me!" He began to say something and she pushed the front of his upturned face with the palm of her hand. Losing his balance, Darol bottomed out and Ziortza stepped over him, running for the stairs. Em chased after her, Darol close behind. Treatle looked at Meredith for a second, then got up and followed them out.

I gazed back and forth between Meredith and the bottom of the empty stairway. Tonic whispered something to Vonning, they looked at me, and Saulie shoved me from behind.

"I'm right here, asshole."

His head was dipped toward me and I could see the teeth at the corners of his mouth. His left hand hung open but his right was a fist at his thigh. The way he was setting up to throw a punch, he might've put it in a letter. I was saying something to that effect when it came.

I ducked it easily enough, but I hadn't counted on his knee. Somehow I'd never imagined prep school guys kneeing people in the face. Such generalizations were always bad business, and I'd remember that. In the meantime, though, I needed to stand up. Saulie hated that idea and showed me how much by glancing one off my forehead just as I'd gotten my feet under me.

There were footsteps and voices in the gathering dark. One of the voices was Maria Shockley's. It said, "Told you stop following me," and I knew that I had to follow her. I heard more footsteps, frantic and fast, fading away above me. My head buzzed a little when I got to my feet, but there wasn't any pain. That would come later.

"You're bleeding," Meredith said.

"It's about time."

She was still at the table, but she was alone now.

"You can still catch them if you can run."

"I can run," I said, "but I'm not sure I will."

"Oh, you'll run, you idiot. It's so you."

"Are you okay?"

"Ask me again tomorrow. Or today or whatever."

I ran.

Upstairs, there was still a crowd and I saw Em in it, at a table with her back to me. Ziortza and Darol were with her, Ziortza's white wig on the table and her hair held back with pins. It was the same color as Em's. Treatle was at their table, talking to Em. His face was close to hers. Then he saw me, smiled, and I went out.

West Fortieth Street was empty and the sky above it a cobalt dome. I walked to the corner and snuck my head around a wall. They were half a block down Tenth Avenue, Shockley banging and kicking the glass front door of Tracy's coffee shop while Saulie argued with her back, his arms spread out in a plea. The storefront was shuttered and you could see through the door that the lights were off, but Shockley kept at it with her hands and feet.

"Someone's going to call the police," Saulie told her. "Is that what you want?"

"When's it ever matter what I want?" she said without turning around. She leaned her forehead against the door, then stepped back and the door opened inward. "Oh thank God," she said, stepping inside.

Saulie followed her in and immediately went out again, backwards, holding his mouth in his hands. The door shut silently.

"Motherfucker!" he screamed, and stumbled toward the gutter. Hunched over, still trying to hold his jaw together, Saulie stalked away down Tenth Avenue.

I had no reason to expect better treatment from whoever had dealt Saulie such a nice crack and decided to go in through the back.

Inside Siberia, Em and Treatle were alone at the table. Em still had her back to me and I saw his arm across it. His hand was in her hair. I couldn't see her face, but I knew that it was pressed against his. I watched his hand in her hair, the fingers clutching at it. I watched her hair, how the light rode on the curls, their weight drawing them down in thick shining spirals. I saw his hand in it, the bitten-down nails. Their faces came away from each other. He blinked his eyes and saw me, then smiled, closing his eyes, and leaned into her again. Her fine long fingers stroked his cheek, nails ballet-slipper pink.

I was a pair of eyes floating down the steps, through walls and through darkness, and there was nothing left to see. Drifting across the basement and into the hallway, I got the padlock on the storeroom door in my hands and tried to feel it. It was heavy, ridged steel, but it was as if I only knew that because I'd felt locks before and my fingers were senseless now. When I grabbed the lock in both hands, pulled my knees up and hung all my weight from it, it was because I'd seen myself doing it a long time ago and my body was getting it done without me.

The crackling sound of the screws splintering out of the wood helped some; so did the feeling of my knees hitting the concrete. I took one of the screws from the steel plate that had come off the door and made a fist around it, held it tight until it broke the skin and my body and mind were on speaking terms again. Then I went in.

Feeling my way through the storeroom, I moved some boxes from in front of the third door on the right, opened it, moved down the corridor through another door and into a bathroom. Across the bathroom was the door to the back of the luncheonette. I went slowly, opening it a crack.

Peeking into the room, I saw a candle burning on a table at one of the booths, the light flickering on a pair of black-soled feet that dangled sideways from the end of a cushioned bench. Maria Shockley was fetal beneath the tabletop. I didn't see anyone else in the shadows.

As I stepped into the room, I thought something moved in the kitchen past the lunch counter and I stopped dead. Watching for a human shape, I saw only the steady blackness and crossed the room to Shockley.

Her neck was hot and damp and there was a pulse in it, though not one a person might hope for. I held the candle near her feet. Flecks of glass shone in the caked blood of her right sole. Holding the candle to her face, I saw that her lips were moving and I leaned close to them.

"A wiz of a wiz the wiz he is . . ." She took a breath, her eyes opening enough to show slivers of white. "If ever a wiz there was . . ."

I heard something behind me, turned, and the something I'd heard launched itself flawlessly into my solar plexus. On my knees, eyes watering, I tried to breathe and managed only a violent gag as I contemplated the high-heeled black pumps and the pretty ankles in front of me.

"Oh, it's you." She sat on the edge of the bench across the booth from Shockley. "You should never sneak around when you're around me. I didn't really mean to hurt you, Sunshine."

The first thing I did was get off my knees and sit on the floor with my legs out in front of me, thinking it might make me a less attractive target than if I tried to stand up. I wouldn't do that until she made it clear she would let me.

"You're just lucky I didn't use the heel."

My breath wasn't all there but I knew I had to say something. In what was mostly a gasp, I said, "Thanks."

The laugh rolled out above me, deep with disdain and afraid of itself. It was even worse to hear when it came from such an attractive childlike face and under such lovely bright green eyes.

"It would've been much better if you were Robin. If you were Robin I wouldn't have stopped."

"That was some punch you gave him."

"Oh did you see it?"

"I saw what it did to him. I was standing up the block."

"It wasn't a punch. I kicked him. He leads with his head—that made it easier, but I could've done it even if all six-three of him was standing up straight. He played too much football in school. Made him thick and clumsy."

Terreya November stood up and stood over me all in one motion, nothing showing in her face or her body. Her arms were thin but deeply cut with muscle and she gave off an air of perfect tranquility, as if she controlled her own body down to brainwave and pulse. I didn't know if I wanted to get to my feet and run away on them or if I wanted to stay where I was, looking up at her.

"I really am glad I didn't hurt you, Sunshine. You're not like Robin, are you?"

I didn't need to know the context of the question to answer it honestly. I said, "Never."

"That's good. I knew you weren't but I just had to hear you say it." She crouched down over my legs, touched my face with her palms, tenderly and as if she were afraid to touch it with her fingers. "Everything a person says is a promise. Did you know that?"

I blinked, waiting to understand the question. Then I said, "Yes. But that doesn't mean anyone will keep their promises."

"Then it's just like I said."

With my chin in two fingers, she moved my face side to side, observing it with a clinical look.

"Your face is pretty messed up."

"Saulie got a hold of it. He hit me when I was sitting down."

"I hate Robin," she said. "But there aren't any rules in a fight—people die in them." She tapped my nose experimentally and I winced. "It's not broken. But I'd get that forehead checked out." Then, as if its relevance to the situation could not be more obvious, she asked, "Have you ever stalked anyone?"

I said, "You mean like the paparazzi?"

"I mean like a stalker."

"No. Never."

Her fingernails stroked my jaw so gently that they could have been just her breath. When she smiled I noticed that she was somewhat bucktoothed and lightly freckled across her nose and the tops of her cheeks. My eyes change shape when they see things they like. I felt them changing.

"I know," she said, holding my face in her hands. "I know you so much, Sunshine." Her voice was husky and confidential. It seemed to promise that the things it said would become true if you believed in the sound of it.

"What do you know?"

"You're afraid of me. You want to run away."

"I'm afraid of you, yes. But I don't want to run away."

"Oh no? Then what do you want to do?"

I let it warm in my chest a moment, watching her ankles,

then her small smooth chin, then back to her eyes: "I want to praise you."

She grinned widely, her copper-red hair drawing light from somewhere and sending it out through her eyes. "That's sweet," she said. "And it's funny too. I'm into damage control and you're into damage."

Shockley made a noise from the bench—a damp, plaintive sound—and Terreya got up and leaned over her, stroking the wet hair from Shockley's face.

"Will she be okay?"

"Of course," sliding herself onto the table. "She has me to take care of her, doesn't she? She may not look it, but I do a very good job considering what she gives me to work with."

I got to my feet, carefully, and walked to her with the same slow caution.

"And what about you?" I said. "Will you be okay?"

"Why shouldn't I be?"

"Last night, this morning, you sounded a little . . ." I would not have said the word *crazy* to her any sooner than I would have uttered Kyle Prince's name in the same room as her. But she did it for me.

"Crazy?" she said. "I guess I was. Kyle made me very upset. But that was yesterday."

"Everything's okay now?"

For the first time, I saw the green eyes wrinkle with concern: "Aren't they?"

"A lot of people are looking for you. Some of them are cops."

It did nothing to her face. "People are always looking for someone. They never find them."

"Sometimes they do."

"Only by accident. Anyway, you'll help me. I know that. You lie for other people, now you can lie for me."

"I lie to protect myself," I said. "The truth is for people who aren't in trouble."

Crossing her ankles, she swung her feet up and down like a toddler on a swing. "You see, Sunshine? It's just like I said."

I held out one hand and she took it in both of hers. Her palms were warm and roughly calloused, the veins thick in her forearms.

"I guess it is."

"You should go home now. I have to put this one to bed." She indicated Shockley with a sideways nod. "And you and I have a lot of work to do tomorrow."

"You mean today."

She laughed a different laugh, plain and sweet, and said, "I hope you're good. I'm not as easygoing as Meredith Fields."

I felt myself smiling and felt good about it.

"Is that all you've got, November? That's the worst-kept secret this week."

"Do you want me to sit here telling you everything I've got right now? Would that be much better? The sun's probably rising. You should go and see it and get some sleep."

I laughed, shaking my head, and told her, "Anything you say."

"I know that too. Oh, by the way . . ." She hopped off the table, tapped a finger on my chest. "What I said before? About you wanting to run away? I didn't mean from me."

"Okay."

"I meant from here."

"The coffee shop?"

"This whole thing. All of it, everyone. You want to go someplace warm and simple."

"If you keep telling me these things, you're going to give away your source."

"Not with that," she said. "You don't even know it yourself yet."

"Well if it turns out to be true maybe I'll take you with me."

"If you think you could ever get me up in a plane."

"You're afraid of flying?"

She grinned. Her hair was a fire around her eyes.

"No, Sunshine. I'm afraid of the sky."

17

Lost Horizon

*E*m hadn't seen me when she'd kissed Treatle, or when she'd let him kiss her, or however that calamity had managed itself, so I didn't mention it when I went back into Siberia and walked up to their table. The place had mostly cleared out. They were sitting away from each other and Em still had her back to me. And Treatle was talking.

Standing behind Em, I listened to Treatle giving her his beauty-appreciation pitch, waiting for him to notice me. Eventually, that strategy began to wear, and I slid myself into the chair beside Em, saying, "How are you holding up?"

"Just hardly," she said, and then her fingers shot to her mouth to catch a gasp. "Gosh, Leon! What happened to your face?"

"It stopped to appreciate beauty," I said, "but beauty was doing sixty."

"Seriously. What happened to you?"

I touched the knot on my forehead and the pain ran through my temples in a nauseating wave. My teeth hurt as well, I noticed, and my chest wasn't having any fun either. With all the different throbs that were playing through me, my body felt much too small, fragile, and it scared me to think how much worse it would feel in a few hours.

"I'll tell you on the way home," I said. "Are you about ready?"

Treatle put his hand across the table, seemed not to know what to do with it, and brought it back to his side. "Dude," he said, "it's cool."

"What's cool, Billy?"

"I mean, it's *cool*." His eyes shifted, beckoning me out the door with all the frantic subtlety of a tattooed neck.

"I heard you, Billy. I heard you both times."

Treatle's shoulders hunched forward. "I mean I'll take her home." His speech was slow and ill-paced, coming apart with each syllable as he leaned his face across the table. "It's cool. Don't worry about it."

"I know it's cool, Billy. You don't worry me."

"What do you mean you'll take me home?" Em said.

He pushed that immaculate face closer to mine and I wanted badly to do something that would age it for him, but I figured he wanted that too—it would help build the character he was inventing for himself.

"What do you mean?" Em said again. "What do you mean you'll take me home?"

He looked at her, blinking, and his body shape-shifted out of the attitude he'd been assuming, leaning back in his chair with a languid flick of the head that suggested he could take or leave anything he couldn't take.

"Hey, I just thought we'd grab some breakfast or something. But it's cool."

"Oh," Em said. "Breakfast?"

"Sure. You eat breakfast, don't you?"

He smiled, she put her eyebrows together. I wiped the sweat from above my lip with the back of my wrist.

"Maybe I'll take a rain check," Em said. "Besides, I don't really think Queens is on your way home at all, is it?"

"You live in Queens?"

Em laughed, covering it with her hand. "Geez, Billy, I only told you twice."

"Maybe I don't believe you."

"Well, maybe I'll have to show you sometime."

Treatle's grin was pornographic. "I don't know," he said. "That's a long way to go for breakfast."

"Maybe," Em said, standing up. "And when I say breakfast, I mean breakfast."

"Well, it is one of my favorite meals."

"It comes right before lunch."

They both laughed. Em excused herself to the bathroom and Treatle was still laughing—soundlessly, right behind his eyes.

"She's a nice girl," he said. "I'm just not crazy about her mouth."

We could have had a conversation then about the nature of beauty, how seeming flaws enhance it by orders of magnitude, and whether beauty is subjective or a state of being that is immune to the eyes of its beholders. And we could have discussed what particular shapes, shades, and sizes happened to sate the mindless hunger of Billy Treatle's pathology, but . . . you understand, I only wanted him to die then.

So I sat quietly, wishing for it, until Em came back. She gave Treatle her cheek by way of good night, and not her crooked mouth, thank God.

We caught a cab and I made up a lie to explain my face to Em as we made our way out of Manhattan. I didn't like it, but I couldn't tell secrets to someone who might or might not be brunching with Billy Treatle.

In the urine-hued gloom of the Midtown Tunnel, I watched Em as she gazed out the window, those eyes taking in the curved walls of broken and moldering tile with the same expression they'd bestowed upon the movie stars. It was as if her eyes, in their vastness, imbued everything with an intrinsic decency—nothing in the world had rotted, there'd been no fall: we were not degenerate.

Spring broke as we moved through Queens, our cab gliding into the wide open stretch of the Grand Central that winds smoothly along LaGuardia Airport and then arcs around Flushing Bay. T-shaped docks of sun-bleached wood with aluminum walkways jutted out of the grassy shore into the World's Fair Marina, bright against the dark blue water. Around the docks, speedboats covered in tarps bobbed faintly in the new sun next to sailboats with their masts bare.

The flat gray ceiling of cloud had shattered under the weight of morning and spread into a fleet of jagged shifting plates, the sunlight falling through the cracks between them in the kind of brilliant shafts you see in the more daunting paintings of the Rapture. The shafts where thin and pink where they fell out of heaven, miles-wide gold when they reached the earth.

I could feel Em beside me and the warmth of the sun beneath my eyes. A hundred million miles of voided space, room enough for everything to die in, and the light fell through it to warm our eyes. I knew that anything I could say would ruin it.

The light was burning away what was left of the clouds, and the winter with them, and the night. I thought I saw what Terreya was afraid of in that sky. All the things you had ever lost were in it, and all the things you ever would.

The cab pulled out of the Grand Central's sunlight and into the solid archway of tree branches that shadowed the slim winding lane of Peartree Avenue. On our right, six-story art deco apartment buildings rose out of the steep slopes of Forest Hills. The landscape sank away to our left, into the shallow basin of marsh ponds that separates Forest Hills from Flushing.

I leaned my face through the open window, felt the breeze and the cool moisture of the budding limbs above us. The driver had his radio on and I tried not to hear it. After a minute, I gave up and sat back next to Em, listening to a news feed out of Haiti. According to my French, there was either an epidemic among that country's horses, or its government had fallen again. Whichever, it was bad news for my paper's editorialists—Corporate had no position on the people of Haiti, let alone its horses.

When we turned onto one of Queens Boulevard's fourteen angry lanes, the sun seemed almost directly overhead, blazing in the lingering haze of the hole it had cooked through the clouds. The driver pulled down his visor. Em put her hand over the tops of her eyes.

She said, "It's like summer already."

"It's pretty great, isn't it?"

"You know, I don't think I've seen a sunrise since I've been here."

"You've got to wake up early, or stay up late."

"No, you have to be outside, and not in the city. I try to see the sunset at work sometimes, but you can't see it from anywhere. All it does is disappear behind some skyscrapers—that's not a sunset."

"You could go over to the river."

"It's just funny you should have to go that far. I think that's what makes all the people there so darn nuts."

"What?"

"They have to take a taxi just to see the horizon."

"You might have something there."

Em had the cab pull over on Queens Boulevard, down the block from the criminal court. Her place was five blocks away.

"It's so nice," she said. "I want to walk a little."

I paid the driver, got the receipt, saying, "Me too."

"You're going to walk home from here?"

"It's only about twenty minutes." We crossed the boulevard at Union Turnpike, going past the door to the district attorney's office, two cops in street clothes hustling a man in handcuffs through it. "I used to come here a lot when I covered straight news."

"Why'd you stop?"

I'd tried to explain that once or twice over the years, and never with much success, but I gave it another shot.

"This Indian woman," I said. "She did a dowry-killing on her daughter-in-law, set a nineteen-year-old girl on fire right in her own kitchen. The city desk gave it two inches on page sixteen."

As we got farther away from the open boulevard, trees and apartment buildings began to shadow us, and I started to feel cold.

"The photographer hadn't gotten to the crime scene in time, but it worked out for him anyway. He noticed all those colorful little Indian shops on Roosevelt Avenue and took pictures of pretty girls in saris. They did a two-page Sunday feature called 'The Jewel of Jackson Heights.'"

I wasn't sure if that explained it or not, but it would have to do. Anyway, Em didn't say anything and we kept walking.

Her building was a pleasantly antiquated arrangement of brown and red brick from the thirties or forties, like just about all the apartment buildings for a mile around, mine included. We were going up the steps to the front door when Em stopped and sat down on one. I sat next to her and she grabbed my hand. My pulse surged past all the ache and fatigue of the night we were putting to bed.

I watched a pale blue vein that traced her temple, the dry lines in her upper lip where the gloss had worn away, the sharp darkness of her pupils, set deep in the impossible color of her eyes. She looked down at my hand, ran her thumb along the crease of my palm, and I knew I wouldn't care what happened to the rest of my life if I could kiss her then, touch her hair. If I could kiss her, if I could kiss her and deserve to do it, the rest of my life could take care of itself.

"Tell me the truth about something?"

"Anything," I said, but the sound didn't take. Em squinted at me and I said it again.

"Why don't you want to tell me how you lost your virginity?"

"What?"

"You said at the club that you'd tell me later, but you never did."

This was not a line of questioning I'd been hoping for, but there was still hope in it. I said, "It just never came up again."

Her thumb tapped against my palm, Em looking up at the trees lining the sidewalk.

"Do you . . . You don't ever look down on me about that stuff, do you? Do you really think I'm so naïve?"

They were two different questions but, looking at her, there was nothing in me that wanted to be clever. My eyelids started beating out rim shots and the corners of my mouth were laughing. She pinched the pressure point between my thumb and forefinger.

"Why are you *laughing* at me?"

"I'm not! Oh God, I'm not!" I laughed harder and she pinched harder and I howled hoping the neighborhood would come out to see us. "You just kill me, Em—you, just all of you . . . That you could even think that, that I could ever look down on you."

"Why wouldn't I?"

"God, Em, don't you even know what you are? You're the best person I've ever met. I've never seen anything like you."

"You're not still drunk, are you?"

"No, Em. God, no."

She spread my fingers out, looking down at my shaking hand.

"You know I, I kissed that boy tonight. I kissed Billy."

I didn't know why she'd told me that, so I let it sit a moment, maybe longer. It sat there in the dark with all the old fear. My face felt like it had been put in a kiln and left there. I remember trying to move my mouth and that the color of the light seemed to change.

"Did you like it?" I said.

"I don't know. I guess."

"That's fine."

"It's fine? What's fine about it?"

My eyes hurt. Her face was shadowy and far away, a face at the top of a well.

"I wouldn't know, Em. I'm not the one who got kissed."

"No," she said, "you're not," and let go of my hand.

"Don't worry. I think I can live with it."

Her lips were rigid against each other as she stood up, looking down at me. "Is there anything you *can't* live with?"

I looked up at her face and English died, the whole language. "I'm sorry."

"Don't be," she said. "I'm too tired and I really don't want to go to sleep hating you, but I'm going to sleep either way. You go live with it."

She went through the door, the door shut behind her, and there was my face in the glass. It was hard to conceive that it was the same face that Em had bothered talking to, that it went with the hand she'd been holding.

It must have been an amusing scene, me shivering on a doorstep with that face in my hands. I'll have to be amused by it sometime.

When I started walking home, it had become one of those mornings when everything seems too bright and too close to the sea, somehow, and you're especially vulnerable to déjà vu and sense-memory hallucination.

I thought a little about losing my virginity, how, to other people, most of it wasn't even sex. She'd been four years older than me, a decade or so to a teenager, and she'd explained afterward that I'd drawn a freak because that's what freaks draw—each other. And didn't I like it? It was good, our secret tribe, with all our secret handshakes. We couldn't be with healthy people, but we would always have us, the members of the end of the world.

What would one of us even do with a person like Emma Lake? Be grateful that she touched your hand and learn to live with it— or without it, or without anything.

No, no one ever stops to appreciate beauty. They only break their hearts on it.

18

Desperado

The broad gray boulevard was paved with enormous octagonal cobbles, pitted and cracked, spaces caked in ash between them. It ran into the sea between rows of stone columns with deep mossy gashes winding down through their fluting. Smashed capitals stuck up in the surf.

I started for the water but something held me still, behind me somewhere, facing me toward the sea.

The landscape was too delicate—white light from the real world shimmering around the edges of the ocean and the jagged outlines of the ruined pillars. I tried to keep the light away and stay in the dream, but it was too bright and I could feel myself falling into it.

It might have been a minute I was sitting up in bed before I heard the knocking on my apartment door, or it might have been five seconds. It might have been five minutes.

But I knew who was at the door. No one else ever popped by at such an hour. No one else ever popped by. I smoked a cigarette in bed and he was still knocking. He would knock until I answered the door. His persistence was steady, stupefying, and would persist until I answered. He liked answers—they agreed with him.

The clock by the bed showed 9:53. I went to the bathroom to put on a robe and checked my wounds. The knot on my forehead had reduced to an acceptable blur, and only a connoisseur would suspect that the red crescent in my chest was left by the toe of a woman's size-five pump. I closed the robe around it.

The knocking continued. It was a changeless, one-two beat, neither loud nor soft, and as hypnotic in its constancy as the rhythm of a mellow heart. I liked that about it but even after I'd splashed my face, I didn't feel ready to answer it. Brushing my teeth triggered a coughing fit that wracked the sleep from my body and lungs, and I still wasn't ready.

But I knew the day was going to be full of things I wouldn't be ready for, and that every one of them would be counting on that.

As I opened the door, a rolled-up newspaper snapped twice against the top of my head.

"May his tribe increase!" August MacCalamite shouted into the apartment as he stepped past me, heading for the kitchen.

Among his more egregious habits was to come up for a morning bracer after a night-long crawl with the courthouse crowd in Em's neighborhood while his car waited in the street. I do not believe I ever did anything to encourage it. Though it sometimes got me a lift to the office, it more often ended with Mac napping on my couch and my leaving a key with his driver to come collect him in the afternoon.

"My God," he said when I met him in the kitchen, "I wish you'd dress better."

I looked down at my robe. "And I wish your cops and your ADAs would take you in in the morning."

"They have wives, they have husbands." He took a pair of rocks glasses from the rack by the sink and removed a liter of scotch from the cabinet above it. "They have homes—safe, substantial homes. They have lovers, they have children."

"You have plenty of children," I said. "And a home. With a wife in it."

His head jerked over his shoulder. "Good God, is *she* here?"

We settled onto the living room couch, Mac bringing along the bottle and glasses.

I told him, "You know I don't drink in the morning."

"But you forget," handing me a glass and filling it, "that it is always nighttime somewhere."

He was wearing his blazer as a cloak, his arms coming out through the front of it as he filled his glass and set the bottle on the coffee table.

"You make some pretty fine points," I said, "so long as no one handles them too much."

Ignoring me, Mac toasted, "To the perpetual night," and we drank. "To the continuation of death," and we drank again. I felt it melting into my lungs as Mac held his glass aloft and intoned: "I drink, therefore I was."

The warmth fluttered my eyelids and I smiled through them at the man beside me who could not be and was. I knew we wouldn't speak again until that first drink was put away, obeying the urge toward ritual that eventually replaces every addict's soul. I wondered how much of mine was left.

Mac's eyes closed, a serene grin spread around his teeth, and I got the feeling he was laughing at me. Then he peered into the shafts of daylight falling through the windows across the room and I was sure that something in him found me hilarious just then.

I finished that first drink and poured another and thought I

saw a quiver of laughter move Mac's ancient cheek and then disappear, though he still didn't turn to look at me. The morning
quiet began to vibrate in my ears as I watched him and drank.
Then it grew louder, more and more familiar, until it trilled against
the dome of my skull.

It was Terreya November, laughing at me.

I listened to the sound of it, thinking of her eyes staring down
at me, and I kept listening, watching Mac squint against the sunlight. It seemed as if they were in on a joke together, that they
had cast themselves into my future and that something in it had
delighted the darkest part of them.

*You people think you know what's going on, but you have no
idea.*

"You," Mac said, lighting a cigarette and shaking out the match,
"look utterly sinister."

"Funny. That's almost how I feel."

"I know that look. I have been intimate with that grim visage
since before the war, since before any war you care to name." His
soft eyes gazed at me over pouched lids as he poured his second
drink. "It is the look of despair."

"I liked sinister better."

He held the glass in front of his face and moved his head to
the rim, closing his eyes as he sipped. Swallowing, he opened his
eyes, looked into mine and said, "Despair."

"Fine."

His cave-deep laugh bounced between the walls, shoulders
rattling beneath the shawl of his blazer. "He would deny it!"

"I might."

"You do."

"So what if I'm a little—"

"Down? Depressed? Dysfunctional? Don't you get contempo-
rary with me, you bastard. I am talking about the end of hope,

the abandoning of all of it, oh ye who'd enter. So you'll goddamn well show it some respect and call it by its name."

" 'Kay."

"So you confess! It is the ultimate sin, you know."

I lit a smoke, shaking out the match. "That won't answer and you know it—I'm no Catholic."

He gave me a smile that liked itself immensely, saying, "And yet you despair. Just be grateful I was here to diagnose you."

"How can I be grateful if I despair?" I got up and opened the windows, put a box fan in one of them and turned it on. Sitting on an arm of the sofa, I took in the breeze for a moment, the scent of pine coming in from the clean apartment next door.

"This is a beautiful place," I said. "Who could despair in a room like this?"

"Every hell has its comforts."

"You try too hard, Mac. At my worst I'm a bit despondent."

"At your worst you're a bit-correspondent. And if you persist in that sin you may die a bureau chief."

"Or a chest of drawers."

"Dead of life," he said, "debt of lust."

"What's that?"

He was speaking softly into his glass now, clutching it in both hands, hoods lowering over the eyes.

"Death of lush . . . Daedalus . . ."

"Mac."

He began to whisper, his body leaned to one side. I put my face close to his mouth and heard: "To know me as shadow, and never with any great basis. And he—what's the man now?"

I didn't know if it was a contemplation of the dead, of himself, or of me, but I felt there was little difference whatever the case.

As I took the glass away from him, the old man snapped up-right, grabbing the drink with one hand and a shoulder of my robe with the other. His eyes appeared perfectly lucid as he said, "If I am dead, how do my fangs still grow?"

I watched the hand on my shoulder. "It's just your gums receding."

Laughing, Mac took his hand off me and returned it to its partner around the glass. "There's a lad! You can be saved, you know. Shall I save you?"

"No thanks," I told him.

"Stubborn, stubborn, stupid young man. What unholy creature doesn't want to be saved?"

"Of course I want to be saved. Who doesn't? I want to be picked up by the collar and shaken up and dusted off and told to be a good boy. But you could never do that."

He took the glass away from his mouth, about to speak, and I cut him off.

"The problem is, you're a male," I said. "You're about as good a male as I've run into, but what's that worth? I could never have any faith in a male. I could never believe in one."

"But," rising to his feet and sweeping his out-turned palms down his body, "here I stand before you."

"Believe me, that's no point in your favor."

"Well," he smiled, returning to his seat and taking up the glass, "then it *is* tough shit for you that I'm the only one here."

Pouring myself another, I said, "Not exactly. I'm here too."

"That must give you endless solace."

"It's endless, all right."

We finished our drinks and I'd gotten up to shower when Mac said, "Tell me about the girl."

"What?"

"Well, isn't it a girl?"

"Who?"

"It is."

"Who is?"

He held up one manicured finger. "Is it a girl?"

Feeling the ache in my chest, I touched the sore spot she'd left there. After a second, I said, "Yeah, it's a girl."

Mac placed his empty glass on the table with a clack and rose from the couch again. "When the time comes, my dear, the Beast will ask you why you have betrayed your country, your kin, and the very last of your benefactors—"

"Then I'd better get a joke ready."

"You? You will look lamely into his omnipotent gaze to mutter with equal lameness, 'It's a girl.'"

"At least it's a faith."

"There you may have something," Mac nodded. "Now go and dress for it."

As ordered, I showered thoroughly, shaved carefully, and dressed slowly—mustering all the grim ceremony I could from a four-hundred-dollar suit.

We were heading west on Queens Boulevard in the back of Mac's town car when he showed me the morning paper. Lane had made the wood. But it wasn't our paper.

"Well," I said, "any press in a storm."

They'd given her the upper left-hand corner, her headshot beneath the line WHEN GOSSIPS ATTACK!

Some header. You *could* swing a dead rat in Manhattan without hitting some media-blogging envy case who hadn't used that line twice a week for the last few years, but only if it had a very short tail. Lane deserved better—writers deserved writers.

As for the piece itself, Robin Saulie's accusations were buried under such a strain of hackwork and gimmickry that the casual reader might never find them. The inevitable "killer scoop" gag I could tolerate. But when the team assembled to write the thing (it was saddled with three bylines) tried to string together "deep dish" and "deep six" and muddled the construction until any chance of rhyme or alliteration fell under its weight, I could no longer suffer their ambitions. I stuffed the paper between the seat cushions.

"I won't ask what human scraped a knuckle on your happy face," Mac said, "but you could wear it more proudly. It's a fitting visage for our little war."

"Sure," I said. "These things have to happen every ten years or so . . ."

The *Godfather* line about getting rid of bad blood finished itself in my mind and died there. A tabloid war suddenly seemed such a small-time prospect. Yesterday, the idea of hours spent kicking libelous turds at the competition would've floated me to work. Now there was nothing in it for me. It was a sideline, a distraction, and there was no way around it.

"Your lack of enthusiasm is cause for concern."

I didn't answer him. The driver was taking the Boulevard all the way in, riding its ugly broadening flatness past strip malls and strip clubs, auto part shacks—all the structures and storefronts advancing in the decay of timeless poverty the closer we got to the river.

"I'm going to get fired," I said.

"Koch fired? Hell you say!"

It took less than a minute to tell him the madwoman story, I'd told it so often. "I know who she is," I said, "and I'm not going to tell them."

"And why would you do that?"

"The way the hacks across town made an item out of Lane, the hacks in our office want to do the same thing to this girl. But whatever happened with her, they're not going to find out. I'm going to lie to them, I'm going to fuck everything up for them."

"I refer to my previous question: why?"

"Because it'll make me feel good."

"Bosh! You've rested too well, your inner rube is showing. There's more to life than feeling good."

"Yeah. But I've done too many of the other things."

We passed through the tunnel and into Midtown, me thinking of the trouble I was in and all the trouble I'd ever been in. Trouble wasn't settling scores with the typists across town. Trouble was something real, and always potentially final—trouble could kill you or leave you wishing for it.

And I was starting to worry that trouble had decided to leave me out of it when the cell began to bleat in my jacket.

"Morning, Sunshine." I felt the breath go out of me. "Did you get a good sleep?"

"I, uh . . . I was just glad to have it."

"You didn't eat breakfast, did you?"

"No."

"Would you like to eat breakfast with me?"

"I . . ." It tightened my throat, the fear of her, and wanting to see her again.

"All that drinking's going to kill you, you know. You play like it's a joke, but it's going to kill you, silly."

Swallowing down the knot, I said, "Maybe."

"And it's going to kill you so much faster if you don't at least remember to eat. Would that be much better? You don't really want to die, do you, Sunshine?"

I looked over at Mac, squinting in the light.

"Well if you don't know, I'll tell you." The sound beneath her voice carried up the promise. "Did you dream for me?"

"For you?"

"The nice thing would've been to say yes—that would've been much better. Am I making you shy?"

"You could call it that."

"But it's okay, Sunshine. Now don't say anything."

She gave me an address and the phone went dead.

"Pull over."

"What?" Mac said. "What is it?"

I felt a grin making a mess of my face.

"It's a girl."

19

The Miracle Worker

The apartment was in the seventies on Central Park West, that strip of prewar fortresses that always made me feel I ought to have more money. The lobby spread out for what seemed a city block on a black and white checkerboard that reflected chandelier light from vaulted ceilings. Black fireplaces were built into the high white corniced walls, and molded archways led to checkerboard hallways on the north and south ends of the room.

The corners of the room were too fluid and I felt a haze around my face. The drive into the city and the subway ride uptown hadn't stood down four morning scotches on a day and a half's empty stomach. I gave the concierge Terreya's name. He rang her, directing me to the twenty-second floor.

The elevator opened on a low hallway of peeling beige paint and bare yellow bulbs. There I was met by a man whose presence made me want to walk away at once. Anthracitic eyes gazed down from a long brown face. His cropped black hair receded from the crown of his skull and his sideburns grew into a beard that ran the contours of his jaw without being so well-groomed as to seem dainty or severe. His body was long, nimble-looking, and decked in a white four-button suit that would not have fit another human being correctly.

"Dr. J.," I greeted him. "I had a lovely time with your wife last night."

Dr. Jerzy Singh had become wealthy as an anesthesiologist, rich as a plastic surgeon, and even richer treating the latest generation of moneyed addicts with an old sodium pentothal therapy. He'd become famous by marrying Cora Heart.

He let out a deep pleasant chuckle, contained deftly by a curled forefinger. "My ex-wife."

"I didn't mean to offend."

"I cannot be offended, Mr. Koch. Hence my success. But we can talk inside."

There was no hint of India in his voice. There was no hint of anything.

I said, "Is Ms. November at home?"

"That is a very philosophical question, very searching. But we should talk inside."

"How about we stay out here, Terreya comes out here, and the two of us go away somewhere without you?"

"I'm afraid—"

"You're afraid that won't be possible?"

He stroked the beard—why else have it? "I'm afraid Ms. November is in the shower."

"You should've gone with my line," I said. "It's got more threat to it."

"Do you think I'm here to threaten you?"

"That's what everyone's here for."

"Paranoia. How delightful. Now, if you'll come inside, we have a great deal to discuss."

"Do you mean you want to discuss a deal with me? Or do you mean we're going to sit around lying to each other while Terreya slips out the fire escape?"

Another hearty chuckle was followed by, "Ms. November on a fire escape? And on the twenty-second floor? An intriguing image—we can explore the symbolism. Now, if you'll follow me."

After all the dirt I'd slung at him and Cora, I could understand his wanting to get me alone in a room somewhere. And I could've understood him working on that project with Terreya if she had been his publicist, but she wasn't his publicist. So there was another reason for our meeting in that particular hallway on that particular morning, and being sharp enough to reach that conclusion was such warm comfort I could've stuck it in my ass to see how it fit.

"All right," I said. "It's good to take a leap of faith once in a while, or just a good old flying leap."

"Faith, flight, fire escapes," Singh said, ushering me through a door. "You speak volumes, Mr. Koch."

The apartment had a sunken living room enclosed on two sides by a hardwood foyer in the shape of an L. Each side of the foyer had a three-step staircase leading down to the living room and a wrought-iron railing fencing it in. There was a kitchen at the far end of the L and a second hallway led off from its corner.

Someone was moving out. Yellowish squares and rectangles of dust patterned the walls, outlining the bright spots where pictures had hung. The living room carpet was threadbare, filthy, and imprinted by the feet of the furniture that once stood on it. The furniture was back against the walls—bulky ponderous armchairs and a matching sofa, a dining room table top beside a bundle of turned legs, an elaborate headboard, bookshelves, and various other antique-looking pieces.

The only furniture that seemed in recent use was a futon mattress with a blanket and two pillows at the end of the room by the heavily curtained windows. Above the mattress was a halogen lamp, providing the only light in the room. A laptop sat blinking on the mattress.

"Terreya asked that I keep you company," Singh offered.

"You're a little expensive to be putting in time as one of Terreya's gatekeepers," I said. "What else have you got?"

He didn't say anything, stepped past me and laid his hands on the railing, staring into the living room. If there actually was a shower nearby containing a five-foot redhead who may or may not have murdered Kyle Prince, I couldn't hear it.

"It must've been a great disappointment to you," I said.

"Excuse me?"

"Kyle Prince."

He still didn't turn to look at me. "Treatment was wasted on him. We must first desire change. What he was is quite exactly what he wanted to be."

"Dead?"

"Yes, he's dead, so I can speak about his treatment, but I don't believe that I would profit from continuing to do so."

Turning, Singh stood away from the rail and massaged the fingers of one hand as if he were finessing off a kid glove.

"You said you wanted to talk. What else do we have to talk about?"

"Why don't we talk about you?"

"I don't see any profit in that."

He walked down to the living room and pulled two chairs away from the wall, saying, "We cannot always see what we are looking at, Mr. Koch." I went and took a seat.

"You asked before if Ms. November is at home. Do you appreciate the connotations of such a question?"

"Did I connote something? I wasn't listening."

Above a smile was the faint heat of his eyes.

"Is Ms. November at home?" he said, crossing one leg over the other at the knee—it always made me squirm, seeing a man do that. "Is Ms. November at home, Mr. Koch?"

"That's what I'm hoping. Last time I came uptown it ruined the whole weekend."

"At home." He was massaging his hand again, this time more deliberately, watching himself do it. "Are you at home, Mr. Koch? Are you at home in your body? In your mind?"

His eyes caught mine again and my face felt drowsy. I blinked against it.

"Where are you at home, Leon?" He was facing me with his back to the dim lamplight. It framed and darkened his features. "Were you ever at home, Leon?"

I leaned toward the darkness, slowly, toward the heat of his eyes. "You ask some interesting questions yourself. And people pay you to ask them?"

"I lead them to answers. Aren't you here for answers?"

"Not to your questions, considering how that worked out for Prince."

He stopped massaging his hand. "Every doctor loses patients."

"How many have you lost?"

"Why not ask me how many I've saved?"

"That's not as interesting."

"But it is very interesting, Leon. It's perfectly astounding when you reflect that I take on the most hopeless cases."

"Apparently some cases are just a little too hopeless."

"There is always a point of no return. Is that alcohol I smell on you this morning, Leon? How close do you suppose you are to your own point of no return this very moment?"

Spots of color began to twinkle in the darkness between us.

"I was just discussing that with my confessor," I said. "He tells me that despair is the ultimate sin."

"Oh?" The light was getting dimmer. No, the darkness was growing, moving toward me as I slid my palms down the arms of my chair. "Do you believe in God, Leon?"

"I believe in sin."

"Of course. Of course you do, Leon. You were sinned against?"

I sat listening to the darkness. "I should hope so," I told him, and my neck stiffened under my jaw. "It's a pretty strong indicator that I'm alive."

"Are you? Do you remember the first time?"

"The what?"

"The first time you were sinned against."

Reds and yellows burst between us in the dark. "Sure," I said, lighting a cigarette. "I kept a scrapbook."

"Well, Sunshine—*this* isn't going anywhere." She was standing on the steps in a purple robe, hair hanging dark and wet, her toenails the color of her hair. "Are you smoking in my house?"

I blinked at her and, before I realized it, was mashing the cigarette into her carpet. Soft, swift footsteps were still in my ears as she seated herself beside me on the arm of the chair. Fingernails tickled the back of my neck, played with my collar, my arm against the warm damp silk across her hip.

"I thought one of you might get something out of the other," she said. "But I guess I'm not really the best at planning. You understand though, don't you? Things go so fast you don't see them."

"Ms. November—" Singh began and she froze him with a glance.

"Anyway, you don't want to play those games with him." Her body slid into my lap and she stroked my cheek with the back of her hand. "You want to play them with me."

"What games?"

"He blames you for breaking up his marriage, Sunshine. Can you believe it?" I could see my face in the bright green of her eyes and felt like I was in a cage full of exquisitely beautiful snakes. I wanted to be quiet. I wanted to *become* quiet—a primal, distant silence.

She took my cheeks between two fingers. "Such a prestigious, educated man, and he *blames* you. He would've treated you anyway, though. Business is business, isn't it? He would've been happy to put you under and put things in your brain so that you'd have to die like Kyle had to die."

"Now Ms. November, I—"

"Shh! But tell me the truth, Leon. Do you think you're just a scapegoat for everybody's most awful, awful dirty stuff? Would that be much better? Or are you what they say you are?"

"No one says I'm anything."

"You're still pretending a little, I think." Her eyes flickered to the cigarette butt at my feet. "Oh my." She spun off my lap, squatted between Singh and me, holding the butt in front of her face. "Did you put a cigarette out on my carpet?"

As she grinned at me, the slight projection of Terreya's two front teeth gave the impression of a whimsical little kid. Her eyes gave the other thing. Together, they made Terreya look like a girl who kept her dolls pristine until she decided to burn them.

"You're all a-shiver, Sunshine. Does Jerzy bother you? Sitting there? I'll make him leave us alone. Won't that be much better?"

"Ms.—"

"Get out."

As if she held a gun on him, Singh rose and moved through the room without turning away from Terreya. She was watching the cigarette butt in her fingertips.

"I'm sorry about that," I said when I heard the door shut behind Singh. "I was starting to think this wasn't your apartment."

"It was my grandparents'. All this furniture too. I had to have it moved out of storage. They haven't lived here in years and years. But it's mine now, half this whole floor." She slid back into my lap with an arm around my neck. "Don't you like it?"

"Yes."

She stared at the cigarette butt, grinding the dead coal between her thumb and forefinger as ash flowed down the sleeve of her robe. "Do you?"

"Very much."

Drawing her fingertip across the tops of her cheeks, Terreya painted matching lines of black ash beneath each eye. Ginger lashes fluttered above the lines of ash.

"My mother hated it." She slipped her hand inside my jacket, removed my pack of cigarettes. "That's why she filled it with so many ugly things—cold harsh tasteless things. Eighties things. I had to have it all hauled away to the dump. Or to someplace. Anyway, it's all gone now."

She took a smoke from my pack, held it to her lips, and I lit it for her. Steady gold bands brightened in the depths of her irises, as if straining to keep her pupils centered. Watching the smoke twirl in the light, Terreya said, "Oh, look at that. You're making me smoke again."

"I'm sorry."

She blew a stream of smoke. My eyes watered.

"I don't know if I can really blame you or not," she said. "We should talk about that. We should really talk about that. But what was I saying?"

"Your mother."

"Oh, Mother. Anyway, she's in hell now. Do you believe in God?"

20
Us

The cell phone bleeped in my jacket, but I didn't move to answer it. It would be Harris asking where I was. My accounts knew not to call the cell during office hours and the only personal calls I ever got anymore came from Em, who I didn't expect to be hearing from anytime soon—or anytime. I kept one hand on Terreya's shoulder and the other on her shin. I didn't know how long they'd been there. I didn't know if Terreya understood that they were there at all.

She'd been saying something about her mother when the words had sped up, got lost under her breath. I'd felt her body tensing against me until it seemed to cramp around the sound of her voice. A sweating blush came into her cheeks and she'd hugged her knees with a gasp, doubling up in my lap. Then she'd stayed there in a rigid sort of coma, her face against her knees, her body a tight warm coil. I'd whispered to her, raised my voice, tried the most tentative strokes of her back, always answered by the same deep steady breaths. When I'd say her name, a shiver would play through her muscles, then she'd go solid again.

Now, with her heels against my thigh and an elbow at my ribs, it felt good to wait for her, watching her dream madness in my lap. She felt like someone worth holding. Holding her felt like something worth doing. I'd woken up in plenty of rooms without knowing why, but I thought I belonged in this one.

Under Terreya's eyes, the lines of ash blurred down her cheeks in moist gray trails of cooling violence.

She'd said her mother was in hell. Experience said there'd be a male or two who belonged there with her. Terreya could finish telling me about it or not. We could trade the long stories or not—those stories that are all so common by now; those stories that aren't supposed to define us anymore, even if they cut off anything else that might have.

The front of her robe hung open around a gray sports bra, her breasts rising and falling with even breaths that whistled through thin pink nostrils. I couldn't tell if this time-out was more an emotional catnap or a genuine schizo lapse. Whichever, it amounted to the same little dodge, the same temporary sample of forever. It was good to be able to go there now and then if you could come back from it. Even better with someone waiting for you.

A shaft of light fell through a crack in the heavy curtains and shone across Terreya's cheek, bringing out her freckles. I was glad Prince was dead. Because either you let yourself die or you didn't. Whatever else was wrong with Terreya, whatever was wrong with me, we were alive, and there was no percentage in the other thing.

Rubbing her shoulder, I felt the sinew hum beneath her robe. With her so close to me, feeling her breath, her pulse, I could sense her strength. There was something expert in her form, as if each muscle possessed an individual intelligence. I could feel it in every taut fiber as she held herself unconscious, what made her more artist than athlete, what elevates some human flesh above the rest of the simple meat—

Terreya *needed* that body.

I held that body closer, pressed my face to the back of her hair. In the shaft of sunlight, Terreya's hair seemed to change texture and hue the longer you stared at it. Whispering her name again, I closed my eyes and woke up in the dark.

◇   ◇   ◇

Across the room, an orange glow lit Terreya's mouth and the tip of her nose.

"I'm sorry I went away on you before," she said around the stem of a pipe. "Sometimes it happens." The coal brightened, crackling in the bowl, and she closed her eyes above it.

My eyes adjusted to the darkness and I could make her out past the glow of the pipe, laying on her stomach on the futon mattress, her feet bobbing in the air behind her head.

"I guess we both were kind of sleepy," I said.

"I wasn't sleeping. It's something I learned in pain management."

"What were you doing in pain management?"

"You picture these knots in these great big ropes," she went on, ignoring me, "and you untie them in your mind. It takes every-thing you've got to focus, every part of your energy to really see the knots—to feel them and be there with them. If you're still here at all, you only feel the pain. If I do it right, I'm on a beach and I can feel the breeze on my neck."

I thought of her whispering into my cell. *Breeze . . . breeze . . .*

She dragged on the pipe, exhaled, and I smelled something sweet and somber in the air, like roses dying. "The drugs only dulled it the littlest bit. And, anyway, they didn't want to make an addict out of me."

If Terreya was going somewhere, she'd get there her own way—all I could do was stay out of it.

"But you," she said, "you were sleeping like the sweetest baby. I think you have a little fever. Really, Sunshine, you're in no shape to be staying out all night."

"How do you stay in shape, smoking that?"

"It's cheaper than beer since the war. Besides, your shape isn't something you *stay* in." Taking another pull, she exhaled the dead blossoms. "It's what you are. And it's always changing. Your shape is all the things that ever happened to you, everything you were and are, and everything you're going to be. It's a lifelong negotiation."

"Did you learn that in pain management, too?"

"I was only nine. My father died in the crash and things started coming to me. I started thinking about them, but I couldn't put them together until much later."

"Sounds like you've thought a lot about them."

The orange light painted a zigzag in the darkness and she was sitting in the lotus position. "Doesn't it look that way too?"

"From most angles, yeah."

"It should. It's my religion. Do you have one, Sunshine? Or do you just have the angles?"

"An angle's just a way of looking at things. A person should have a few of them."

"I can see all of yours." Standing up, she touched the belt of her robe and the robe fell down around her. Against the gray of matching sports bra and Jockeys, her skin seemed luminescent. She wrapped a blanket around herself and sat on the edge of the mattress, her feet peeking out in the dark.

"Your shape is only jagged," she said. "You're only these jagged little edges and angles. You think you're hard and sharp but you're only just brittle. Did somebody tell you that was enough?"

"I'm not sure I know what you mean."

"Your friend from last night, the one with the rack, the one with the eyes—I bet she knows."

Her head moved forward and she put wrinkles between her eyes, like she was trying to see something behind mine. "What would you do if you fell down, Sunshine? What would you do if someone dropped you?"

"I don't tend to cuddle up in people's hands."

Smiling at that, she said, "Brittle boy. You've spent the last twenty-four hours in mine. Don't you like it? Or am I not squeezing hard enough?"

"If I was really all that brittle you'd have cut yourself."

The smile widened with her eyes. "There go those angles again. What will you have when you run out of them?"

The feeling running through me then, you could call it fear or want—I didn't have to pick just one.

"Maybe you'd have the truth," I said. "Or maybe just something that sounds like it."

"Isn't that always enough, though? When you think something's true, what more do you ever need?"

"But if you're wrong," I said.

Curling her toes, she rubbed her feet against each other, the blanket falling away to her knees. "I am not wrong about Jerzy Singh."

"I didn't know we were talking about him."

"He did something to Kyle," her legs folding under her as she turned away, taking a handbag from behind the mattress. "I had Kyle for two months and he was just the sweetest boy. Jerzy took him for two weeks and sent me back this thing that couldn't live." One hand took a white oval from the bag and squeezed it over the top of the other. Her hands made a squishing sound, caressing each other, then spread an oily sheen down the length of one shin.

"What did Singh do to him?"

"I don't know," she said, watching her hands work the lotion into her calf. "He shoots people up with truth serum and then he *talks* to them. Who knows what he says."

"You can't actually brainwash a person with truth serum—that's movie stuff."

"Don't tell me about doctors," her hands sliding the shine over the heel of one foot. "I was finished with doctors when Jerzy Singh was still doing anesthesia." Her fingers gripped her toes with a crack, slid between them. "I thought if I got the two of you talking he might give something away."

"So now you're done with me?"

She watched me through the tops of her eyes and the white bottle arched across the room. I caught it in two hands. "Wouldn't it be much better if you did this for me?"

I watched her legs, her face, then her legs again. "Is this the part where I'm going to praise you?"

"You mean you don't want to?"

"That—" I watched her legs again, her eyes. "That can't be what I mean."

I crossed to her and knelt at her side.

"Do my shoulders."

I smelled coconut when I popped the cap on the bottle. Rubbing the lotion into my palms and gazing down at the curves of her shoulders, the slope of her back, I was afraid to touch her, that this was part of a test and that I'd disappoint us. I might have been touching her for two seconds when Terreya said, "Harder."

The word seemed to come from a distance, with nothing personal in the sound of it, no qualifying tone at all. It was perfectly ordinary that someone should tend to her body when it wanted tending. "Are you really going to do my shoulders while you're staring at my ass?" she said. "Some people are in such a hurry they never get anywhere."

Her shoulders were much smaller than my hands, and much harder. There was heat between my palms and her skin when she spoke again. She said, "What's her name?" Reaching back, she put my hands to the tendons between her neck and shoulders. I sat beside her on the mattress.

"Whose name?" The tension hardly yielded to my fingers.

Her body slid against my palms as she pushed up on her elbows, smooth wings of muscle standing out below her shoulders. Tapping the bowl of her pipe with a brushed steel lighter, she said, "The one with the eyes," and blew a stream of smoke, laying her face against the mattress.

"She isn't here," I said, tracing heat along her spine to the small of her back.

"I don't believe you. I can feel her all over you." With a twist of her torso and waist, Terreya's thighs were straddling my lap and she was staring into my face. "Tell me she isn't here."

"I–"

Her hand on the back of my head, she moved my face into the curve of her neck. I could taste her sweat on my lips as her other hand went up the back of my shirt, warm against my skin.

"Tell me again she isn't here, Sunshine."

"She isn't here."

"You lie," she whispered, and touched her tongue to the front of my lips. "You lie," she said into my mouth, giggling, and tore her fingernails down the length of my back. I screamed.

"Shh," she cooed, the pad of her thumb on my lower lip. "Why don't you make us a drink now? For the pain."

In the kitchen I pulled a yellow plastic shade away from the window. I felt the sunlight on my face, the burn of her mark in my skin, and took a fifth of Black Label from a cabinet above the refrigerator.

"Need any help?" She was leaning against the doorjamb.

"I think I'm bleeding."

"But it's a clean bleed, Sunshine," displaying her fingers like a kid before dinner. "My hands are immaculate."

"Is that what you used to do to Kyle?"

"Kyle isn't here."

"Tell me that again."

She let out her laugh, ageless and tinged with hate. "Do you want me to cliché you to death? Want me to say he was everything? So what if he wasn't? He was part of it."

Rinsing a glass in the sink, I poured off a shot and swallowed it. "What do you want from me?"

She looked past the question, toward the window, eyes wincing against the light. "Isn't it so distracting? The world out there? I always try to pretend I'm really in it, but it gets so hard sometimes I forget pieces. Or I remember glimpses of things, but the things themselves go away."

"Do you remember why you called me in the first place?"

She crossed one foot in front of the other, balancing it on a curled toe and sending tiny wrinkles into the curve of her arch. "A person has to call someone, don't they? I've never had a lot of people to call. Have you?"

"No."

The skin around her neck and above her breasts was a mottled pink blush. Her fingertips left white trails through it. "But you have people you can talk to. I mean, if you wanted to find things out? You have your sources?"

"They're not always a lot of help."

"Were they any help last night? Did they help you then?"

"No."

Her eyebrows were fine, straight lines that angled down sharply at the ends. Most of the ash was gone from under her eyes. "Maybe they can help me though."

"How so?"

The wrinkles tightened around her eyes and she tilted an ear toward the ceiling. "But first you can help me get this one back to bed."

Even as Terreya said it, Maria Shockley appeared behind her in the doorway. She was slouching her shoulders and tugging on the bottom of an oversized *Synchronicity* jersey that composed her entire outfit. Her reddened, watery eyes switched back and forth between us, settling on Terreya.

"I did it again."

"Oh, sweetie." Stroking a sweaty tangle of hair from Shockley's cheek, Terreya told her, "We'll get you cleaned up."

Shockley pulled the collar of the jersey into her mouth, chewed it for a moment, and stuck out her lower lip.

21

Emerald City Blues

erreya took her trembling ward by the shoulders and I followed them from the kitchen down a hallway and into a bedroom furnished with a collapsible plastic wardrobe, bookshelves built into one wall, and a box spring–mattress set. Shockley's purple premiere dress was a heap in a corner and she stood over it holding herself, swaying vacantly at the knees, while Terreya and I stripped and flipped the mattress and gave it clean sheets from the wardrobe. Unsure whose modesty I was trying to protect, I inspected the bookshelves while Terreya lay Shockley on the bed, undressed her, and set to cleaning her with a handi-wipe. I also didn't want a better look at the scabs running lengthwise along the tops of Shockley's thighs.

"Don't be embarrassed, sweetie," Terreya said.

Actual books were sparsely represented on the shelves, most of the space taken up by leather-bound volumes of *Vogue*, *Cosmo* and other glossies. But there was also a paperback called *The Body in Pain*, an edition on corporal punishment by the name *Thy Rod and Staff,* a battered *King James* beside an equally worn *The Wonderful Wizard of Oz,* and a mammoth hardcover called *The Ashley Book of Knots.*

"You've got an eclectic taste in literature," I said without turning around.

"Are you making fun of me? The magazines are for business and the rest—you could call them keepsakes."

"I see."

Bedsprings creaked and I thought of the song I'd found Shockley singing at Siberia. Removing *Oz* from Terreya's collection, I noticed the dust jacket was held together with strips of Scotch tape. In a corner of the lemon-yellow flyleaf someone had printed "12/83." Beneath it, in a florid, swooping script, was inscribed:

My Sunshine,
> *This is the most wonderful book in the wonderful world, full of imagination and love and the most clever ideas. That is why it is my gift to my most imaginative and clever and best best girl! Haven't you always been mine?*
>
> > *Forever,*
> >
> > *Gene*

"Isn't it sweet?" she said. Turning, I saw flat eyes so dark they weren't green or any other color, and felt the lids over mine begin to quiver. Shockley was curled fetal with her head in Terreya's lap, Terreya stroking her hair with automatic motions that didn't register on her face. "He always had such the sweetest *words.*"

Staring down at the loops and swirls, I snapped the cover on them, hoping I wouldn't leave Terreya any worse than I'd found her.

"Why would you keep a thing like this?"

She put a finger to her lips and smiled behind it. "This one's almost sleeping," she said, and fluttered her eyelids against Shockley's moist, gaunt cheek. Shockley squirmed and giggled through a shiver.

"Sing to me," she muttered, and Terreya began to whisper a melody that was only a murmur in the flow of her breath.

If ever oh ever a wiz there was . . .

The words whirred gently, just on the tops of her lips.

. . . because, because, because, because, because . . .

I found myself mouthing it, feeling the familiar shape of it through my lips, the double U's, and the *causes*. Nothing on earth is so lovely that it cannot be perverted.

Shockley's eyes were slips of white when Terreya slid off the bed and spread a comforter over her while I flipped through the book—no other notes, no underlined passages, not even any wrinkled brown tearstains.

"Mother only kept him a year," Terreya said, spooning behind Shockley with an arm around her cocooned body. "Gene was not an earner."

"You don't think Maria needs a hospital?" I asked, wanting to stave off the specific details of the year that took the color from Terreya's eyes.

"She'll go once nobody has to carry her in. Then we can call it elective surgery. It used to be it was much better to admit you were an addict than to say you had your ass done, but everyone's priorities are so deranged these days."

"Why didn't Kyle go to one? When he got fired in LA he went into rehab full time. Singh isn't exactly serious treatment."

"But he's the kind of treatment no one finds out about. I wanted Kyle to get help—for real—but if anyone found out about what he was doing then no one would've ever hired him again." She put a hand over Shockley's exposed ear. "Someone would've *told* on him if he went into rehab again. Someone like you," she said, adjusting the comforter around Shockley's neck. "Maybe that's why I thought of you when I saw all that blood. He would have been okay if he could've gotten real help, if there weren't so many of those people around—those, those . . ."

"Caligulas?"

"You know about that?"

I nodded and she went on.

"When I first met him he'd only been back here for a few months and he was—I'd never known anyone so *offended* by people. The way they go after each other, the way they climb, it made him sick. He thought it would be much better here but he had to start using again even just to look at people."

I looked down at the battered copy of *Oz* in my hand. "And you think I'm one of them?"

"Everyone is one of them." There was no anger in her face, no accusing glare—only the weary calm of someone who had spoken a truth and wanted it acknowledged in kind.

"I don't believe that," I said. "Are you one of them?"

"I could be. You spend your whole life hating them, all you have is that you know you'll never be one of them, and then you figure out that it only takes a second to change your mind—it only takes a second to be one of them. You said you believe in sin? Kyle did too, but then he goes and does the worst thing there is in the world."

"You think suicide is the worst thing a person can do?" I said. "You've seen the worst. You've had the worst. You know what it is."

"I know that something changed Kyle. I want to know how and I want you to help me find out. I can't go around asking people—we were a secret, Kyle and me—and now there's the police. But you can ask, you can find out what happened to him. You can help me."

"Not if you're going to stick to this delusion that you had yourself a perfect little saint. If Kyle hated his business he could've found another. There must've been something pretty worthwhile in it for him."

Terreya split one sentence into three: "You. Fucking. Lie." Anger tightened the corners of her mouth and froze there.

"Sure," I said. "But not now. And where do you get that crap about suicide being the ultimate sin? It wasn't any Sunday school sermon that made you weaponize your body, Terreya."

She leapt off the bed and had crossed the space between us before I finished saying her name. "You lie."

"You're lying to yourself."

Her lips and eyes shut tight as she shook some thought from her head. She said, "Listen to me, Leon," and I liked it, finally hearing my name in her voice. "It is getting very hard to keep talking to you when you won't—you won't even, you won't even try, you ..." The rise and fall of her shoulders sped up with her breath.

"I don't think you deserve any of what's happened," I said, letting the book drop from my hand, "but I bet Kyle did."

"You fucking lie!" she shrieked. Bookshelves rattled along my spine as I fell back against them, ahead of her fist. I wouldn't have taken it standing up if I could have—and I couldn't have.

Terreya crouched in front of me on the balls of her feet, while I passed time on my knees.

"I only wanted you to tell the truth!" she was saying. "I only wanted you to help me!"

There was moisture budding along the rims of her bright green eyes and I could feel the shape of her in my chest, in the energy of the pain she'd put there, even as I tried to breathe through it. When a breath stayed down long enough for me to use it, I said, "Do it again."

"What?" A tear slid over her cheek through the faint dust of ash.

"Do it again." It fell from the curve of her jaw onto the mottled blush of her chest. "I'm here for it. Do it again."

Reds and yellows burst around her face as she shook it side to side. Her tears pooled down from wide open eyes that clicked helplessly around the room, as if looking for a friend, a witness, a way out. All the heat in my body seemed to surge into my cheeks. I could feel my heartbeat beneath my eyes as Terreya's squared on them. Her eyes were so steady then, so clear, they seemed to touch and taste what they saw. Sniffling, she bit her lip, and her hand moved toward my face the way hands move toward the things they fear. Her touch was gentle and trepid and I never felt it, only saw the pink blur of her thumb as it passed beneath my eye, pulling away a tear.

I didn't blink against the ones that followed, letting them roll hot down my face, easy, empty of shame—watching Terreya through the tops of my eyes.

Her gaze was soft and drowsy. She ran her thumb under her eye and smiled at the drop on it, holding it toward me and drawing it along my lower lip. The salt warmed over the tip of my tongue as I felt the smooth edge of her nail against it, then the tiny ridges of her thumbprint.

"Do you think I'm a murderer?" she whispered, slowly pulling away her thumb.

"I don't know."

"But you still think I could be?"

"Yeah."

She slid her thumb back into my mouth, watched it slip back and forth between my lips with the dangerous charm of a tipsy girl eyeing her car keys. "You knew that I could hurt you, you knew I might have killed Kyle, and you came to me without telling anyone."

"I might have told someone."

"No," she said. "That's just not you. But what *is* you?" She cocked her head at the question, took her thumb from my mouth.

"I don't know."

"I do. You're the boy who can spend years bullying me on the phone all day and flirting me up at parties every night and then not even know my voice when it's saying it's going to hurt you.

You're the boy who makes me cry and then sucks the tears from my dirty little thumb."

"You said your hands were immaculate."

Standing over me, she held my face in those hands and said, "But I'm *delusional*, aren't I? Maybe I'm a liar. Maybe I'm a killer. What are you?"

"I don't know."

"Lonely, I guess. Do you believe in God?"

"I don't know."

"That's no way to live." One hand moved to my neck, tilting my head back. "How do you know if you're even alive?"

"It doesn't matter." I put my hands behind my back. "No one knows the difference if you talk fast enough."

"That's the trouble, isn't it? That mouth of yours?" Her palm slid over it, her fingers pinching shut my nostrils while my fingers locked around each other behind my back. "This pretty mouth that lies," she said. "This pretty mouth that defames and defiles. Give me a reason to let it speak again. Give me a reason to let it breathe again."

When she took her hand away, I said, "Because I'm going to help you."

"Why?"

"Because I know how much you like me. This is twice you didn't aim for my face."

22

Year Zero

Terreya gave me her version of the night Kyle Prince died. We agreed that she would take the story to a lawyer and prepare a statement while I tried to dig up anything about Prince's recent "change" that might bolster it. It had taken some effort, but I'd convinced Terreya that there was no way for her relationship with Prince to remain a secret much longer—that her best chance against the police was a preemptive press release in which a grieving young woman is being hounded by a vicious old cop without any real evidence to back him.

From a PR angle, even the rope burns—strictly speaking—didn't amount to evidence. She had tied him up to protect him from himself, suicidal and high as he was. It had been a mistake to leave him alone for an hour or two, but she'd had a job to do. Who can afford to lose their job?

Terreya dropped me off at mine in an obligatory Range Rover. Maria, dressed in a fresh new jogging suit, slept with her head in Terreya's lap.

Harris was off on a lunch date when I got upstairs, and Lane was on my ass.

"You must think fuck-all nothing of me," she said.

"Of you? What the hell are you talking about?"

"I warned you to stay out of all this about Kyle and you spent all night getting into it. Everybody knows about it, Lee. Is there anyone left you *didn't* tell?"

"A few," I said. "But it's all working out. What are you so afraid of?"

"I'm afraid for you. I was trying to protect you."

"From what?"

She was staring into her monitor, her lips a tight, grim line. "From getting fired, for one thing."

"That was always going to happen," I said, taking my seat and switching on my computer. "I keep feeling less and less distance from the people we're covering, and I hate the people we cover. I'm starting to feel like one of them."

"You've already made yourself one of them." She still wouldn't look away from the monitor. "You're reckless, and you're in the story."

"Then I'll be glad when they can me."

"No waiting there, Leon. The publisher wants to see you."

Our publisher wasn't called Pol Pot merely because his first name was Paul and he carried before him an impressive gut. He'd had to earn that nickname through decades spent traveling the globe assessing news outlets for acquisition and purging them of their staffs. The walls of his office were hung with framed front pages from newspapers I'd never heard of—declaring scandals I'd never heard of—and it amused me that other countries should still have news of their own.

Pol sat behind a steel desk that resembled something you'd dissect a body on, looking every inch of what you wanted an old bastard to look like. His eyes were sharp at their corners but serene in gaze and hue, somehow too intelligent for the puffy contours of the face they were in. They seemed especially betrayed by the nose beneath them, gone bulbous and raw from a hundred capillaries that had never stood a chance.

"Smoke?" he said, as he prepped a cigar.

I shifted in my seat and looked at him more closely. It was too soon to get fired. I needed at least the rest of the day to issue promises and threats with the implied backing of the page. Thinking up a string of lies was taking much too long.

"Good God, mate, do you smoke or not? I'm sure I've seen you out front."

"Um, yeah," I said. "Okay."

"Well, light up then, make yourself at home—this is practically Tasmanian soil." He pushed a ceramic ashtray across the desk, tapped Corporate's logo, and said with confidential pride, "They don't make these anymore."

Despite all the lurking doom, it did feel good to light up in an office again, to exercise a friendly vice in the workplace as humans had done for several civilized centuries. Perhaps my career was over, perhaps all for an opium-smoking ninja girl with rabbit teeth, but here and there people still managed to live well. I'd seen them doing it—I wouldn't forget.

"Do you like it here, Leon?"

"Of course."

It was enough that he smoked cigars and wore a slept-in blue dress-shirt with the sleeves rolled up and red suspenders, but God bless the fat fuck if he didn't produce a pair of genuine bifocals from his breast pocket.

"I believe you," he said, furrowing over a one- by two-inch clipping he'd taken from a folder on the desk. "But, then—why this?"

Taking the piece, I recognized it as my own, an item from a few days back about a USO show. "What, uh—what about this?"

He blew smoke, eyed the cigar distastefully, and damped it out in the tray. "It's quite a bit of work. You are the author of that bit of work?"

"Yeah."

The clever eyes were distorted by the two thicknesses of glass, expanding and contracting depending on how I looked at them. "Come on, mate. Must I do all the work myself?" Regardless of how I watched the eyes, they just sat there looking well rested. "Go on then, read it and tell me where it goes wrong."

Working the thing over, I couldn't find a sore spot in it. It even made me a little queasy, how utterly it toed the editorial line—right down to "our fighting men and women."

"For the love of—you really don't see it, do you?" Pol said, perusing the folder it had come from. "It's right there in the lead, Leon. Try reading it aloud."

With a humble throat-clear, I began, "'With the way the war's going, our fighting men and—'"

"'With the way the war is going!' What exactly do you imply by that?"

"Imply? I wasn't implying anything."

"Weren't you, mate? Weren't you really? If you say the war is going a certain way, but you don't say for certain what way that is . . ." Setting down the folder, he eyed me over the tops of his glasses. "Well, say it to me now. What way do you suppose the war is going?"

"I can't say I've been paying much attention."

His eyes received it with a deep, crinkling bliss. "And there's the essence of my quandary, Leon: you don't care." When he took the bifocals from his face I hoped he'd use them as an effective prop, but he simply dropped them in his pocket.

"I don't ask you to believe in our positions," he began again, rubbing the bridge of his nose. "For a reporter, it's probably better all around if you don't believe in anything at all. But when you could care less about either side of an issue, it's just a bit disturbing to see you make a habit of launching these penny-ante sneaks against ours."

"I didn't even notice it."

"No? I seem to recall a similar problem with you just last month."

"That Chinese thing?" I said. "I was told to drop it and I dropped it."

The story had involved an arrangement between a Chinese diplomat and a strip club, and fifteen thousand dollars. It had been killed before lunch—an arrangement involving Corporate's satellite TV division, the People's Republic, and a billion people who still can't watch the BBC.

"No one here needed to be reminded that China was a sensitive case," Pol reminded me, "but you made the calls anyway—using the name of this newspaper. That's our *brand*, mate!"

"I was following a tip."

"You were getting done all the damage you could before anyone here had an opportunity to intervene."

That had been about the size of it. "Honestly," I told Pol, "you're giving me too much credit," and slid the clipping toward him. He returned it to his folder.

"Is that my permanent record?"

"It's a record, but do you know what I've learned after thirty-one years in the news business?"

"No such thing as permanence?"

"There he is!" making his hand into a pistol and putting one through my chest. "What offends me about you, Leon, is not that you attack our positions, but that you attack them when there's no evidence that you personally take any position on anything. It suggests that your problem isn't with our politics but rather our existence itself. And I'd say that's rather a sour attitude for a man to take after we've sponsored his lifestyle for the better part of a decade."

"The better part of it was a long time ago."

"That's only because you still haven't learned to live well. Take this, for example." He handed me a sheet of printer paper from the folder, its text in the familiar lone rectangle of a news item waiting to be fitted to a page. "There's been some interesting buzz about you the last couple of days, Leon—call it increased background chatter."

I saw my name within the text, and a set of bylines from the other paper at the top of it. Pol explained that it had been faxed for comment to our publicist that morning, a jovial enough creature who'd rep bubonic plague if it had the credit.

"I suppose they held it a day so as not to hit you and Lane Martin in the same editions," Pol speculated. "It's certainly too rich to have tacked it to the end of her story with a 'Meanwhile.'"

"What are they saying now? I'm gay?"

"Oh for a simpler age, mate." The centers of his eyes sharpened with the corners. "They're saying you're impotent."

I felt not so much like I was sinking but being pressed on all sides by the air itself. Reading it through, I hated that I'd ever been young enough to want my name in print. And I wanted to hate Meredith Fields while I was at it, but I couldn't get that far. There were no victims between us.

"Well," I said, "at least it's poorly written."

"I'd ask after its veracity if it was any of my business or the point, but of course it's neither. What matters is what we do about it."

"Do? What's to do? It's just some more wind in the whisper mill."

"Of course it's not!" Pol leapt from his chair, or stood from it fast enough to give that impression. "This isn't the kind of thing that gets laughed off or goes forgotten. It's certainly not a thing you could disprove publicly."

"Well, I'd give it a shot with a member of the competition," I said, "but I doubt there'd be any run on volunteers at their end."

"This is the kind of thing that breeds speculation, Leon—and that breeds follow-ups. They'll hang this over you in perpetuity. It'll come up every time you so much as squeak. Are you honestly telling me you don't care about *that?*"

"I'm not telling you that."

"Good to hear it," he said, returning to his seat. "So I assume you'd feel some tremor of gratitude toward me and toward this newspaper if I got the story killed—which I have."

He didn't need to explain how. Both papers were owned and operated by people who had families and who could never conceal as much about themselves or those families as they'd like to. So all parties could mutually assure the destruction of one another's reputations if the old tab war ever became unmanageable. But I'd never heard of that kind of power being tapped to protect someone as low on the list as I was, and I said as much.

"I can't fire you over this, but I also wouldn't like to have it floating about," he said. "You're supposed to be out there finding scenes to get behind, engaging in the blurry dreams of the excessive elite. You're supposed to be living your life right through the bloody roof, Leon. So you'll understand if I wouldn't like my advertisers believing that the legman for our celebrated chronicle of daily decadence is in reality nothing more than a jejune little monk."

"Thank you," didn't roll off my lips. Nothing did.

"And now that I've done this for you," he said, "of course I'll expect to see a new you around these offices. That is, you'll think twice about biting this company in the ass the next time the opportunity arises."

I thought to say that you couldn't buy loyalty, but of course you could. And mine felt pretty well paid for.

"No ass biting," I told him. "Got it."

Father and son, he was walking me to the door with a hand on my shoulder when he said, "I don't suppose you've any idea as to the font of these accusations?"

"An old friend went on a little campaign against me yesterday. But that's over now."

"Anything to do with the Kyle Prince trouble?"

"Something, but that'll be over soon too."

"That's over now," he said as his hand left my shoulder and he stood between me and the door. "We had to fire Delores, Lane Martin's a page-three spread for the enemy, and you'd have been their next meal. *And* I've got the police pestering my Editor. One dead slick isn't worth that amount of trouble."

"Okay," I said. "But it would've been neat to know what really happened for once. You know, instead of two sets of lies boiled down through their publicists and our lawyers."

His nose twitched with pink laughter. "I've got as soft a spot as anyone for the vainglorious pursuit and the quixotic gesture, but you're going to let this one die where it lies."

I gave him my word and I shook his hand, trying to remember when either had meant a goddamned thing.

"You're good at what you do and there's no reason why you shouldn't have a good home here," Pol sent me off with. "But he that troubleth his own house, mate . . ."

"Ah, home," I said. "The place that there's no place like."

23

Timing is Anything

With both Pol and Lane telling me to get out of the Prince business, there wasn't anything I could do from the office. Besides, Emma Lake was in there somewhere, and I was relieved to get outside without having to face her. Or so I'd have liked it to go.

Instead, Em was standing fifteen feet across the plaza when I got outside, one shoulder to me and one to Sixth Avenue.

I remember that she was smiling behind her long fine fingers, her face in the sun and the sun on her bare legs—smiling with no sign in the auburn and gold of her eyes that she'd had reason to miss any sleep. I don't think I would've felt the sunlight then if I'd have stepped into it instead of skulking behind the building's front columns with the ESU men and their machine guns, but Em was dressed for it: a pink scarf that would've evaporated in a minor gust, sheer floral blouse with fairy-puff short sleeves, a sage-green skirt to her knees, and pink suede flats with little pink flowers at the toes.

All of that, in all of that sunshine, and all of it for Billy Treatle.

He stood opposite her, dressed in something interesting, his hair doing interesting things. He was saying things, too, and he was saying most of them to her breasts. I was too close to the building to hear anything except Corporate's news channel pundits piping in through hidden speakers—one of them making Jesus out to be a maniac, the others agreeing with her.

I waited to see if Em and Treatle were coming or going, waited to see if I might follow them or make a scene or make Treatle one with the traffic. I didn't know what I was doing. That became especially troublesome because I was already doing it, stalking out from behind a column and heading for them with a sullen devotion to I knew not what.

Three insane strides and it was over. I stopped and stood still as their faces came together. When they came apart, Em started to say something and Treatle spoke on top of it. When she began again, Treatle nodded his way through some of that, cut her off again, shrugged, pecked at her cheek, and started to walk off as soon as she'd turned toward the building.

The muscles in my jaw felt heavy when she was near enough to speak to.

"He didn't watch you go," I said.

"Excuse me?"

Up close, there was darkness beneath her eyes and edging in around the curves of her face. I hated that I'd put it there, and that anything else I might say was only likely to make more of it.

I told her, "It's nothing."

Nodding, she looked off to one side without turning her head. "Well, that's new and different."

Her looking away scared me—once someone has to hide their eyes from you, it's never long before they can show you them again without feeling it. Those eyes barely touched on mine when they moved again, watching something behind my ear. A voice said from there:

"Tardiness is a mode of sloth, Mr. Koch."

The hairless detective angled himself between us, sporting yesterday's beige suit and a smile you could misread in any direction. "You keep showing up at these advanced hours and you're just liable to lose your job."

"Don't worry," I said. "I'm always in the last place it looks."

"And here you are right where I left you, but just a little worse for wear." He touched my forehead, the pain reminding me of the bruise Saulie'd put there. "Just a little worse for wear. Excuse me, Miss . . .?" he said to Em.

"Emma."

"Emma . . .?" His mellow gray eyes measured her face like it was one they'd seen before and were happy to see again.

"His name is Detective," I cut in. "He's the cop who thinks Kyle Prince was murdered and that I know who did the murdering. Now he thinks he'll talk something out of you about it."

Em bit her lip at that, narrowing her eyes, gauging the face that gauged hers.

"I was talking to a charming young woman," he said with leisurely charm and without looking away from her.

"You weren't talking fast enough."

"Come now, Mr. Koch," he said, "it's all these petty pleasantries that get us through the days and nights." He turned back to Em and demonstrated. "A pleasure to meet you, Emma. James Hood."

"Emma Lake," placing her hand in the hand he offered with the easy confidence of someone who'd never had to fear a functionary of the law.

"A pleasure. How do you come to know our friend here?"

More petty pleasantry followed. Hood was good at it. He was one of those men you wanted to talk to if you weren't me—all composed competence, a man who could take care of things, protect them. It depressed me that he spent it on something as arbitrary and artificial as the law.

Watching the crescents sneak in around Em's mouth, the forward jut of her eyeteeth, I let myself zone, listening to the sounds in her voice. There was the blue shadow of vein tracing her temple and the gentle brown bounce of her hair as she spoke, all the shapes and motions that were hers. I wondered if it would inspire anything but pity or fear if she knew that I thought of her as *her*. It certainly inspired as much in me.

"He means well," she was saying, "but he just has to walk into a wall every now and then." They were laughing, Em leveling her conspiratorial squint at me.

"Now don't stand there looking so evil," Hood advised me. "She's just got you pegged."

"She's got all that," I said.

"You should see all the good it does me."

Hood smiled at her and I forgot for a second that he was a cop. Then I remembered.

"Made any progress since last night?" I asked. His smile didn't wither. Neither did he turn it away from Em.

"Do you know what we have here, Emma?"

"Yeah, I wish."

"Just one more of these young men who doesn't know when to come up for air. How's a woman put up with it?"

She beamed at him through the tops of her eyes. "She doesn't."

Gathering a breath and some courage, I let out, "He thinks I know at least one woman who puts up with it. And when he's done playing with you he's going to start getting all bad cop on me because I'm not going to tell him who she is."

The warmth withdrew into his face, his features thickening over it: "You know who she is." His posture stiffened with his face.

"Of course I know who she is," I said. "And of course I'm not going to tell you. She's a confidential source. If you arrest me for obstruction or get me subpoenaed as a material witness we both know all you'll get for it is bad coverage and wasted time. The

ACLU and what's left of the free press will make this season's poster boy out of me and you'll be all over the news for not being able to break a case without shitting all over some of the more popular amendments."

My monologue hadn't moved a muscle on him, but I felt like Em was the only thing keeping his hands off me.

I pressed on. "The fact you're here talking to me again suggests that you don't know who anyone is or where anyone goes. But that wouldn't necessarily keep you from getting to her, the way people keep their secrets around here. So she's meeting with her lawyer and working out a statement this afternoon."

The brown curves on his forehead that should have been eyebrows lifted. "Nothing like a prepared statement to bolster up some good suspicion," he said. "What might this one have going for it?"

"I don't have to tell you that. Maybe I don't even know."

"Only reason you're telling me word one is to stand me still or send me walking. I might be persuaded to give you a little bit of one or the other, but not in exchange for nothing."

"For one thing, it'll have plenty of alibi witnesses on her side," I bargained, "and the total lack of witnesses to the deceased's deceasing on yours. Oh, and your lack of motive while we're at it. All that plus a known dope fiend fiending harder and harder the last few weeks and a girl who tried to protect him when Robin Saulie started predicting his demise all over the place—that's to explain your rope burns."

The curves changed shape as Hood's eyes lit under them and his face loosened enough for a smile that I didn't like. "Now that last part's interesting. Those burns don't feel explained to me."

I explained them further, how she'd tied Prince to his bed and left him alone, adding, "She was in shock when she found him. She's got—you understand—a delicate temperament. Her leaving the scene, calling me—most of it's lost to that shock. And explained by it. I'm the only one she spoke to in the after-blur, and guess what kind of witness I'll make for you or any ADA who thinks she's lying about her state of mind? That's if one could ever get it into court, and of course we're betting none could."

"Just a step back now," Hood said, gesturing me to slow down with his palms, my face buzzing from all of my chatter. "If she tied him up in his bedroom, how does she account for his turning up dead in the kitchen?"

"Lucky for her she doesn't have to. Whether he got loose or someone got him loose, maybe you'll have better luck looking into that than you've had with the rest of it. I'd say Robin Saulie has a weird knack for knowing which of his friends won't make it through the night."

I didn't like to keep bringing him up, but he'd taken a prime position in my mind ever since Terreya and I had decided on a strategy. Her list of people who knew about her and Prince was a short one, and Saulie was the only one on it who'd been interviewed by Hood. Saulie's failure to name her would make a nice second suspect of him if Terreya needed one, but I wanted to know why he'd been protecting her before we used it against him.

Hood's fingers slid over the smooth dome of his skull, traced the line of his jaw. "He's also got an alibi."

"Doesn't everyone? Look, I don't even care who killed Kyle Prince. I only care who didn't."

"Let me have one of your cigarettes." I supposed he could smell that on me, and who knew what else. His face crinkled behind the smoke at first, then evened out, luxuriating in a rare indulgence. "I'm going to enjoy that statement," he said. "I am going to enjoy that statement in full. Right down to its every last hole."

"It doesn't matter. The statement's not for the police," I said. "It's for the press." I laid out the angle for him—the grieving girlfriend against the NYPD—in case he'd missed it. "So that's where we stand."

Either something I'd said had warmed all the friendly back

into his eyes and cheeks or he was forcing it there. He looked at me so happily I thought he'd wink.

"That's where *you* stand," he said. "But don't step too hard on it or you're liable to fall right through."

"All you've ever had to suspect her on were the rope burns and the fact that she didn't come forward when she found him. In an hour you won't have either one."

"An hour's a long time, friend."

"Try one of mine."

"No, that pleasure is yours. Yours and your new playmate's. Let me ask you something, though." Here I heard the first faint snicker of a story being torn to pieces. "She told you Prince had been abusing his substance of choice with an ever increasing vigilance lately. She ever tell you how?"

It was Hood's face in front of me, but Terreya's was flashing over it—her darling, lying face.

"How?"

"Shooting, snorting, smoking? What was the man's favored method of delivery?"

He had the corpse, so he had the answer. All I had was a choice of lies to be caught in, so I scrapped them and cleared the sudden heat from my throat, admitting, "I didn't ask."

"That's fine," he laughed. "I like that. Looks like you've got everything sewn up right and tight on your end, or someone's just got you sewn."

"What are you talking about?"

"Got his blood work back this morning, follicle tests too. Kyle Prince wasn't on anything stronger than Maalox, Mr. Koch. Only thing in his system was what the pictures used to call truth serum. Someone was treating the man. And the treatment worked."

"That doesn't make—" almost blurting her name. Centering myself around a breath, I shook my head and told him, "That doesn't make the girl a murderer."

"It makes her a liar. That's a fine thing for a source you're protecting."

"You might have a point," I said, "but it's neat to have more than one of them if you're going to charge someone with murder. If heroin can't explain why he got fired anymore, why should it still explain his getting dead? Prince was just an ugly list of ugly problems. You're not going to nail them to his girlfriend."

"But you're happy enough to nail yourself right to her and I'll be happy enough to let you. Her lying is about to run her at a wall and I'll be happy enough when I find you there with her."

Telling Em it had been a pleasure—her eyes in a daze like the one I was trying to will away from my brain—he shook her hand, held it, and leaned his face close to hers.

"I'd ask you to talk sense to your friend here," he said in a low, almost sympathetic voice. "But why should anyone else get to wasting some hard-earned breath?"

I was watching him walk off down the avenue, mixing in with the late lunch swarms, when Em grabbed my hand. "You don't look good."

Closing my eyes, I breathed, concentrating on her hand in mine, the cold of her fingernails, the warmth in the pads of her fingers.

"Why did you kiss him again?"

Pinching her favorite pressure point and shoving me in the chest, Em laughed, "You're really hung up about kisses."

"Some of them mean something."

She shook her head, bouncing her spirals. "You're sneaking around for some girl that maybe killed someone—"

"And I've barely slept, and I haven't eaten—"

"And you've been drinking instead." Tilting her head, she watched me out of one eye. "And all you're worried about is did I kiss some stupid boy?"

"If he's just some stupid boy then why did you kiss him again?"

"Why are you still covering for that girl when you know she lied to you?"

"A lot of people lie to me. Not all of them mean to."

"So if they don't mean to, that makes it okay?"

"If Treatle doesn't mean to be a sociopathic little shit, that makes it okay? Why did you kiss him?"

"Why do you still want to help her?" Anger made Em's eyes and mouth seem small. That it was anger at me made it more than I could look at. I looked at the ground between our feet, felt my lips hardening in a miserable little kid's pout. "Don't look away from me."

Something was new in her face then—in the self-possessed cast of her features, the vivid depths of her eyes: the woman she would grow into, the sanity and the strength.

"You want straight answers out of me," she said, "but you've hardly spoken straight to me since I've known you. It's always around some corner with you. What are you waiting for?"

"Things are bad, Em. Things are getting out of control."

"And I don't care about any of them. Let's just have things be okay between *us*. You hurt me this morning and I hurt you back. But we don't have to keep doing it. You can make me mad at you or you can make me sad, but it doesn't mean I want to hurt you for it—or for anything bad to happen to you." She touched her lips together. "Don't you know that?"

I said, "Yes." My lips snagged on it and I said it again.

"This girl you're trying to help, do you know that about her?"

"I don't know it, Em. But some part of me just believes in her."

"Maybe it's the same part of me that likes kissing Billy."

"I don't get it."

Something seemed to shift in the vastness of her eyes. "I mean, there's nothing to be afraid of with him, nothing to get my hopes up, nothing to disappoint me. So I let him buy me lunch and I let him kiss me."

"Since when did you get so cheap?"

"You want to buy me dinner?"

"I . . ." I watched the ground again, Em laughed, and I watched her face.

"I'm not as delicate as you think I am, Leon. No one's that delicate."

"It's just that things are so ugly right now, Em. Not just around me, but in my head."

"I'm not afraid of it. You're always trying to protect me from everything, but you can't protect me from that." The warmth of her breath tickled my ear as she giggled, "Meet me after work. We'll go Dutch."

24

The Rummage Sale

ood could have been lying when he'd said that Prince had died clean and sober, but he'd told the truth about the rope burns the night before, and it was also true that Prince had been in treatment. But it didn't make sense for Terreya to have lied about it. That is, I didn't want it to make sense.

Wandering through the clotted wreckage of Midtown, I called her up to chat about it.

"Where are you?" she wanted to know.

"Strolling."

"It's no good teasing me, Sunshine."

"It's no good you lying to me." She asked what I was talking about and I asked if she'd been to see her lawyer yet.

"Not just yet. What is it?"

"You might want to hold off on that statement. The police tested Kyle's blood. You do know they do that, right?"

"So?" Her voice was small. "It would be much better if you stopped teasing me, okay? What is it?"

"Kyle hadn't been using when he died. There was nothing in his system."

There was a pause, a breath, and then the shrieking of her familiar refrain. "You fucking lie!"

"Why would I lie about that?" I said. "What would I have to gain?" But I wasn't talking to her. I could hear gasps and sobs from a distance, Terreya crying, "He's lying! He's lying!" in between them.

"Hello?" said a woman.

"Maria?"

"Yes?" It took some trying, but I got her to understand who I was. "She's kind of throwing up right now. I can hear her through the door. What did you say to her?"

I told her.

"No, that's not right," Maria said. "He had to be on *something*. He wouldn't have done it if he was himself. He couldn't have. He was using."

A false dilemma. It was the kind of logic my stories had always come from. But it did weary.

"Did you ever see him use?" I tried.

"I'm not sure, maybe not. But it doesn't matter." I heard knocking through the receiver and, "Reya, are you okay in there?" After a moment, she said, "Maybe you could come here? I never know what to do when she gets like this."

"Just stay with her and don't go anywhere, okay? Now, listen," I tried again. "Why are you so sure Kyle couldn't have killed himself without getting high?"

"Killed himself?"

Listening to her breath, I waited for more. When none came, I asked, "Well, what else are we talking about?"

"Where are you? Can you come here?"

I was very sick of addicts, and very much wanted a drink.

"I have to go talk to some people if I'm going to be any help to Terreya. Now if you know something—"

"Who is there to talk to? Can't you just come here?" I told her where I was heading and she responded instantly, "We'll come there then."

"Don't come anywhere. Just stay with Terreya. She'll be okay," I said—though I didn't know who I was saying it for, or how it could possibly be true.

◇ ◇ ◇

The front room of the restaurant on East Fifth-fifth was particularly desolate, even for after three on a Friday. The swarm had come and gone, leaving me free to sift through the remnants of their careless chatter with the staff. I might get nothing for it except a few minutes alone and a buzz, but I needed those too.

At the bar I asked for a Red Label and the manager. I was working down the first thing when Massimo Ciccone came out of the back room with Hilary Dale, who had a column at the other paper that was most generously described as flavorless.

"Leon," Dale said as he stepped to the bar. "Popular sort like you drinking alone?"

He'd come up from a Maryland debutante page a year before and had brought with him the wavy middle-parted fop of a petulant fifteen-year-old prep. "Not so close, please," I said. "You'll get smarm all over my jacket."

"Guys, guys," Massimo stepped in, the bats over his eyes nervously flapping their wings. "We won't like to have a scene."

"If there was a scene here, your friend would be kissing better ass than the one on you."

"Getting any ass at all yourself, are you? I'm hearing lately that, well . . ." He faded the sentence into an expression of pleased disdain that jiggled the nexus of jowl and neck that had eaten his chin. "I'm hearing lately that that isn't quite a priority with you."

"Try writing down your quips before you trot them out, Hil—

they give you trouble. Besides, that story's been killed. Doesn't anyone tell you anything?"

He grinned at that, his upper lip straining over a row of translucent gray teeth that wouldn't have fit in his mouth had they not been inverted shark-like. Behind the oval lenses of his glasses, Dale's eyes undermined that grin with the cringing apprehension of a man who suspects there is a unanimous opinion of him that might soon be spoken to his face.

"It may be a dead deal for the paper," he said, "but it would be—heh—it would be a hell of a shame if it made it out to the blogs."

"And you're just amateur enough to do it."

Laundering libel about celebrities and politicians through the blogs and then putting it in our papers as "Internet buzz" was basic for any print journalist. But most of us had refrained from using that tactic against one another, since most imaginations could extrapolate the eventual consequence.

"What do you suppose would happen—" I started and stopped. Reasoning with Hilary Dale would be as fruitful an exercise as reading his stuff. I turned to Massimo. "This is who you go to for an image fix? No one trusts a gossip page you have to flip through the business section to get to. Really now, Massimo, you gave up on me too easy."

"What's that he said?" I watched the jowls bleat silent fury around Dale's lips. "You went to him first?"

I sipped my drink and said, "Stop steaming up your glasses. Why should he be any different than anyone else?" The old petty was a warm embrace. "I think I was a little hard on you last night," I told Massimo. "I was just off on a bitch. But that's no reason we shouldn't do business."

The bats soared toward the low line of his hair. "We could, eh . . . Business?"

"Sure, why not?" I saw the manager coming out of the back room and got up to meet him halfway. "Just give me a minute."

Massimo and Dale were exchanging hisses as I walked away. The manager took me to a table toward the front—beyond earshot of the few remaining diners—and seated himself to my right. I asked what he'd heard about Kyle Prince.

"This is a place for watching," he smiled, "not listening."

The table hadn't been bussed since its last batch of patrons. Fried calamari glistened in a bowl before me, fat emulsifying on jagged crusts.

"It comes to the same thing," I said. "They want to be paid attention—that need applies to all the crap that comes out of their mouths."

Despite the distance of our nearest fellow humans, he leaned his elbows on the table, saying low and evenly, "Certain things are meant to be overheard, certain things are not. My talent is in knowing which is which, and you can't say I haven't always been good to you guys with the part that's meant for you."

"That part won't do me any—"

"Besides," he went on, squeezing closer to me along the table, "I'm all paid-up for the month."

That was a point I couldn't sidestep. He'd bought a month's worth of sightings. If I wanted decent information on top of his cash, he'd have to have something for it. For a second I thought he wanted some portion of his money back, and that offended me. I might practice checkbook journalism, but only in one direction.

"Of course," I nodded. "What's on your mind?"

"Have you met my niece? Catherine?"

"Should I have?"

"Have you should, have you will. She's an actress. She's very talented."

"Of course."

Next to the squid, a plate contained the remains of a burger, its discharge of inner surprises stagnant in a petrified ooze that touched a pile of wispy fries. That would fix my appetite for a few more hours.

"She's in her second semester at Tisch," he was saying when I cut to his chase.

"NYU—of course. I assume she has her headshots?"

"Of course." I assured him that there was always room on the page for another pretty face and a few lines of meaningless praise. He said, "Wonderful, I'll get you her picture on Monday"—and started telling me the relevant banter from the lunch rush.

"Something about Kyle getting fired must have been a real snafu," the manager said, pushing the burger plate away from him.

"Why do you say that?"

"Some girls from the agency were in, not endeavoring to keep down their voices."

"You think they wanted to be heard?"

"That could be, or—you know how it goes with the kids. They get excited and don't know or don't care what travels."

"What traveled?"

"Kyle's agency's hiring outside PR." His voice dropped, intimidated by its next words: "Kevin Rose."

Rose was emergency toxic cleanup. Individuals—like Jennifer Morales—used him to ease themselves into or out of rehab, deflect child custody hearing revelations, or spin the occasional battery charge. Companies had one use for him.

"They're being sued," I said.

"Keep your voice down," he reminded me pleasantly, sliding even nearer. "Nothing's filed yet, but they're thinking soon. They haven't even officially retained Kevin yet. There was a meeting last night, a breakfast this morning."

"Panic. Who's doing the suing? Prince have family?"

"That I don't know. They said something about a girl."

Something about a girl could be any girl, but I figured I knew the one. My scotch was a pale yellow shadow around slivers of melted cubes. Finishing it only made me need more. "Couldn't you dig me up a specific?"

He chuckled at that. "Couldn't the girls? You know their mode of talk." I was staring somewhat hypnotized at the curling dead tentacles as his voice took on a high-pitched trill: "'She was totally freaking. The girl's totally freaked.' It would stop their little hearts if they ever got their minds onto a specific."

"Who's freaking?" said a woman's voice. The manager was out of his chair and kissing her cheek before I'd fully turned to see her. She was still wearing the jogging suit Terreya had put her in, along with a new pair of sunglasses and plain black baseball cap.

"You should've come when I asked you to," she said. "She's much worse now." I blinked at her. "Come on, we gotta run. Fast."

"You look wonderful," the manager told her.

She scrunched her nose at him, munched a fry from the burger plate. "Could you bring me, please, a Diet Coke and a Cobb salad?"

"Of course."

"Thought you said we had to run."

"And I thought you said Reya would be okay. She's having one of her blackouts."

"She'll wake up. You really shouldn't be here."

"And you should? You said you'd help her. You keep saying things."

Thinking this might be the only time I ever had Maria alone, I told her, "Well now's your chance to say something. You were trying to tell me something before. Kyle did something he wouldn't have done sober, and not the suicide. What was it?"

She was looking at me, then beyond me.

"Ask her yourself," she whispered, then, "Please not this fucking cunt."

"Maria!" Dale announced and I pushed in the chair on my left, keeping my hand on its back. "This is interesting company you're keeping."

She returned his gray smile with a smirk. "Why do you have to talk to me? Did I talk to you?"

"I, um . . . Just being polite. I'm here, you're here, you were looking my way."

"I look *ways* all the time. It doesn't mean you need to interrupt my lunch and insult my friends." Maria fed him cold dismissal over the tops of her sunglasses.

"Now I know why you get such glorious press," he said, sulking away and out of the restaurant, leaving Massimo abandoned at the bar.

Poking a squid with her finger, she said, "And I know who you work for, pussy." To me, she explained, "Matt's people own his ass."

"Well," I said, "someone's got to."

"Who owns yours?"

"Mine's strictly a rental."

As if to prove it, Massimo pulled the seat out from under my hand, ignoring Maria. He whispered, "We have a deal?"

"Not yet we don't."

I told him what I could do for him, for how much.

"You, eh—" He looked across my body at Maria, tried to pull me closer to him.

"You can talk in front of her. I just did."

"I—you want that I pay you?"

"You pay your publicists, don't you? With me you'll get something to show for it. Send Ziortza with it tonight—she'll know how to find me."

Blackhead pinpoints winked in the Roman nose as he considered the proposal. I moved my face away from them.

"Leon, I eh—I don't like this deal so much. Ziortza, this is no girl for trusting with money."

"All the girls trust you with theirs, don't they? We couldn't do business if I didn't think it ran both ways."

"We need to go," Maria cut in. "Reya'll kill us if she wakes up and we left her alone with that chauffer."

"What's wrong with the chauffer?"

The corner of her lip slipped under her teeth: "He's a man."

"You've got to tell me what's going on."

"We need to go."

Massimo put a hand on my wrist as I stood up. "You've got the offer and a few hours to consider it," I said. "You think Hil'll be as generous after what you just pulled on him?"

Of course Ziortza would keep the money for herself. I hoped she'd go home with it, but she'd probably blow it over the weekend. Either way, Massimo would be deprived of it—along with the items I'd promised.

Walking to the Hummer at the curb, Maria asked, "Do you always take money to write nice things about people?"

"I don't always do anything."

"Do you ever take money to write evil things about them?"

"Every week. It's called a salary."

25

The Man in the Kerosene Suit

 couldn't do anything about Terreya's blackout and I couldn't get Maria to talk about Prince, but I could get a lift up to Kevin Rose's place in the SUV—so I settled for that. We pulled over in the east eighties with Terreya's head in Maria's lap, Maria pluming opium smoke down through her equine nostrils. If all those two ever did was take turns getting each other high and putting each other to bed, it was as good a relationship as I'd ever seen.

"I'll never figure how Reya gets by on this," Maria said.

"What do you mean?"

"Do you ever have one drink and then stop?"

"Not if I can help it."

"That's what this is for me. It—" She flared her nostrils, surveying the bowl of Terreya's pipe as if its contents had personally betrayed her. "It teases."

Getting help or not getting help was her business, so I left it to her. "I don't know how Terreya gets by at all," I said. "I've only spent a day with her and this is twice she's gone catatonic. How does she keep it together to do business?"

"This is new." I saw the orange coal in her brown eyes, the darkness behind it. "Except when we were kids, she's always had these fits under control. She'd have them when she wanted them—when it was safe. The way other people meditate."

The SUV filled with the depressing floral scent, putting an ache behind my eyes.

"How long have you known her?"

"All my life, give or take. We grew up together—across the park. It hasn't been this bad since we were little, when it first started. The last week's been as bad as I've ever seen it."

A week, Hood had said the night before, was how long Prince's behavior had been getting him noticed at work. Exhausted by the sound of my own questions, I put to Maria: "What happened last week?"

She put the pipe between her knees and stroked Terreya's hair. "You should ask her. I shouldn't talk about her behind her back."

"I'm trying to help."

"So am I."

"Great." I opened the door to go.

Grabbing my wrist, she twisted it in an awkward version of one of Terreya's holds, but I let her pull me to her. Even the clumsiest violence can demand my attention.

"Don't ditch her." Her lips barely parted around the words, the sounds taking on a deep tight emphasis by passing through clenched teeth. "At least wait till she wakes up. Then you can ask her."

"I have other people to ask right now and I can't wait for Terreya to come out of it. Asking her questions would probably just put her out again anyway."

Maria's nails would have cut through my skin if she hadn't bitten them off. "You said you'd help her. You made a promise."

"I know," I said. "But remind me again sometime."

◇ ◇ ◇

Kevin Rose had been in semiretirement for as long as I'd known him, taking on the occasional new client according to some personal formula of economy and whim. He'd always told me what I wanted to know if he figured I'd find it out sooner or later anyway, but that's not to say it was ever a straightforward process.

"You can never get out of this fuck-ass business," he said as we stepped onto his corner balcony, twenty-nine stories above the earth. "There are always too many people waiting to stuff their slimy little cocks into one orifice or another the second they think they don't have to be afraid of you anymore." We sat in deck chairs around a short glass table. "And no one's afraid of you once you've stopped conducting business. So you've got to keep fucking conducting it. Even if conducting business makes you batshit fucking crazy."

He never raised his voice when he spoke that way. He never raised his voice.

"The business I'm conducting—" I started. That was naïve.

"Like those old lions on the National Geographic," he mused, or began a long musing: they spent their lives protecting the pride, breeding the pride, only to be chased off one day by some young thing. "Then you get to watch your pride from the outskirts." His eyes were watching his pride from an outskirt, squinting in the reflected sunset of a mirrored skyscraper across the avenue.

He wore a cabana shirt, khaki shorts and sandals that didn't agree with his broad flat nose, his grand bald pate or the white hair gelled behind his ears sharp enough to display every line of his comb. "You die out there," he said, the red rage of dusk on one half of his face. "You die out there on the edges of the thing you made."

One end of the island was a fury in orange and red, the black outlines of buildings disappearing in a mute scorching glare that grew hotter and brighter as it descended the horizon. Across the sky, the moon seemed to have risen upon that heat to set itself halfway into the night, caught between black space and blue atmosphere—ready to fall through either one.

"You build a house, these cocksuckers at least know you built it," Rose was saying and I nodded, sipping quietly at a margarita his maid had given me. As much as I hated to hear grown men poeticize the larger carnivores, I preferred it to their discourses on the nobility of house-building. "Maybe I'm just another full-of-shit old cocksucker myself," he continued. "Maybe it's something about the spring . . ."

I'd opened the door to these intimacies the previous summer, when I'd looked over some notes for his memoirs for him—I thought there might be money in it. There might've been, too, if he'd published them. But he was still waiting for a few more people to die.

The maid came out and refilled my glass. I touched her hand as I thanked her. More thankfully, she brought Rose a joint, which usually softened his focus.

"After you," he said, offering it.

"I've got enough paranoia working today, thanks."

He gave me a look that brought all the fire of sunset into his eyes. "You think you can ever be paranoid enough, you fucking three-year-old?"

"I think you'd better smoke that thing."

I went to the railing to let him do it in peace. Peering over the edge, I felt the building surge forward behind me and the street rushing up through my senses. I sat back down, black spots buzzing my eyes.

He was crushing the roach in an ashtray on the table when I tried, "I don't know what you've got to complain about, Kevin. You've got all the clients you could ever want."

"I've got all the fucking clients I don't ever want. And I don't want them more all the time."

"You've got a new one I'm interested in."

He nodded, watching the flames across the avenue. "Vile Prince. Why would I tell you anything about that expired cumdrop that his agency didn't already tell the police?"

"What did they tell the police?"

He waved a hand in the air, dismissing refuse. "Erratic behavior, suspected of drug use."

"The police know he wasn't using drugs."

"What the police know couldn't hold my morning BM. And you haven't answered my question. Why should I give you anything my client didn't already give them?"

"The police can't do anything to them or for them," I said lighting a cigarette. "I can."

"Fuck them. What can you do for me?"

"What's on your mind?"

"Jenny Morales. I thought I was going to see something nice about her in that shit paper of yours today. Her asshole of a father's a friend of mine."

"You can still see something nice about her. What do you want to see?"

He said he would think of something, then told me what had gotten Prince fired. Three weeks ago, Rose said, two female assistants had filed a complaint against Prince with human resources.

"This business is so cunted-up," he elaborated, "who knows sexual harassment from getting a cocktail? Stupid shit it was, strictly four-button suit rookie stuff—throwing a twenty at a girl and asking for a shoulder rub, a 'Fuck Me I'm Irish' pin, an invitation to a hot tub . . . This half-a-woman little prick didn't know what the fuck coast he was on." Curling his lips, Rose spat, "Motherfucking LA."

"And they fired him for that?" If I sounded incredulous, it was because I'd never heard of any company, let alone a talent agency, doing the right thing without the actual application of legal action.

"Fire him? They gave him two weeks of lunchtime sessions with that piece of shit voodoo fuck Jerky Singh. Fucking 'aggression therapy.' "

"And it didn't take."

"And it didn't take. The girls made a second complaint this last Tuesday, in the afternoon. Tuesday night it happens. One of the girls—not one of the girls who'd been making noise, just another assistant, another girl."

He took a moment to put it together more neatly. I was glad that the girl in question wasn't Terreya, but there was always another girl, with always another of these stories, and there always would be.

I looked at the cold open eye of the moon, that unmovable stare. Kyle Prince flashed across the white of it, flashed frozen and dead, bathed wet magenta, cradling himself in one hand.

"She'd stayed late," Rose began again, "and she's fixing herself up in the girls' room . . . She's doing her makeup, she's washing her fucking tits—whatever they do in there."

Lighting another cigarette, I saw there was only one left in the pack and hoped it would be enough to get through the rest of the interview. "Kevin," I said. "What happened?"

He shrugged, wiping a film of sweat from his upper lip with the pad of his thumb. "Kyle Prince comes trotting out of one of the stalls with his fucking chinos around his ankles and a monkey fist on his pud. He's whacking off all over himself."

Shrugging again, he turned back to the burning skyscraper, working his roach with a Bic, as if there could be no more to the story.

"What did he do to the girl?"

"Sprayed her skirt up a little before she could get the door open."

"He didn't touch her?"

"I told you what the cocksucker did. If that constitutes a *touch* is for the lawyers to figure out." He sucked at the yellowing wedge between his fingers, coughing smoke. When his lungs cleared, he added, "Or it would've been, if he'd lived."

"It still will be," I pointed out. "The agency's being sued."

Flicked across the railing, the sparking wedge looped in a gust and disappeared beneath the balcony. "Not by her. She'll get her payday. So will the two who made the complaints, and pretty much any other brat who comes along with a plausible enough story about him. I'm only needed in case this leaks to the press in spite of the confidentiality agreements, which these things always do."

"Especially when the publicist leaks them."

Smiling, he took the margarita from my hand and set a glass-ful of cubes on the table between us. "Wait around to prove your value and you'll be waiting a long fucking time, Koch."

We sat with that as the last flames withdrew along the mirrored panes. Then the moon was alone in the pale dome of sky and we were sitting in its shadow. I'd always been waiting and my value had always felt the same. Waiting and proving value was getting old, along with me.

"So Tuesday night he attacks the girl," I said. "Wednesday morning they fire him and the agency gets someone to tell Lane that it was for doing drugs?"

Rose blinked his eyes at the disrupted silence. "It's better all around than talk of fucking sexual harassment."

"Was it true when he got fired in LA? Was he shooting up back then or was that just a cover story too?"

"That was over a year ago. No one remembers and no one cares. Don't make trouble for yourself, Koch."

"That was Lane's story too," I said. "A movie studio and a talent agency put the same one over on her two years in a row?"

Rose put his hand on my shoulder, saying, "You've always been sort of a good kid." I leaned closer—it was a long time since anyone had called me a kid, even longer since they'd called me a good one.

"What I was saying before, about watching things happen from the edges?"

"Yeah?"

There was white light in his eyes. He turned away from it. "Just you stay there, all right? At the edges. Don't get yourself in the middle of this bullshit. This Kyle Prince—these agents, these re- porters, the fucking flacks, any of these people. They don't know the difference between who they are and who's a movie star. That's the sickness of these people." He was touching his own chest when he said it. "They don't know the difference."

"Well, when you come down to it," I said, "what difference is there? People are all pretty much the same crap."

At this, Rose laughed in my face, his cheeks sweating in the moonlight. "Are you just out the womb, you fucking newborn? The difference is people *love* movie stars—they figured out how to make eighty million sniveling shits *care* about them. The rest of us in this business, no normal person knows who the fuck we are, not even our names. And anyone who does is such a goddamned basket case that they should get shock treatment until they can't remember when to wipe their own asses."

I was formulating some response to that when he went on, "Let me ask you something. What goes through your mind when you see people on TV?"

"I guess it depends on the person," I said.

"Not one fuck it doesn't. What goes through a normal person's head is, 'That's one hot bitch!' or, 'Change the fucking channel, I can't stand that guy.' What's in your head though, what you're thinking, is: 'Have I met her? Have I met him? When'll I meet her again? Do these fucking people know my name? What else am I gonna have to do to make these motherfuckers remember my name?' That's what a sick fuck thinks, Koch, and that's what we think."

Taking the last smoke from my pack, I lit it, watching the coal, the gathering dark, the glow of the city beneath us.

"But we do pretty well for all that," Rose said, settling back in his chair. "This is a fucking beautiful place I've got."

It was. And, going through the final form, he could spend a Friday evening there, confessing himself to a man who was, by any meaningful definition, a perfect stranger.

As if I'd spoken it out loud, he said, "I'll tell you one thing. My funeral's going to be a gala like you've never fucking seen in your life." Grinning in the dark, he explained, "Everyone's gonna be there."

"They wouldn't miss it." I got to my feet.

"Listen, Koch, just don't make yourself sick. Don't . . ." He put his chin to his chest and his body slouched forward behind it, his head shaking side to side. "Don't be a fucking asshole, all right?"

"I won't," I told him, thinking how no one would miss Prince's funeral either, and it occurred to me that I'd been putting together quite the little burial party of my own.

26

My Beautiful Laundress

The bright chill of evening followed me into Lane's apartment, me following Lane as she casually related that Robin Saulie had checked into St. Vincent's that morning with a broken jaw.

"I thought you'd get a kick out of that," she said as we stepped into the living room. "What's wrong?"

The only spot on the floor that wasn't covered with stuffed animals, Pokemon figures, and coloring books was the one occupied by their owner, who was currently on her belly with one hand on her cheek and the other doggedly working a sky-blue Crayola against the eye of a Powerpuff Girl, the blonde one.

"Look who's here, Bess."

"Beard-o!" A mess of white curls scrambled around her face as she went for me and I crouched to receive her, a soft sweaty hand grabbing the spot where a rather stupid goatee had once resided. A few months after I'd started working on the page, Lane had gone on a six-week exchange to Corporate's flagship paper in Tasmania, where she met a salvage diver and came back pregnant with Bess. She left the diver in Hobart—they don't travel well.

I said, "Hiya, Bess."

"Are you coming to my party?"

"Your party? That's not till next month."

"You tell me, round-eye," she said in what was supposed to be a Chinese accent.

"Oh for fuck's sake, Lee," her mother said. "Are you the one who taught her that?"

"You tell me, round-eye!"

"Bess, stop that!" Lane laughed.

"Well, are you?"

I told her, "I'm hip, I'm with it." She was turning five, and I didn't want to lie to her. Before she could ask me again, I asked Lane if we could have a drink.

In the kitchen, Lane poured me a scotch and herself a vodka-grapefruit, asking, "So what's up?"

"What happened in Los Angeles last year?"

Her lips set that familiar grim rigid line in her face. "I told you to leave that alone."

"Well I didn't. And I know that Prince didn't get fired over drugs. He didn't even have a drug problem. Is any of this news to you?"

Sitting at the kitchen table, she put her fingers to her temples, closing her eyes. "Have you ever been to the Beverly Hilton?"

"No."

"There's a little tiki bar behind the hotel. It's pretty nice, actually." There was a pack of Marlboro Lights on the table, she took one for herself and I eyed the box until she offered me one.

"Kyle brought a production assistant there," she continued, shaking out a match. Again she closed her eyes, either trying to see it more clearly or trying to black it out. "It was just after closing, he was giving her a ride home."

Opening her eyes, she stared up at the ceiling. The eyes strained, brimmed with tears.

"Two busboys from the restaurant were crossing the parking lot. They had to smash through one of the back windows."

"Ma?" Bess was standing in the doorway. Lane turned her face away.

"I'll be out in a minute, kiddo." She choked down a sob, let it out as a cough. "Go put on one of your movies, okay?"

When Bess had gone, Lane got up and dried her eyes on a paper towel. "I don't have time to cry. I've got fuck-all right to anyway."

"What happened to the girl?"

"He didn't manage to penetrate her. He didn't even leave a mark, but she scratched up his face pretty well. And she was smart. She didn't go to the police, she went to a lawyer."

The rest of it was just as familiar. The girl had refused any deal with Prince's studio that didn't include his dismissal, and the studio had wanted to avoid being associated with the kind of press that accompanies a sex assault.

"I didn't buy that he was suddenly some kind of dope fiend," Lane was saying. "He's someone I talked to every week. And when I visited him out there, I never saw him do anything harder than a line or two."

"So he told you the truth?"

"A little of it," mashing her butt in the tray. "The girl told me the rest—I made him give me her number. And you know what, Lee? She was *okay* with it. She tells me, 'I've got job security, I got my rent paid for a year—I'd've blown the guy for less.'"

She started on a laugh, but there was no sound to it, like it had gotten caught at the back of her throat.

"But what about all the girls he got to before that one?" I said. "What about the ones who'd be next? People like that don't stop."

"There you go with 'those people' again. It's one person."

"One predator."

"He swore nothing like that had ever happened before. He said it was that city—it made him crazy. He promised to go away and get his head together. The girl was okay, he was getting help—"

"And what were you getting? What's the rate for laundering an attempted rape?"

"First dibs on every story coming out of the studio," she said automatically. "And Kyle Prince on a string."

"I like him better on a rope."

There was nothing between us then but silence. Through it, I could hear the *SpongeBob* theme from the next room and I knew what I would do next. I would get Em and we would go back to Queens and we'd watch cartoons. Terreya's little saint, Lane's neurotic innocent, was just another sun-drenched monster and they'd both lied to me about it. So my part was finished. But just as I was contemplating what was monstrous about Kyle Prince, I realized that my part wasn't finished at all.

Either Terreya never knew what was really inside of Prince—that he was just another sociopath conning his way around—or she was drawn to him by the same hopeless dark spot that drew Em to Billy Treatle. I had to know which it was.

And something else was wrong.

"People like that don't kill themselves," I said. "Climbers, users, all the worst people we cover—they hurt other people. When do they ever make a move against their own interests?"

"When they lose their minds." She took a sip of her drink, held it in her mouth a moment, and it seemed to pain her, swallowing it. "When they can't have all the things they want—when they catch one too many bad breaks in the press."

"That little fucker had everything anyone could want, and you cut him every break you could."

"We all make deals we have to live with, Lee."

"That's the problem. Kyle made a deal with you and he intended to live with it. Where did Robin Saulie get the idea he was going to kill himself?"

Eyeing the cubes in her glass, Lane said, "That's what I honestly don't know." She watched my face. "You don't believe me."

"Well, you've been so honest with me so far."

"But I really don't know, Lee. And that's what frightens me. I don't know what happened, what went wrong. But even if I did there's fuck-all I could do to fix it. This isn't the kind of thing you can run a retraction for, and I don't want anyone else getting hurt."

I knew what she wanted to do. If something doesn't make sense in journalism, you simply leave it out, you fudge it. When entire wars and genocides could be fudged, what's one person? Loose ends got tucked away and forgotten at the speed of doing business. Beneath the monotone tautologies of the perpetual newscast, you could always hide another body.

"This wouldn't be happening if you'd just told me the truth all along." As soon as I'd said it, I remembered how silly it had sounded just yesterday, when Lane had asked me for the same thing.

27

Get Happy

Em was alone at the bar across from the office, her coat on, a purse in her hands, and no drink. "Aren't you thirsty?" I said coming up beside her.

Her cheeks dimpled at the sight of me and a chill rushed up through my diaphragm in a sudden surge of vertigo. She smirked at me with a bounce of her hair.

"Well, how did it go today?"

"It went pretty far, but I've still got some people I need to talk to."

"So where are we going?"

Friday nights always offered a dim palette of DJ showcases, club previews, tastings and readings—events that couldn't hope for coverage except in the weekend editions. I had a feeling we'd have to wade through a lot of them before I found the people I was looking for, but Em didn't seem to mind when I explained this to her.

"It's interesting to watch them," she said.

"Watch who?"

"All these people who don't know how much they hate each other. Or if they do know, it doesn't make any difference. I still can't figure what they think they'll get out of it."

"Power."

"Over what? Each other? Wow, that's a prize."

"What else is there?" I said.

"Aside from money?"

"Is that what you want?"

The bartender came by and Em ordered our drinks.

"Well, at least it's normal to want money—a nice house, nice clothes, nice *shoes*," she said, pinching my hand. "But wanting power is crazy. There's nothing you can *do* with it. Is that really what you want?"

"I've never really known what I want. I'm starting to figure it out, though."

"And?"

Our drinks came and I took the top off mine, thinking it through. "I want to stop feeling disgusted with myself," I told her. "After that, I might get the rest of what I want. And, no, you're not going to make me tell you what that is."

The creases deepened around her mouth. We didn't say anything, finishing our drinks. Then Em informed me, "Ziortza says you asked her out—she wants to meet us later. Also, she said you're blackmailing her boss."

Before I could respond, Mac's voice called out, "There's the lad!" He leaned against the bar between Em and me, saying, "If it isn't the monk of Manhattan!"

I'd forgotten about the item Pol Pot had gotten killed.

"When first I'd heard of it," Mac went on, patting the sleeve of my jacket with four stiff fingers, "I thought, What? Is it fear of disease? Was our Koch a casualty of some long-forgotten auto catastrophe?"

"Maybe I was wounded flying the Italian front."

Rolling his hooded eyes, Mac said, "That's been done. You? You fear our city's very blood, and I don't mean its more virulent strains of AIDS and the clap."

"I fear those too."

"No, you fear the whore's whore, the original. Infidelity herself."

Em was eyeing me behind the shoulder of Mac's blazer. "Why would infidelity be a *her*?" she said.

"For our friend here," Mac told her, winking, "everything's a her. The elements, the colors, the gods themselves—all feminine. This has instilled in him certain female tendencies that make him behave like a goddamned priest—albeit a whiskey priest."

"You keep trying to turn me out a Catholic."

"You'd prefer the Wandering Jew?"

"How about Lot's wife?"

When we got outside, Em said, "Was he talking about that impotence story?" and it stood me still a second. "What?" she said. "I hear things too. Even Ziortza heard it."

"And aren't I lucky it got killed."

On the back of my hand, I felt the graze of something smooth and cool: a fingernail, ballet-slipper pink.

"Was it true?"

"There are levels of truth, and Meredith must think she hit a few of them. I can tell you about it if you want."

"You don't have to," she said. "I think I get it."

She pushed spirals of hair behind her ears.

28

Giants on Their Faces

We picked up Ziortza and made a few rounds of the Friday night ghetto. A few times I'd tried to check in with—or up on—Terreya, but she never answered her cell phone.

"This is getting slummy," Ziortza said, coming out of our third or fourth venture, a listening party for a rapper whose name I'd feel silly mentioning.

"They've got to be out here somewhere," I said. "They're all single and none of them have the nerve to stay home with it."

"It's slummy."

"Take some of Massimo's money—it'll cheer you up."

"I take it all the time." Her eyes and mouth were done in blues and whites, or looked that way under the moon. "It never cheers me up." She pouted wearily under a choppy black wig with sharp bangs. She looked like Meredith.

"Look," she said, "do you have any of these people's numbers?"

"I have all their numbers, but they're not likely to take my call. Besides, I was counting on the element of surprise."

Rolling the night-painted eyes, she took a cell from her child-sized denim jacket, saying, "Give me Cora's number."

When I went to fetch it from my own phone, I realized it was the day-old replacement and contained no numbers whatsoever. This left me feeling somewhat unarmed, and elicited another rolling of Ziortza's eyes.

"Fine," she said. "I'll get it."

She'd been working her touchpad and her mouth for about three minutes when I heard her say, "Is that Cora? Hey, it's Lisa from Angela's office at HBO." Winking, she grabbed Em's hand and shook it above her shoulder, girls together at a roller coaster's peak. "We met last week at—what was that thing?"

The tactic didn't take long to work its effect, Ziortza reaching the end of her circumlocutions with a "Most *yes!*" and an invitation to drinks at a Union Square restaurant in its second night of previews.

She kept one hand on Em's wrist while she reached into a burgundy leg warmer with the other, producing a fold of twenties. "I'll get the cab," she chirped, pecking Em on the cheek. Anyway, she was a vast improvement upon Billy Treatle.

The restaurant was the usual fusion—post-traumatic future with a touch of medieval. Vaulting, wrought iron, black velvet and steel were served in a whirlwind with Cora Heart's table at its constricting center. It was quite the table.

Cora had Jim Vonning at one elbow, Tonic Blackwell at the other. Charlie Gaines was there, too, and so was Meredith, and Treatle was between her and Tonic. It seemed to me that the hours I'd spent looking for Cora had been wasted energy, that if I'd gone straight to my own bed I would've woken up with these people.

As always, there was plenty of empty space for late arrivals, and waiters brought chairs for us to fill it with.

"Hey, booger!" Tonic said. "What happened to your face?"

"I slipped in the shower getting out of a cab."

"Didn't I see you wrestling around with Robin Saulie last night?"

"Did you?"

It went around the table while waiters brought us drinks.

"There isn't enough man-on-man violence anymore," said Vonning. "You can't stand young Le Treat here. Why don't you pull his chair out from under him?"

There were Treatle's empty eyes, empty glasses, shellfish husks on dirty plates. Meredith's blue-and-black bangs shifted over her eyes and I supposed that she was all talked out. I wished we all were. The dead, the disgraced, the betrayed—what more would it take?

"I thought you were staying in tonight," Treatle said to Em.

"Is that what I told you?"

"For fuck's sake!" Tonic laughed. "How many throws are you going to try for at one table?"

"He hasn't tried you on yet," Gaines said.

"That's all of what you need," Meredith told her, sipping something green through a stirrer. "A schoolboy murmuring his life story to your vagina all night."

"What did you say?" All the boyishness had run from Treatle's face and he put his hands on the table, turning toward her.

Vonning smiled, telling him, "Sit down, gorgeous. If Meredith wants to depants you, you might at least pretend to take it well. Like young Koch over here."

Treatle said, "I thought I was taking it well," and Vonning turned his smile on me.

"But you'll have to try to age better than he has. My God, you're looking ancient tonight."

"You said that last night."

"Did I? It's in bad taste to remind me of the past. I think you've been spending too much time around unhealthy minds."

"It would be unnatural to spend it with the healthy ones."

"Thank God! I thought there was something wrong with my glands."

"Sooner murder an infant in its cradle," Cora cut in, looking at me, "than nurse unacted desires."

"Up-up-up! She's getting literary. You'll want to pay attention to this, Le Treat. For your memoir. It's in bad taste to make a work of art without anyone discussing art in it."

"Cora," I said, "I need to talk to you about your husband. Do you want to do it here, or should we go to the bar?"

She aimed her dark blue pointing eyes at me, the eyebrows that arched too high. "Are you threatening me, Leon?"

"I'm just trying to maintain your privacy."

"You could do that by going away."

"Did Jerzy ever treat Robin Saulie?"

"Why are you asking me?"

"Because I don't think I'd have any luck getting it out of your ex, and I sure as hell can't get it out of Saulie." She asked why I wanted to know, and I told her, "Kyle Prince tried to rape a girl in LA last year and he attacked another girl in his office bathroom the other night. After that, Saulie—who's not usually known for the depth of his perception—correctly predicted that this rather self-obsessed person would suddenly up and kill himself."

Taking a brown clove from a leather case, Cora lit it with a match, dropped the match into a plate of leftovers, saying, "And?"

"And Prince was one of Jerzy's patients. If Saulie was being treated by that mindfucker too, I think it might explain his sudden power of foresight."

Tonic's cell phone materialized at her ear as she uttered a string of yelps, leaving the table in a gust.

"Clutch many straws lately?" Cora said. "Jerzy couldn't convince water to run downhill."

"He convinced his way into your bed," Vonning said. "A dubious achievement, but there it is."

"Oh shut up, James. Don't you see what he just did?" She looked at her watch. "Ten-thirty. That fucking Blackwell can still get it into tomorrow's paper."

"Perhaps she's just gone to powder her labia. And what difference does it make to you? You detest the little Sikh."

"I detest more what it'll do to my alimony if that cunt runs him out of business."

Vonning suggested she write another book.

"God help me."

"Oh, *that* old chestnut."

The clove jittered at her lips and I noticed she had the brittle bleached fingers of an obsessive hand-washer. "Why are you doing this to me?"

"I'm not doing anything to you," I said. "I'm doing it to your husband."

She damped the clove in an oyster shell. "Jerzy's harmless. He tells people how to get to Sesame Street."

"I thought we were talking about art," Vonning said. "Le Treat's suddenly so quiet. I think the whole Kyle tragedy has him down. Why don't you write that it happened to you, Billy? No one will accuse you of avarice."

I watched the kid's jaw tighten and his eyes lose their slackness. His features bore a vicious confidence, then cooled into a shy, slanting grin. "It's sad that I should even have to consider where my art comes from," he said. "But, you know—isn't ugliness just there to make us love beautiful things? Too many people are too cynical about art."

"Excuse me." Em was standing away from the table. Her eyes were bright and her hands were shaking. Ziortza touched her wrist and Em pulled it away. "I just need some air."

Treatle began to rise and Em told him to sit down. Swaying at her hips, she looked down at her purse in her hands. "I'm sorry, I—"

She went out of the restaurant with her red jacket still hanging from her chair. I took it out after her and found her standing on the curb, looking out at the park across the street. A shudder went through her shoulders as I put the jacket over them. I saw a couple with their arms around each other come out from under the trees in the park, walking along the path and passing under the statue of Gandhi. It was a nice clear night for them.

"What's wrong with me, Leon?"

"Nothing on earth, Em. What do you mean?"

She twisted her lips. "I let him, I let that thing put his tongue in my mouth."

"You're the one who explained it. There's nothing to hope for with someone like that—nothing to be afraid of."

Holding her purse against her stomach, she watched her shoes. "There was more than that. There was something, something I wanted."

"Sometimes we want to make ourselves sick."

There were her eyes again, and all of their vastness. "Why?"

"That part doesn't matter very much. All I want is to stop doing it. Some people never can."

"Can you?"

"I'm learning."

We were watching the park by the lamplight when Gaines came up beside us, rubbing ChapStick on his lips. "Let's move the dramatics to a cab, guy. The party's ambulating."

The party came out of the restaurant as he put the lip balm away, Ziortza walking over to us and the rest of them getting into a cab.

"We'll catch one across the park," Gaines decided. "The ones over here are all pointing the wrong way."

Em had just gotten her jacket on when Ziortza slid an arm around her elbow. Gaines nodded at them as they walked ahead of us. "Aren't you gonna hold my hand?" Crossing the park, he stopped us under the bronze Gandhi. "Get a load of this joker. Bad case of sciatica."

He watched the girls for a second, then squinted more closely at the wrinkled black face streaked with glassy light. "Is he—ah—is he *dead*?"

Em let out a short wet snort, covering it with her hands, and Ziortza shoved Gaines in the arm. If you had to have an act, Gaines had a good one. And you had to have an act.

In the cab he asked me, "So what do you make of Toxic and this Le Treat nemesis?"

"He makes enough of himself," Em said.

"Great-looking kid, though. And his story doesn't hold together—he'll be in the *New Yorker* in six months."

Meredith's usual talkative mood had returned by the time we found her and the rest of the group in a booth on Okay-Shiny's third circle.

"I should've known what to expect the time my cat died," she was telling the assembled as we squeezed among their ranks. "He didn't even call."

"I never did like that cat," I said. "And he was dead two days before you mentioned it."

"She was a she. Don't ever call her *he* again."

I think that was the first time I ever hated her. That automatic expectation that I should do what she wanted had once thrilled a part of me, but it was a part of me I was getting very tired of.

"Is that what you were paying me back for?" I said. "That fucking cat?"

"You didn't like her? Did you like it when my heels would dig in? When I'd smile over you and you'd try not to scream?"

I didn't feel their eyes on me. There was no reason to feel them.

"I want a beer," Em said. "Come get a beer with me, Zee?"

When they'd gone, I said, "*Like* is an odd word for it."

Meredith lifted her drink, made a face at it, and put it back down. "Why didn't you ever make love to me?"

Vodka and mixers were on the table and Gaines went to work mixing them and passing them around. We were all very composed, which is not the same as having dignity.

"I was staying on the edges," I told her. "And just because we never had sex doesn't make me impotent."

"We never had sex? Isn't that so sweet and Clintonian of you?"

"Maybe he was saving himself," Tonic said.

"Yeah, that's what my life's been about. Saving myself."

"I think it is." Meredith's eyes had that look of being too close together. "You're not really human. I see it every time I try to follow your eyes. You're never looking where it looks like you're looking."

"I guess it depends what you think I should be looking at."

"Oh he's perfectly human. Perfectly miserably clawingly human," Cora said, lighting another clove. "That's why he was holding out for something higher-profile than you. Isn't that the trouble with all of these *men* we bother with? They all believe they rank a celebrity bed. That's why they're always so thrilled to see them falling on their faces." Flicking a thick rim of ash onto the table and gesturing with her chin, she said, "Take this one, for instance."

I looked behind me. He was making his way through the circling crowd, leading with his face, a dark purple lump on the hinge of his jaw.

"Have you ever in your life seen a dog straining harder on a *leash?*"

29

Jubilee

aulie leaned into our booth in a panting red sweat, grabbing the corners of the table as if he were going to heave it up over the rail and into the pit.

"You need to learn to keep your fucking mouth to yourself, asshole." The words shushed and slurred through wiring that locked his upper and lower rows of teeth against each other.

"Are you giving lessons?" I said. "Or will you send me to the guy who screwed yours shut?"

Putting his face out over the table, it seemed to me he was offering that dark throbbing knot for a target, when Cora said, "Get away from here, Robin."

"I'm not talking to you, bitch." Turning back to me, he said, "Where is she?"

"Where is who?"

"Don't fuck with me, Koch. You were having lunch with her. People saw you."

"Oh, Maria?" I said. "Isn't she lovely? But I'm afraid our relationship is none of your business."

"You're my business when you spend all day talking shit about me."

"Funny. Maria never mentioned you."

"That's my fucking woman, Koch." A trickle of drool escaped the corner of his mouth as he said it.

I looked away from him, at Cora and Vonning on either side of me, across at Tonic and Gaines, at Meredith, then down into the pit and across that, too. Em was staring back at me, her hands folded around a beer on the padded railing. Ziortza was talking at her ear and the great glass box of the Credit Lounge gleamed above us at the center of the rings. I had the sensation it was about to shatter, raining black shards on us all.

Saulie pressed his fingers into my shoulder. "I'm talking to you, Koch."

I slapped his hand away with the back of mine without looking at him. "Do what Cora told you. You don't know what the hell else to do."

"Get up."

"And then what? How much more of your life are you going to spend prancing around like a jock?"

"Get up."

"So you can kiss him hello?" Gaines laughed. "Put your heels on and sit down, you big girl."

"I'm not talking to you, Charlie. Get up."

"Oh just sit down," I said. "You can tell me what Jerzy Singh has on you."

His head tilted dog-like to one side and he pushed up his brow. "The witch doctor?"

"Come on, Robin. It's all coming out anyway. Be a gentleman and get it off your chest."

"I don't know what the hell you're talking about, asshole."

His face looked too stupid to be containing any secrets. I felt a sudden panic streaming into my pulse. Looking across the pit to see that Em was still there, something caught my eye in the swarming throng behind her—a flash of shining skin that disappeared in the swirl before I could fix on it.

"What exactly do you want with us?" Cora asked Saulie.

"I don't want anything from you, bitch."

"You're all the bitch that can fit in one body," Vonning told him. "You absolutely take it like one when a woman won't be bothered with you."

The sweat seemed to form a protective seal over his face then, the red skin twitching beneath it, threatening to break out in open hysteria: "Maria loves me."

"Because she mercy-fucked you at Sundance?" Meredith groaned through a yawn. "That was three months ago."

The repeated mentioning of Maria's name had sent Treatle's face searching the crowd, ticking side to side and straining on his neck so that you'd think there was a rash around it.

"I heard she was half asleep in that tub," Vonning was saying. "Did she notice that you were there too?"

"We'd've been happy," Saulie said, watching the edge of the table between his hands. "We'd've been happy if people like you didn't go talking a lot of shit. I had every right to it, I deserved it, but people like you . . . you—"

"We bitches and faggots?" Vonning asked. "That's some philosophy you've found yourself. Is it *Fight Club* or Nietzsche?"

"What? You think I can't have her just because she's in movies?" He put a hand over the lump on his jaw, holding his face and his mind together for another second. "Because she's in *movies*?"

Treatle's searching motions hit a more frantic rhythm, as if Saulie was reminding him that he was running out of time to get all the things he wanted as soon as he thought of wanting them.

I especially hated the blank hunger in his eyes while Em was out there for him to see.

"I'm going to go mingle," he said, getting up.

"That's good," someone told him. "Mingle along."

Em was still at the railing and I saw that flash of skin in the crowd again, moving toward her. My pulse beat in the sides of my neck as his head and face came out from the swarm. Last I'd seen him, he had disappeared into another crowd after telling me that Prince's blood work had come back clean.

Coming up beside Em, Hood smiled, shaking her hand.

"I think I know why Maria doesn't want you," I said to Saulie. "She's not into murderers."

He backed away from it. "You're full of shit."

"I know that. But I also know you're the only one who had any idea Kyle was going to kill himself. And I know you lied to the cop that asked you who Kyle's girlfriend was."

"I was just trying to keep things quiet for them."

"Sure. Except you didn't give a shit about either one of them. How did you know Kyle was going to die if you didn't kill him?"

"He was . . ." His hand returned, delicately, to the engorged jaw. "He was a pussy like the rest of you. He couldn't take it."

"You think you're going to sell that to a cop?"

"Fuck the cops and fuck you, Koch. I'm all cleared with them."

Nodding across the pit, I said, "Then what's he doing here? He's not looking for me."

The various stages of grief played across Saulie's face in immediate succession. At the end of fifteen seconds he was sitting on the floor talking to the palms of his hands.

"She burned me," he was saying. "She so fucking burned me. Why does everyone *do* that?"

"Who burned you?" I said, crouching beside him.

Saulie put his hand on my shoulder, laughing and watching the ground. "Terreya."

The breath went out of me, the air bursting with yellows and reds.

"She told me to call the paper," he said. "She's the one who said Kyle wouldn't be able to take it. She said if I could keep it out of the papers about him getting fired the rest of it would blow over." He covered his eyes with the heels of his hands. "She said everything always blows over."

I had my breath back, but there was a heavy, exhausting pain behind my eyes. "Why did you do it for her?"

"She said she'd get Maria to talk to me again. She said she could get me back in with her. How do you think it made me look, getting ditched like that?"

I said, "How do you think you look now?"

His eyebrows came together and he wiped his mouth with the palm of his hand. "Yeah. Maybe I better go brush my hair before I talk to that cop again. That guy scares the shit out of me."

"Don't worry about it," I said. "He's not looking for you."

30

Nearer Thy God to Me

The faces in the crowd appeared very white and far off in the periphery as I made my way toward Em and Hood. Soon my legs were heavy and it was hard to keep working the floor beneath them. Then my face felt heavy, too, and other faces rushed in close and dark, and here and there familiar ones seemed about to speak but would turn suddenly away, their features stuck at unnatural angles.

Stopping, I grabbed the railing and tried to breathe down those sensations. I knew that if I looked into the pit I'd more vividly picture rats feeding, or hornet larvae, or a sunflower head with a thousand florets writhing clockwise and counter-clockwise, dark within the bright petals—so sickeningly round and tight together.

Bended elbows overhung the two smaller terraces above me, jaws flexing at the hinges, and Ziortza appeared among them, waving down at me before disappearing into the chattering faces. Such a noise came from those faces that I thought there must be a silence at the heart of it, a quiet steady core, unchangeable in the swirl. I listened for it as I started along the ring again, and I could hear it inside me when I'd gotten where I wanted to go.

"Evening," I said to Hood.

"That ever pleasant evening was long ago," he said without looking away from Em. "What we've got here is our own little witching hour."

"How did you find your way here?" I asked. "I guess your luck is changing."

"Luck?" The gray eyes turned down at the corners, and he smiled for Em. "If it's luck that brought me to this place, then you can keep it."

The eyes leveled on me to see what felt like a blank yet somehow obscene expression.

"Prince's woman called me herself," he said. "That is, she called a desk sergeant an hour ago saying she was wanted to make a statement regarding the Prince case, and this is where she wanted to make it. She left a cell phone number—no name."

Taking the green notebook from his coat, he read carefully and without emphasis: "'I guess I'm the girl you're making such a fuss about. It would be much better if you would please just leave me alone, but if you really are just going to keep insisting . . !'" The book slapped shut in his hand and he tucked it away in his coat. "So she wants to meet me here. I thought I'd show just a little bit on the early side, take in the color. Interesting kind of a voice she had." He looked up at the rings above us. "Made me think of if an animal could talk. Maybe a little fox or some kind of cat."

"Something like that."

He stared into the pit, sniffing the air. "I'm guessing you to be a regular around here."

Whatever I might have said to that vanished as the cell phone trilled in my jacket.

"There you are, Sunshine. Is that him? That little bald man?"

I watched the black gleam of the Credit Lounge. "That's him. What is it you're doing?"

"Oh he's adorable."

"Isn't he? What are you doing?"

"Just what I always do. I'm always here, you're always here—everyone's always, always, always right here!" I listened as her breath quickened and slowed. "Well, you might as well bring him up now," she said. "Everyone's here."

The close confined heat of the fourth and fifth terraces brought a sweat to all our faces as we rounded them and it looked even hotter in the tight dim alcoves of the VIP tables. On the fourth terrace, I saw Matt Block alone with three white men in Tibetan robes, hemmed in by his bodyguards. On the fifth, there were three commentators from Corporate's news channel—one of them scratching at the blotches on his cheeks, and all of them laughing in one another's faces.

We went up another flight of steps and through a corridor, at the end of which I saw the bodyguard Gaines had maced the night before, and three others just like him—blocking the door to the Credit Lounge.

"Private party tonight?" I said, taking the keycard from my wallet.

One of them shrugged, the four of them stepping away from the door. Its lock lay on the floor in a rectangular steel hunk, an LED flashing red on its face and wires trailing away from its back. A blue glow showed through the hole in the door where the lock had been and, stepping past me, Hood pushed open the door. The hallway filled with cold blue light and I turned my face away.

Em and I followed Hood down the six steps and into the small blue-lit square. A low, round, black marble table took up the center of the room, a circular couch in black leather arranged around it. Smaller versions of the table and ottomans matching the couch ran along the four tinted walls, the crowds on the terraces beneath them muted and cast in sepia.

There was a portable bar in a far corner of the lounge and Maria Shockley was sitting on top of it, wearing a skirt that was bundled into her lap and pressing a napkin high up against her exposed thigh. A hypodermic needle lay next to her on the bar.

Hood moved forward slowly, saying, "Miss?"

I stayed by the stairs with Em. I'd never been inside the Credit Lounge without a mob and it was so cold I could see my breath ahead of me. Em shivered by my arm and I wondered what shadow Terreya would pop out of this time.

"Miss?" Hood said again, stopping beside the couch.

A shape rose up in back of Maria. "Just Terreya," it giggled. "Terreya November. It says Teresa on my driver's license, but it's much better to be Terreya. Teresa's just a little dead girl."

Quick soundless footsteps carried her to Hood and she offered him her hand with a publicist's ready confidence that anyone should naturally take it. Hood took it, Terreya saying, "Teresa's just so *Catholic*, don't you think? I haven't been Catholic in years. And besides, I never drive anywhere anymore—where would I go?"

Hood said nothing as they shook hands and she smiled up at him. She looked childlike in a hooded sweatshirt, last night's cargo pants, and dark low-top Chuck Taylors. But Hood seemed to stiffen and lean away from her when their hands dropped, as if sensing something animal in her, like what he'd said about her voice. And I thought I saw something animal between the two of them—an instant and elemental understanding that neither should assume they were the one controlling this space.

"Why don't we all sit down?" Terreya negotiated pleasantly.

"Why don't we?" Hood said.

"Come on, Maria."

Maria came to her and they sat at the center table across from Hood, facing Em and me while Hood showed us his back. I felt like

Hood had become a protective wall then, a barrier against Terreya. She patted the couch next to her.

"Aren't you coming, Sunshine? Oh look, you brought a friend."

"Emma," she said.

"The one with the eyes." Terreya showed her rabbit teeth. "Do you look at my Sunshine with those eyes?"

Leaning her face forward, her features darkening, Em said, "I work with him."

"Work, work, work," Terreya said, looking past us. "Is there anything but? But I really would appreciate it if you would sit down now."

Grabbing Em's hand, I kept us where we were.

Terreya looked at Hood again. "After everything that's happened," she said, "he won't even sit with me."

"I don't know everything that's happened," I told her.

"Oh would you like to know? Would you very much like that?"

"Yes."

Her buck teeth dug into her lip, then she closed her mouth over them.

"Did you ever feel . . ." She shook her head, closing her eyes. When she opened them again, she took Maria's hand and started tracing its lines with a fingernail. "Did you ever feel like you're in a time trap? How years can run forward or back however they want to? It's almost pretty when they do it, the loops they do." Looking at me, she seemed suddenly shy, like I was an actor calling her out of the audience from the stage in her mind. Her gaze fell away, eyes closing again, her hands folding around Maria's.

"It would be much better if it were only the years," she said. "But I know it's the days that will kill me now. The days never pass anymore. They just—they trade places."

"Terreya," Hood said. "Are you sure you want to tell me what happened right now? Mr. Koch had told me you were going to talk to a lawyer. You can still do that, you know. I believe it might be—"

"I've believed in just everything," she told him. "I've believed that grown-ups are there to protect children. I've believed that I'd made myself strong enough to keep living." She beamed at Hood, her eyes a tranquil turquoise in the blue light.

"I once believed I had found just the best boy," she went on. "Then I believed that some creep doctor had played with his brain and changed him."

Her sneakers squeaking against the leather couch, Terreya crouched there, fingers spread on the marble before her, and she lowered her head to them. "But it turns out I'm still just a stupid little girl."

"Let us just take this back a step," Hood said, leaving his hands folded in front of him. "I'd like to know more clearly what you mean by that. Can you tell me?"

Nothing moved in her body, but her eyes clicked on Hood. I could feel the energy coming off her, the potential. I could feel the pressure of it in my joints.

"I had a sweet, decent boy for two months," she said. "And then I had a rapist." Her energy shut down around the word. I saw her knees quivering under her thighs as she reseated herself. You couldn't see her face blanch in the blue light, but you could see it slump forward and her shoulders begin to tremble.

"A rapist?" Hood said, gently.

"Kyle got fired for attacking a girl in his office Tuesday night," I told him. "And he tried to rape a girl in LA last year. Both his employers threw money at it."

I think I felt Terreya's laughter before I heard it, a nervous spasm in my teeth, in the fluid in my ears—an animal premonition of an earthquake.

"You know he didn't rape any of those girls, Sunshine." Mascara trailed away from her eyes, but they were vivid and hard. "He only raped me."

I felt the shiver of Em's body beside me, and the harsh empty coldness of the room. No one spoke and Terreya's eyes shined blue in the cold silence. Em's shivering stopped, but there was still the coldness.

It had happened last Thursday night, Terreya said, in Prince's apartment. She'd been waiting for him to get home from work and had put herself into one of her knot-untying fugues. She didn't explain those spells, those trances, and Hood didn't ask her to.

"I woke up and he was there," she said. "There he was. I thought it must be a flashback—I used to have them. Kyle had always understood about my spells. I'd told him where they came from. But it really was him behind me. And he said I was faking, it wasn't real. There he was and he was behind me saying that I only got like that to get attention."

Maria put her face to the marble, hiding it in the hinge of her arm. Terreya's face was distant, unreadable.

"I'd always told Kyle that the worst part was when I'd come to with that man's *breath* on my neck, to come out of it and—to come out of it and he was still *there*. And I'd hear my mother in the other room . . . I'd hear the TV . . ."

She looked across at me. I felt the hate and the hopelessness of her eyes in my own.

"Kyle did it anyway. And he was telling me I was faking, that I was teasing him. He said that's what we do. I should have killed him as soon as I woke up," she said. "As soon as I threw him off me I should have broken his neck and called the police. But I couldn't think. I thought I loved him, it was hard to start hating him, and he was so apologetic at first."

She said she didn't see him again until that next Wednesday, the night he died—though he'd begged her and begged her before that.

"Until he raped me," she said, "I guess I thought all those other girls had been lying. Then he did that to me and all week I thought about killing him. Then I realized that it would be much better if he killed himself. I mean, he's the one that made it have to happen—it wasn't my fault. And it felt like such a perfect thing to have happen. So I told him I was coming over. I told him we would play a game."

Wednesday afternoon, she said, watching me, she'd called Robin Saulie—"To lay the groundwork. I knew that even if Lane got second thoughts from that call, you wouldn't. Your hate is your religion, Sunshine. Anyone has eyes enough to see it."

"I don't hate you," I said.

"And that's as far as you'll ever get, Leon. You don't love me either. You don't love anything." Her blue gaze focused on Em. "Do you think he loves you?"

Showing Terreya the fullness of her eyes, Em said only, "I'm sorry for what happened to you."

Terreya shrugged and told Em, "I didn't touch Kyle even once that night. I want you to know that." She said it again, she told it to the room.

"Our game was with ropes," she went on. "My Kyle tied naked to his bed, and me whispering in his ear. Before I cut the ropes off him, I told him he could only have me if he was truly sorry. He said he was, but I still wouldn't let him loose and he kept getting angrier and angrier. And he kept getting more and more excited. He started saying again how I'd been faking, he started saying I should be grateful." She ran her fingers down the inside of her wrist, staring at it. "He said that I should praise him."

When she first cut Prince loose and gave him the razor, she told us, "He just kept staring at his wrists. He said they were *his* veins, his life was in them, his drive—he couldn't do it. He said he could feel the blood in them, that he'd worked so hard to be what he was. How could he betray that? And I—I dared him to show me the blood."

He hadn't cut any veins on the first try, she recalled, or the second or the third.

"It took a lot of cheerleading," Terreya said, her eyes still on her own wrist. "I told him he could have me as soon as I saw some blood. Then I told him I'd call an ambulance as soon as he cut the other one. I told him how it would be good press, getting rushed to the hospital—something to humanize him, make people think he was sorry for what he'd done to all those girls if it ever came out. Then he cut the other one, and then I didn't think I'd call an ambulance after all. I thought it would be much better to just let him see me walk away. That was in the bedroom."

Running his hand over the back of his head, Hood took a long unmoving look at Terreya.

"He could have saved himself," he said. "There was a phone in the bedroom. We found a cell phone on his coffee table, another landline in the kitchen, and no blood on any of them. He just set himself on the kitchen floor and—" Hood looked at his own hands, his wrists, shaking his head. "The man didn't even care that someone would *find* him that way."

Taking a black oblong handle from a pocket in her cargo pants, Terreya said, "Eventually, it's much better not to care about anything at all." She flipped the straight razor out of its plastic cradle, saying, "See?" and nothing quivered the smile on her face as she drew the blade upward from her wrist to her elbow.

"Goddamn it!" Hood screamed, scrambling to the other side of the table and lifting Terreya onto it. "Someone call 911—got both my hands full right now."

Em took a cell phone from her purse and called for an ambulance while Hood removed Terreya's sweatshirt and Maria fainted onto the couch. I listened, frozen, to Terreya's dead laughter as the detective tried to save her.

31

Emma

When the EMS men showed up they had a pair of uniformed cops with them. Hood took the cops aside, speaking to them by the stairway while the medics worked on Terreya and strapped her to a gurney. Her hands left streaks of blood on the white sheets, black in the blue light, an oxygen mask misting over her face.

"She's stable," Hood told me, watching Terreya in her stretcher. "I'm going to follow her over to the ER. You should go home now."

Maria stumbled to Terreya, touching her lips to Terreya's forehead, then sobbing against her chest.

"What are you going to the ER for?"

"To arrest her, Mr. Koch. Promoting a suicide is a felony."

"He raped her."

"Promoting a suicide is a felony," he said again. "Throw in duress and deception and it's murder."

"Prince made his own duress, a lot of it, for a lot of people. And what deception are you talking about? All you've got is Terreya's statement, and she made it in such a state that you didn't even write it down. You think she'll ever make it again?"

"Whether an indictment can be made, that's a problem for the DA's office. I heard her confession."

"Maybe you just heard a bad dream, Detective."

"It's enough for a prosecutor to take to a grand jury. Might even be enough for a conviction."

"Well that'll be great for you, if she lives that long."

Eyeing the floor, Hood sucked in his cheek and nodded his head slightly. Then he watched Terreya across the room, staring at the ceiling and breathing into the mask, arms bound to the sides of the gurney.

"Maybe she did commit a felony," I said. "Do you really believe she committed a crime?"

Running his hand over the back of his head, Hood went to Terreya.

"Mr. Koch told me this afternoon that you were going to consult a lawyer before giving a statement," he said, buckling his coat. "I'm suggesting you do that. The statement he described to me had some fine points and it had some holes in it too. A decent lawyer will get around those holes for you."

Even above the oxygen mask, Terreya's eyes were the same unmoving blue they had been since I'd walked into the room.

"But I told you the *truth*," she hissed, her breath wet against the plastic.

"Now why don't I believe you? If you'd really had anything to do with Kyle Prince's suicide, he would have saved himself after you left the room—so, clearly, there's something faulty in your statement. Clearly, that wasn't the truth. Go talk it over with a lawyer, Ms. November. A good lawyer will explain how the truth works."

Nodding to Terreya, Hood went to Em and took her hand, telling her it had been a pleasure. He looked at me.

"This all might have ended less bloody," he said, "if you hadn't been so helpful, Mr. Koch."

"Sure. And there were so many people I could've trusted along the way."

Sunrise seemed to spread itself on a horizon of frosted glass when we got outside, but it was warm even under that faint early haze, and all the colors were what they naturally should be. Terreya's eyes were green again. She strained against the gurney straps as I climbed into the back of the ambulance, telling me to take the mask off her face.

"You're off the hook for Kyle," I told her. "And the doctors will take care of you."

She shook her head, smiling. "I told you I'm through with doctors. Once they sew me up I'm going home."

"You need to be someplace where they can take care of you."

"If I went into a place like that," she said, "I wouldn't even know who'd come out."

"It might be good for you just to get a rest, a little quiet time."

Shaking her head again, she whispered, "Come here," and I leaned my face to hers. "All I've got is me. I have to carry this—I can't go rest, I can't listen to the quiet." Her eyes closed as she leaned back into the gurney. "Now kiss me good-bye."

I kissed the side of her mouth, felt her breasts against me, her breath on my face and, for a second, the touch of her tongue on my lips. "I can't rest," she whispered. "I can't change. And I don't ever want to see you again."

I climbed out of the ambulance, watched it rolling away down the wet empty street, and I could still feel her against me. But under that, despite my higher aspirations, I felt simple relief. She was my last account.

Em and I didn't say a word, just started walking together. We walked on and on away from there and I didn't need to think about how it felt to be walking with her. I just walked with her, the rest of the city waking up with itself. I knew I could always think about it later.

Her hair bounced when she walked and it smelled of cigarette smoke.

Through Chinatown and the few blocks that were left of Little Italy, men were out in aprons hosing down the sidewalk, bringing up from the concrete a scent like the rain.

The sun was high and strong when we went through the West Village, Em tying her hair back and me taking off my jacket. We passed under a row of magnolias and dogwoods on a short narrow street of brownstones I thought I'd never seen before. The trunks of the trees were twisted and seemed too thin, but fullgrown blooms of pink and white exploded all along their branches.

Across from Washington Square Park, Em tugged my arm and I followed her out onto the grass. Taking my jacket from me, she smiled with that impossible color of her eyes and lay back, putting my jacket behind her head and kicking the shoes off her feet. I'd never seen her toes before. They were funny looking, the second and third toes on each foot longer and much thinner than the rest, as if one toe had been split into a pair of them. Em squinted up at me, laughing, grabbed the grass with her toes and punched me in the arm.

I felt the cool dampness of the grass through the back of my shirt as I lay next to her. It wasn't until I'd closed my eyes that either of us said anything.

"I was thinking about you and Meredith," she said.

"When did you find time to do that?"

"There was plenty of it. What happened with her, I bet you think it's all pretty complicated."

"It felt complicated."

"It wasn't. You didn't trust her. She wasn't your friend."

"I haven't trusted anyone that way in a long time."

"Well, it takes time." Her toes brushed my ankle. "Lucky for you, you have some."

Of course I'd heard that one before, but never from anyone I'd believed in. I lay there listening to the morning noise, and to the silence beneath it. We could last on and on or we could end in an instant, but we could last on and on—these eluding shapes, these vast, impossible territories.